The Shadow of the Clouds

Fahimm Inhonvi

tara-india research press

Tara-India Research Press
B-4/22, Safdarjung Enclave,
New Delhi – 110 029.
Ph.: 24694610; Fax : 24618637
bahrisons@vsnl.com
contact@indiaresearchpress.com
www.indiaresearchpress.com

Work of Fictional Writing **2005** by Fahimm Inhonvi

ISBN : 81-87943- 47 - 5

2005 © India Research Press, New Delhi.

All rights reserved by publisher. No part of this publication, unless used for Research and Documentation, may be reproduced, stored in or introduced into a retrieval system or transmitted in any form, or by any means, electronic, mechanical, photocopying, recording or otherwise, without the prior written permission of the publisher of this book..

The Shadow of the Clouds
by   Fahimm Inhonvi
1.   Fiction - Indian.   2. Romance– Family.
I. Title.   II.   Fahimm Inhonvi

Printed in India at Focus Impressions, New Delhi – 110 003.

*for my father, the late Nasim Inhonavi
and for my wife, Bushra*

One

Resting her head against the seat she was looking thoughtfully out of the window. She had never come alone so far away from home, and though the colour of the sky was the same, it was a different world from the one she had known- life was just life there; here it seemed a story.

The bus was on the narrow, meandering mountain road and the teeming, silent woods held a vague promise, their promiscuous shadows full of a nameless enchantment while, through the intermittent gaps in the scenery, she could make out the misty silhouettes of the hills looming in the distance.

It was the beginning of December and there was still time for the winter to become harsh. The sunlit morning was full of warmth though the air was cold and it was making her shiver. But she didn't close the window, for she liked the wind touching her and playing with her hair- it was messing it up but she hardly cared- she had always been a little careless with her beauty and now, after what had happened during the past few weeks, she had become completely indifferent to everything except the swirling emotions in her heart.

There were few passengers in the bus with her, for the tourist season ended with the autumn. Faisal, her father, had tried to persuade her to wait till the winter was over. It would be too cold and bleak, he had said. As if anything mattered. As if anything could have stopped her. She would have come even if it were raining hailstones.

Fahimm Inhonvi

It was not as if she didn't have any misgivings. Don't go, her heart had said to her, don't travel the road of memories, memories which are not even your own...But she had refused to listen, not paying any heed because someone else was calling her...Calling her with a voice so insistent, so sad and irresistible...Someone whom she had seen so long ago and forgotten, someone who had loved her across time, who had left to her whatever little he had—a small, lonely house and a run-down, desolate bookshop, and...and what else she knew not. Only God knew what she was destined to find. But whatever it was, it was her bequest and she was going to claim it!

Two

"It was in 1839 that an English businessman, Mr. P. Barron, discovered this beautiful spot. Barron had heard about it and knew that the locals deliberately misled Europeans who tried to find their way there. So he forced one of the guides to carry a large stone on his head until he revealed the path to the lake and very soon he was gazing at a scene so breathtaking and wondrous that it can never be effaced from memory: for there, in front of his eyes, surrounded by lush, green mountains, was the lake... "By far the most beautiful sight I have witnessed in the course of a fifteen hundred-mile trek through the Himalayas," was how he described it.

This lake is situated at an altitude of 2000 metres, is 29 metres deep and has a circumference of 3620 metres. It is said that some time in the past it was even larger but a hill on the northern end crumbled to fill a part of it. That was how the Flatt, where people congregate now, was created..

Nainital has a population of 50,000 and there are more than a hundred registered hotels to receive the great number of tourists that visit mostly during the summer and the short autumn. The nearest railhead is Haldwani, a town in the foothills, from where you can take a bus or taxi for the two-hour journey up the mountains....

Tahmina put down the tourist guide and leaned against the window. The lake must be very beautiful, she thought and that's why he loved it so much. She could feel the yearning for it in her heart and knew she was going to fall in love with it too.

She was almost halfway there and it was turning very cold now so she pulled the woollen muffler a little tighter around her neck and zipped up the black leather jacket she had bought in Dubai. The young, chic salesgirl had said it would keep her warm even in Siberia and here, even at such a slight altitude, with a clear sky and bright sunshine, she was shivering in every limb. How cold must it get, she wondered, when the weather got wild, with dark, rumbling clouds and rain and snow. And though she tried to suppress it, the thought of such weather excited her. She had seen so little rain in her life, for in Dubai, where she had lived since childhood, it rained only occasionally and she had seen mountains only once before when they had gone to holiday in Kashmir. But that was so long ago and at the time there had been nothing in her that could have responded to the beauty of that fabled vale.

She glanced out of the window and was struck by the sight of a tree whose leaves had been singed a flaming orange by the autumn. The bus was passing through a gorge and the silence seemed to echo through the woods. How lovely and peaceful it was, she thought. She could feel the mystery of the mountains settling inside her with its stillness.

All that had happened to her appeared so unexpected and inexplicable. Without any premonition, without any preparation, life had flung her into a storm.....A storm so sudden and traumatic that it had churned and upset everything in her. Nothing was in its place anymore and many things had been wrecked forever...I will never be able to put it all back together, she thought. What's broken is broken and one can only build something else in its place. Yes, everything has changed for me, everything....Even I have changed, she reflected. Nothing before had stirred her so deeply and darkly, nothing before had made her weep and shout and hurt those

The Shadow of the Clouds

whom she loved. And she did not even know from where these emotions had come, so tempestuous and searing! But they had also made her strong and impetuous, ready to fling herself into the storm that life had sent her...

Three

Her life had until a few days ago been so placid, so ordinary. How easily she had grown up, unruffled, without even a hidden sorrow. Nothing had hurt her, nothing had made her intense. It was as though she was waiting to come alive, like a candle waiting to be set to flame.

A shy, thoughtful girl, spontaneous with her feelings, she was, most of the time, as yielding as the clouds. And though there was a streak of impulsiveness in her too, she was never wilful or obstinate. Even when Faisal or Amna, her mother, refused anything she wanted, she wouldn't sulk or throw a tantrum. All she would do was to switch off the light on her face for a while and they would accede. But even such occasions were rare. Like any girl though, she had her seasons of gloom and silence but they would pass soon.

Faisal, whom she addressed as Abbu, was now a very rich man. He had been born in Delhi, starting his career over there as an assistant manager of a hotel. But as soon as he inherited some money from his father, he had bought a small restaurant of his own and never looked back. He was a smart and hard-working man and things had worked out well for him. He had bought a hotel in Delhi, then one in Chandigarh but there were partners and eventually he had to sell his share to them and start out on his own once more. At a loose end, he had, by chance, come to Dubai and liked the place so much that he decided to settle there. He held a good job in a five-star hotel and within a few months had brought his family to live there too. Then a few years ago an opportunity had come his way and he and two of his associates had pooled their savings to buy a decent hotel for themselves.

When Faisal had brought her to Dubai, Tahmina had been just six while her brother Kashif had been eight. She had gone to school there, then to college and then, one and a half years ago, she had opened a boutique in her father's hotel, while Kashif had gone on to the US to get a Business Management degree.

She had visited India only a few times before because her mother hadn't liked coming here too often, though Faisal made at least one trip a year to visit his brother in Delhi. It was only when there was some special occasion, like a wedding, that her mother would condescend, bringing Tahmina with her. Even then they would stay mostly in Delhi; only once had they visited Mumbai, another time Jaipur and many summers ago, they had gone to Kashmir.

Through all these years, Faisal had been an ideal father, mixing his love with discipline so sweetly and finely that despite fulfilling their every desire and whim and providing them with the best of everything, he hadn't let them get spoiled. A man of few words, he always did everything very quietly, without making a show and was one of those men who seemed to be full of hidden strength, so that you always felt safe when he was near. Perhaps this was what made him so attractive to women. And those eyes of his, which always seemed to be saying something, making you forget he was not a very handsome man. But what she liked best about him was the way he dealt with people, with kindness and understanding and the manner in which he always held back his feelings, both his anger and his love. It was natural for her to love him best, and she did so with a deep and abiding affection and she knew too how much she meant to him.

Her mother, on the other hand, was so different...Her whole world revolved around her husband. She was totally, obsessively besotted with him, to the extent that she seemed to be alive only when he was near her. Her whole day was spent in waiting for him, and then, when he would be coming home, she would dress for him, making herself bewitchingly beautiful. She would often praise him, especially to Tahmina and Kashif, saying such silly things sometimes that Faisal would feel embarrassed. One of her pet paeans was to say what a real man he was, a man who knew how to achieve what he desired. And Faisal would say, in that naturally modest and self-deprecating manner of his, that there was nothing special in him, that it was all Allah's kindness and munificence.

And it was worse when they had guests, or at parties. She would not leave his side, flirting with him, behaving almost like a day-old bride. And if he were sitting away from her talking with someone else, she would gaze at him with unconcealed, ardent admiration, unmindful of what anyone would think of this display of her infatuated love. It was really very embarrassing for Tahmina but Faisal didn't seem to mind.

Tahmina did sometimes wonder about her mother's almost neurotic behaviour regarding Faisal but she had never given it much thought, for in other ways Amna was very nice. And what was more, she had such a fetching beauty, and had so much grace that it was a delight to just sit and watch her. Sometimes she would seem languorous (when Faisal was away), sometimes vivacious (when Faisal was near), and it was so adorable the way she would remember something one moment and forget it the other and then make funny faces.

She also had very good taste, intuitively knowing what would look good when and where so that every little thing in their home was nice and cosy and as beautiful as she was. But her exquisite taste was most evident in her clothes, in the way she dressed and in the little touches she applied to herself, like the light henna on her palms, the elusively alluring perfumes she wore, or the way she made a strand of her tresses to come loose and hover over a side of her face.

But there was nothing frivolous about her and she never put on any airs. On the contrary, she was a very warm-hearted and unaffected woman who prayed regularly and was always ready to share anyone's sorrow and happiness. But yet again, sometimes Tahmina had also felt a coldness, a hardness in her....And there were moments when she would turn very remote, appearing to be lost somewhere very far away, and if any one spoke to her or disturbed her, she would become very cross and remain sullen for hours.

For some reason she had cut off all her ties with the land where she had been born and grew up, visiting India only for Faisal's sake....It was true that both her parents were dead and her only brother was living in Dubai, but there were other relatives whom she had all but forgotten. And then there was her hatred for books...

No one was able to understand or comprehend this strange quirk of hers—any book she would find would be thrown out of sight, and Tahmina and Kashif had to be careful to keep their books in their rooms. She was of the view that books were nothing but volumes of trouble.

"What's wrong with them Ammi?" Tahmina would ask her.

"Oh! They just irk me," Amna would reply.

"Why does Ammi hate books, Abbu?" Tahmina would ask Faisal.

The Shadow of the Clouds

"Oh! They just irk her," he would reply.

Her mother's irrational aversion to books really puzzled and exasperated Tahmina, because, in a strange twist of dispensation, she loved and adored them. She had never been very studious but she liked good fiction, especially mysteries, and never went to sleep before curling in bed with a good one. But this had been only a slight irritation between them and on the whole, she loved and appreciated her and felt indebted to her for the beauty and grace that she had inherited from her. For, as Tahmina had grown up, unfolding, as girls do like a flower, she had revealed as much beauty as Amna. And yet, for all the resemblance between them, Tahmina had a beauty of her own too.

Amna was still in her early forties and because women's beauty evolves imperceptibly during the long summer of their youth, a mother can often match her daughter like a mirror. So the difference between them was not so much of age as of the variations by which beauty hides and unveils in a woman, depending on the different stages of her life and experiences, on her moods and inclinations.

Apart from becoming a little fuller, Amna had not lost any of her vivacity and because she knew how desirable she was, her beauty was vivid and almost seductive in its revelation. In contrast, Tahmina was more slender and her eyes were larger, more iridescent and had a melting quality in them. And because she was shy and thoughtful, her beauty had turned inwards, hidden somewhere in her heart and feelings. And as she had yet to learn the magic she could weave, there was nothing of effrontery in her beauty, nothing incendiary or distracting. But this incipient and promising beauty of hers was somehow more attractive and enticing. And the loveliest thing about her was the way she smiled, biting a little bit of her lower lip and tilting her face to one side. She would look so impish then, which she was not, and winsome, which she was.

One and a half years ago, when she had graduated out of college, her father had suggested she open a boutique in his hotel. Tahmina had liked the idea and had become involved in her work, choosing and buying clothes and suggesting designs. Actually Faisal wanted her to gain some experience of work, to learn about business and how to handle people and money. That's why he had made it a serious business venture. The shop in the hotel was rented out in her name and the money Faisal had lent to start the boutique was to be repaid in monthly instalments.

Initially the shop had broken even and it was only since the last few months that it had started showing some profit but as Tahmina had no use for the money, Faisal kept it aside for her in the bank. Tahmina had, however, never thought about these aspects. What she liked was the daily activity of her work and the light-hearted camaraderie with the three girls who helped her in the boutique. And the real thing to contemplate for her was marriage. It dangled like an adventure before her.

Last year, her brother had become engaged when he had come home for his vacation and his marriage was tentatively fixed for early next year when he would be back with his degree. The engagement party had been great fun and Tahmina had stolen many hearts. There had been such frenzy after that, with many families asking for her hand and if it had been in Amna's hands, she would have settled Tahmina's match somewhere. But Faisal had been reluctant, saying he did not want to lose her so soon. And though Tahmina hadn't been too disappointed with that, she had also not felt any sort of happy relief. For the truth was that marriage excited her and she would often wonder what it would be like to have a man for herself, to go away to live with him and to make love to him.

And it was not just the ferment of her sexuality that filled her with such conjectures and fantasies. She was often bored and somewhat restless and could feel obscure stirrings in her heart that made it yearn for something strange and forbidden. She convinced herself that marriage was the only way to find something new and interesting in life.

Till now there had been no man in her life, though she had her little secrets and was not as innocent as she appeared. There had been boys towards whom she had been attracted and had even stolen glances with some of them, but that was how far it had gone. If she had lived in some other place, perhaps she too would have had a romantic fling or two, but it was difficult in Dubai. There were no opportunities here to meet someone, to come to know him and fall in love with him. Even otherwise, it was never easy to defy the prohibitions or cross the limits of the milieu in which she had been brought up. For though she had lots of freedom, could drive her car and go out with friends, there were frontiers never to be crossed.

Yes, religion had never been something oppressive in her home but her parents, particularly Faisal, had been very specific that they respect the limits defined by their culture and traditions. And though Tahmina or her mother did not have to wear the veil, Tahmina could never think of going out in jeans or tops, or doing away with her dupatta. And she had never resented these things, had never felt the need or desire for anything forbidden.

Four

The bus had stopped, she realised suddenly, coming out of her reverie. Many of the passengers were alighting and she glanced outside; there was a small, ramshackle tea-stall perched on a ledge on the side of the mountain. It looked so picturesque, with its tin-roof, wood benches and earthen stove. She decided to step out to buy a glass of tea and was immediately accosted from all sides.

A strip of a boy in a clean, red sweater and woollen pajamas was at her side, urging her to buy strawberries he was selling in small, quaint cups made of leaves. An old vendor was asking her to purchase peanuts, while a woman was offering steaming pakoras. Tahmina was not a little surprised at all this commotion but she somehow managed to evade them. Reaching the tea-stall, she stood near the blazing stove, feeling the comfort of its warmth as she sipped her tea.

She noticed that none of the women passengers had come out of the bus; their men were handing them whatever they asked for through the window. Tahmina could not help feeling a bit awkward, standing surrounded by the men who were staring at her. Feeling discomfited, she finished the tea in a gulp and climbed back to her seat.

The boy selling strawberries followed her inside. He looked charming with his apple-cheeks and tousled hair, and her heart went out to him. In a sudden gush of love she wanted to reach out and touch him. Instead, she bought a few cups of strawberries and he smiled gratefully at her. There was so much beauty, so much peace here but Faisal had told her that most of the local people were poor, living a life as hard as the mountains. But perhaps they drew their strength from reserves unknown to her. From faith in God perhaps.

The bus started again. The brief interlude had diverted her from her thoughts and she was once again observing the mountain scenery. How bracing and wonderful the mountain climate was, and how full of beauty, the trees so lush even in winter. And though snow had not yet fallen here, she had seen a report in the newspaper about heavy snowfall in the higher reaches of the Himalayas. It usually had its effect further down and so the cold would intensify soon.

If her heart had not been so heavy and distressed and if she had someone to share the experience, she would have loved to see the snow falling here. But what did it matter, she had not come for the snow or the beauty of the hills, though she had been touched and affected by it, for even now it was scalding her heart.

Yes, she had done right in insisting she would travel alone, not letting even Faisal dissuade her. "Don't go alone, let somebody come with you…Wait till the winter's over, it will be too cold and you are not used to it…" but she had paid no heed to his expostulations. He had been so worried for her, she recalled; the first thing I will do on reaching Nainital will be to phone him, she resolved. How relieved he would be! How could he love her so much, she wondered, when after all she was….?

No! I will not think about that! To divert herself, she started to look out of the window once again. The road had become steeper and more sinuous now and she sat watching the sky with vacant eyes, trying not to remember or think, and after a little while, she started feeling a slight dizziness. Suddenly, a spasm of nausea shook her...Oh God! she thought, I am going to be sick, just like her uncle had warned her. She took out the half-cut piece of lemon from her bag and started licking it, but it tasted so sharp and tangy and made her feel worse. Then she remembered the medicine her uncle had given her at the railway station in Delhi, where he had come to see her off on the train, and she started fumbling for it in her purse.

She soon felt better and the waves of nausea and dizziness caused by the twisting and turning mountain climb slowly subsided. And though it had become quite chilly now and she was sitting huddled into herself, she was feeling fresh and comfortable. They would soon be reaching Nainital, for the last milestone had said it was just a few miles away, and she became pensive once again.

What would it be like, she wondered, and what more surprising discoveries waited for her there? And what else was going to happen to her? Perhaps nothing, nothing more than what had already come to pass on that morning three weeks ago. How will I ever forget all that, or may be it was all a fragment of a story, a figment, a dream, she thought. But she very well knew how real it all was. She no longer was what she had known herself to be. She had to accept that, however difficult and painful it might be.

Abbu had asked her to be brave, and I will be brave, she resolved. Till now she had been too distraught. It had all been so sudden and bewildering. And though she didn't want to think about it all, it kept on coming back to her.

Perhaps it's better to be so, she reflected, for now that she was alone and had come so far away, now that she was soon going to reach her journey's end, she was becoming

Fahimm Inhonvi

conscious of a need to disentangle her thoughts and feelings, to get a hold on herself. After all, life had taken a new turn and everything was still so vague and hazy that she had no idea of what she was going to do with herself. All she could feel with certainty was that dark clouds were hovering above her and she was under their shadow.

Five

That morning three weeks ago, she had awakened a little late. The night before Faisal had asked Amna to come along with him. He usually came home from the hotel around eight, while Tahmina returned early from the boutique. They would then have dinner sometime around nine and afterwards they would either sit together for a while or go out for a drive. But that evening Faisal had come home from the hotel an hour too soon. Tahmina was having a bath when he came in and by the time she was out, he had left with Amna to go somewhere.

The maid had told her he was in a great hurry; he hadn't even sat down to have tea. He had just mumbled they were going for dinner to someone's house and that Tahmina was not to wait for them for supper. Tahmina had wondered a little, for it was so odd of them to go off so suddenly, but she had become busy chatting on the phone with her friends and then sat down in the living room to watch TV.

One of the Indian channels had been airing a programme featuring romantic songs from Hindi movies and she had become engrossed in them. She had always loved these songs full of love and longing.

The programme had finished at nine, and, feeling hungry, she had sat down to have supper while the maid had kept her occupied with her silly banter. Going to her room after that, she had said her prayer for the night; that was something she rarely missed, for though she had never cared about any rituals, she had become used to saying her prayers before she went to bed. She had never been passionate or fervent though, and the only time she had prayed with any intensity was when Kashif, her brother, was leaving for USA. She had asked God to keep him safe and happy. How sad she had been to see him go and the house had seemed empty without him for so many weeks.

Later, lying down for the night, she had begun reading a new book she had come across, getting so engrossed in it that the midnight gongs of the watch in the living room had startled her. Were they back? But no, she would have noticed the doorbell. She had wondered where they had gone. She remained restless even after switching off the lamp.. There was nothing to worry about, of course, but a feeling of uneasiness had persisted….. She had been unable to sleep till she had, at last, heard the bell ring and listened to their voices in the dark.

Her first thought in the morning had been to go and ask where they had been so late last night. Glancing at the watch and noticing she was late and that Faisal would be waiting for her at breakfast, she had hurried out of bed.

A little while later, as soon as she had stepped out of her room, a feeling of foreboding had come to her…An unfamiliar silence pervaded the house. She had hurried towards the dining room, but there was nothing. As usual, Faisal was waiting for her, looking down at the newspaper spread out on the table. Relieved, she had greeted him.

His voice had sounded hoarse as he replied to her, without looking up from the newspaper, and once again she had that feeling of uneasiness.

"Where's Ammi?" she had asked, turning sideways to look towards the kitchen.

"She's still sleeping, don't wake her, she's not feeling

The Shadow of the Clouds

well," he had said rather hurriedly. Sitting down on the chair beside him, she had asked, "What's the matter Abbu, your voice seems strange and where had you gone off to last night?"

"Why have you woken up so late today?" he had asked in return, still pretending to be absorbed in the newspaper.

"I kept awake last night waiting for you two to return. Where had you gone? And what's the matter with Ammi?"

"We had gone to someone's place for dinner. Now, please, ask Nazima to bring the breakfast and..." He had paused and lifting his eyes, had looked at her. It was only now that she was able to understand the desperation of love she had seen in his eyes at that time. "Get ready, quickly, we have to go somewhere."

"Where? What's going on, Abbu? Where do we have to go so early in the morning? Tell me, please, is something wrong with Ammi?" She had become seriously worried by then. "I'll go and see....." She had started to get up.

"No, Tahmina." He had held her by the hand. "Don't disturb her. There's nothing wrong or serious, it's just that we were very late last night and she is feeling tired. You just finish breakfast and get ready to come with me. I will explain on the way." He had said, trying to smile reassuringly at her.

She had fallen silent, feeling sullen and upset, certain that something unusual or untoward had taken place. Faisal was disturbed, she could see that plain and simple. How could he imagine he would be able to hide anything from me, she had wondered. Gulping down her tea, she had gone straight to her room, hesitating a moment before her mother's door. But she had stopped herself, for she had never disobeyed Faisal.

Once in her room, she dressed quickly. Then she went down to the kitchen to ask the maid to be careful about Amna.

She had found Faisal waiting for her in the hall, leaning against the wall near the window, watching the road. Turning at the sound of her steps, he had smiled at her wanly.

They had ridden the elevator in silence and walked out towards the car. Fastening her seat-belt, she had asked him, "Where are we going, Abbu?" It had become difficult to hold herself back any longer.

"Nowhere in particular; we'll just go near the sea and talk. I want to tell you something..."

"What, Abbu? Why all this suspense, what is it, please? Tell me....Give me a hint at least," She had gone on imploring while he had continued to drive silently till they had reached the road along the sea and he had parked the car in his favourite spot, facing the shimmering waters of the Arabian Sea.

"Well, now, Abbu...."

But he still remained silent, sitting and gazing at the sea, smoking his Marlboros.

"All right, take your time," she had said exasperatedly. And he had turned then to look at her. His face so ravaged with pain had almost made her hysterical.

"What is it, Abbu, please, please, tell me . . ."

And he had told her. He had told her so simply and so starkly that she was not his daughter at all, that her father was someone else, someone who had died five days ago.

Six

She didn't know how long she had sat there, listening to him, silent and forlorn, too stunned to say or feel anything.

She had sat with his hand in hers, staring at the sea, its water shimmering in the stark sunlight. And then the shimmering had been in her eyes and she had wept, quietly at first, barely conscious of the warm tears that flowed down her cheeks, wetting her lips and trickling down her neck. And then she had lost all restraint and sobbed and raved like a child while he had put his arms around her, whispering. And then she had become wild and delirious, jerking away his arm, pulling away from him so violently that she had crashed into the side of the car. He had tried to hold her again, but she had pushed him away.

"Don't touch me, leave me alone, for God's sake!" she had cried. "Leave me alone, go away!" And she had hid her face in her hands, her sobs racking her body, tormenting yet consoling her. She didn't know how long she had wept, stopping only when she had spent all her tears. She had felt her eyes aching and her whole being blazing with a fire in which everything in her had turned to ashes and she had asked him then, asked the silent, suffering, forsaken man who was sitting next to her. She had felt how desperately he wanted to touch her, to console and comfort her, to do something that would make him sure that she belonged to him. But it was as if all the tenderness had gone away from her; all she had for him were questions, stark, bare, simple questions:

"Who was he? Where had he lived? How did he die?....."

She had wanted to know every little thing about him and Faisal had answered her every question, as simply and honestly as she asked them. Except for the wretched question of why her mother had left her father, why had he let her go away? But he wouldn't answer her that. Perhaps he really didn't know, but it was more likely he didn't think it proper to tell her.

"I don't know." That was all he had said.

"Didn't you ask Ammi?"

"No. What's the use of rummaging through the ashes when a house has burnt down?"

Yes, she had thought, you are right, Abbu, what could one hope to find in a house that has burnt down. But if that were your house, you would want to know what fire destroyed it.

"Was he very hard up, Abbu?"

"I think so. I offered to help him out financially once but he refused. Said he didn't have any need for money any longer."

"Did you...Did you know him well?"

"I met him only once. That was after my marriage to Amna. In fact, he had been the one to invite me to come over to Nainital. He wanted to talk with me about you...I assured him that I would love you as my own daughter and never let you feel any difference. I have done so, haven't I?" He had asked, looking at her. "That was when we had decided to keep you in the dark about all this. Both of us were afraid the truth

The Shadow of the Clouds

might hurt you, particularly when you still had to grow up. But he did request me to keep him posted about you, about how you were growing up and I continued to do that."

"How was he then...I mean, how was he when you went to meet him?"

"Oh well, he seemed a man at peace with himself, very soft-spoken and gentle. I had gone to meet him at the shop but he asked me to come over to his house. It was there, at the house, that I could not help feeling sad that things hadn't worked out between Amna and him, because, though he tried to hide it, I could feel the sense of utter loneliness that pervaded that house......."

"He didn't marry a second time, did he?"

"No. He wanted to live alone."

"And Kashif, Abbu...?" she had asked.

"His mother died when he was just two. She was my first wife, Rahila. My mother was alive then and she used to look after him. Then, by chance, someone told her about Amna, who had been divorced recently and so my mother approached her parents and they agreed. That's how we were married. Kashif was too young to comprehend or remember anything but a few years ago, I told him the truth about you. It hasn't mattered, has it?"

They had started for home around one in the afternoon and on the way she had asked him, "You have told Ammi, haven't you?"

"Yes, we discussed last night whether to tell you or not. It was so difficult to decide because we knew it was going to hurt you but......" His voice had trailed off.

"Can I talk with her about......About all this?"

He had slowed down the car to look at her.

"You want to do that, Tahmina? All right, but please wait, please don't disturb her just now...You realise what she must be going through right now..."

" Yes," she had replied quietly.

"You know it took her a long time to forget, and, suddenly, everything's come back. She was so heartbroken when we married and now......Please, darling, you must be sensible, though I can understand what's going through you."

"Don't worry, Abbu. I won't hurt her," she had promised.

But she had hurt her all the same.

Going straight to Amna's room, she had found her sitting on the sofa, her eyes red from weeping. She had gone near her, silently resting her head on her shoulders and started to weep again. Amna had stroked her hair and comforted her.

"Why didn't you tell me before, Ammi?" Tahmina had asked finally, her voice so hoarse that she could barely speak. "Why did you two leave each other? Tell me. And why did you let him live alone, so poor and troubled....You could have told me earlier; I would have gone and looked after him. I would not have let him die like that, so ill and alone....My poor father, you could have at least told me when he was so ill. How unfortunate I am, never to have seen him, never to have touched him, or even heard his voice! Tell me, Ammi, tell me why? Why did he leave us? What happened? Didn't he love you, Ammi?"

And Amna had replied, at last, her voice so low and soft

The Shadow of the Clouds

that Tahmina had barely been able to hear her. It was as if she had been speaking from some place very deep in her heart.

"Yes, he loved me, he loved me so much...."

And after that she had not spoken another word. Tahmina had grasped her shoulders, shaken her as wildly as she could, but Amna had not said a word more, she had not even shed a tear. She had just sat there, her empty eyes staring somewhere far away, lost in her grief and her memories.

Seven

Tahmina had remained in her mother's room till midnight, praying for her father's soul. Amna had gone to sleep sometime around seven, soon after Faisal had given her a sedative. He had asked Tahmina to have one too, but she had refused. "What for, Abbu?" she had said. "Nothing would change if I went to sleep, would it?" But she had let him persuade her to drink a few glasses of orange juice, for she hadn't eaten anything since morning.

Later on, unable to sit up any longer, she had leaned against the bed and closed her eyes while everything that Faisal had told her about her father had gone on repeating itself in her mind like a pattern on a cloth. What agonised her most was the realisation that her father had a very hard and lonely life when all through these years she had been living in such comfort and happiness. Also, her father had been ill for so long, with no one except strangers to care for him. And though Faisal had told her, had explained with such desperation to her why it had to be so, she had still been unable to quell the feeling of resentment welling up in her against her mother....No compulsion, no grudge or any sense of propriety could mitigate the sheer neglect of a man who was, after all, the father of her daughter....

How could she have been so cruel and indifferent about someone who had once been her husband, who had, as she had confessed, loved her! Even if she hated him, as she must have, even if she had not wanted his name to touch her lips, even if she abhorred books just because perhaps he loved them and made a living out of them, even then she should have done something for him…..Oh, yes! No bitterness or rancour could justify her apathy towards him. And even if, as Faisal had told her, even if he himself had asked to be left alone, forsaken and forgotten, Amna could have cared and found some way. And then the way she and Faisal had kept her in the dark, never telling her that her father, her real father, was alive, living in the same world as she was!

She had remonstrated so vehemently to Faisal for this, but he had expressed his helplessness, saying he had promised her father never to let her know about him, not till he was dead and gone. But…..But this would have been right if he had been among loved ones, happy and in good health, not when he was alone and ill and poor….

She had wakened from her thoughts by the touch of Faisal's hand. "You're awake?" he had asked her.

He was sitting on the rug beside her. "Come on, get up and lie on the bed. I'll bring something to eat for you," he had said, taking hold of her arm.

"It's all right, Abbu. I'm comfortable here." She had glanced at the watch. "It's so late. Why haven't you gone to sleep?"

"How can I sleep when my Tahmina is awake?" he had murmured. "But you must have something to eat and take that sedative I gave to Amna."

"No, Abbu, I'm not feeling hungry. And don't worry, I'll go to sleep without the sedative."

"As you wish," he had replied, "but come to your room. I have something to give you."

The Shadow of the Clouds

So she had gone to her room with him and he had given her that letter-the letter she had read so many times since that night and kept it with her all the time. Even now it was tucked away in her dress, near her heart, her father's first and last and only letter to her.

"This letter is from your father, for you," he had said softly, handing her a plain envelope. "He wrote it a few days before he died and Mr. Pandey was kind enough to courier it to me... He used to work for your father at the bookshop," he had explained. "He was more of a friend than an employee and looked after him during his illness."

She had not been able to open that envelope for a long time. She had simply sat there on the bed, her head tilted on Faisal's shoulder, with the envelope clutched in her hands while her eyes had turned moist again.

It was only later, when Faisal had left her alone, that she had found the courage to tear it open.

Eight

My dear, lovely Tahmina,

I don't know how to begin, there's so much to say. But then, everything in life is difficult before it turns easy, so I'll just go on penning everything that comes to mind.

You must be feeling perplexed and angry with me and there will be so many questions that would be troubling you. But no, let me first of all tell you how lovely you are, as beautiful as the flowers that bloom by the lake here.

You won't know perhaps but I had asked Faisal to keep on sending me your photographs every year so I could see how my daughter was growing up. It's one of the many things for which I am grateful to him. He loves you as much as I do, perhaps even more, and he has brought you up far better than I could ever have. So you must always keep in mind that you belong more to him than to me.

Anyway, you'll naturally be wondering why, after having hidden myself all these years, I am intruding into your life now? What difference would it make if I went away as I have lived, a stranger to my own daughter. So many times has my heart put this question to me and assailed me with doubts. Wouldn't it be better to leave her alone, happy and contented as she is? Why throw stones to churn the waters and shatter her peace? After all, what do I have to give you except pain and sorrow. Yes, my heart has asked me all this and I confess I have not been able to find any clear answer. Except that you had to be told one day. It would be too dishonest if this truth were kept away from you. And then, there is also the fact that if I go away without calling you mine even once, my spirit would roam the streets like a madman.

It's now more than nineteen winters since you went away from me. And though I have tried not to remember you too often, your thoughts kept on coming into my life just like the sunlight that streams into my room through the window every morning. And all the while I kept lingering on, waiting for the moment when I could call you my own. Yes, that's what has kept me alive so long, to see you happily grown up, to pray for you and wait till the time had come when I could tell you all this without causing any irreparable harm to you. I didn't want to spoil even one moment of your childhood, for it never does any good if some shadow falls on the days when we are growing up; it can darken our lives forever.

I know that you'll suffer even now, a suffering still much beyond your years, and I am sorry to have hurt you, particularly when I have not been able to give you any happiness. But I console myself with the thought that all of this would, perhaps, make you strong and different too.

I don't know why life robbed me of the happiness to rear my own daughter, but it was certainly not because I didn't want to be responsible for you, or that I didn't want to touch you and hold you in my arms or watch you laugh and cry.

I lost you, perhaps, because I always prayed for you to have a happy and contented childhood. You can never know what it is to grow up in a house that is blighted by unhappiness and despair. And I would also certainly not have wanted you to grow up poor and I was as poor as a church mouse at the time you were born.

The Shadow of the Clouds

There's a saying that it's better to be fortunate than to be wise. I was neither. I was always lost in my thoughts and my books, in the lake and the mountains here. I have found solace and friendship in these things and something of wisdom too. But it's a wisdom that has lost its use in this world, or, perhaps, I was unable to make any proper use of it……..

I was unable to earn money or to deal with the inexorabilities of this world. I was unable to change myself, or to fit my sail to every wind. Naturally something must have been lacking in me and my life has been full of mistakes. But I have still to understand why all this happened.

I go over my whole life, I have turned its every page, but I am still unable to fathom or understand life's judgement on me. I liked and desired all that was good, simple and beautiful in life and yet only bad things came my way. I was never able to make friends easily but my heart would go out to anyone who was hurt or alone. I wanted to succeed and bring joy and prosperity to my family and the people who worked for me but I lost even that which I had, including my daughter.

More painful than everything else was the fact that because I mistook what people really thought or expected, I was always being misunderstood by others, even by those for whom I had only love in my heart. Things would have been different perhaps if I had been different. But it was not to be, for we are as God has made us. So I hold no grudge against life and I wouldn't like you to feel any such thing either. In the end, it's enough for me to know that you and Amna have a good man to look after you, that you have a beautiful home and a secure life. What does it matter if these things have not come to you from my hands?

Anyway, you must be wondering by now that if you and

Fahimm Inhonvi

Amna were so dear to me, why did I let you go away then? But human beings are full of contradictions, more mysterious than the stars that glimmer in the sky. People do not understand this, they do not even know what is in their own hearts and yet they in judgement upon others. The truth is, in real life everything gets mixed up and sometimes we are guilty of doing things we would never dream of.

We loved each other, your Ammi and I, but what separated us was something outside of us, more strong and forceful than our love. And even if there has to be an apportioning of blame, let it come to me. And I'm not saying this out of any false magnanimity; I made a lot of mistakes and hurt her in more ways than you can imagine. I think that's part of being human too, that you sometimes hurt people you love most of all. I only hope she has forgiven and forgotten all that by now.

We were so young then, when we married, and she was lovely and comforting. She had filled my home with her grace and beauty and was like a candle in the darkness of my heart. We would have found much happiness with each other if we had been left alone to create our own world, or if things had not gone as awry with me as they did.

We lived together for eight years and our early days were full of love and friendship. And the roses that blossomed in her then, their fragrance continues to linger in my life even today. But in the end, only silence was left between us. I think it happened because we were different from each other too: she was as brimful of smiles and sunshine as I was full of shadows and if she was a rose without thorns, I was as tangled as a root. Perhaps, that's why God decided to take us away from each other.

The Shadow of the Clouds

So don't burden your heart by thinking too much about us and do not search for answers, for there is not an answer to every question. It's enough for you to know that we wouldn't have been able to keep happy with each other and if you can't be happy yourself, how can you create happiness for others? It's not too hard if one of your parents goes away from your life, but it's terrible if they are both there but unhappy with each other. Their silence and their voices, their bitterness and coldness seeps into the young lives of children. No, it was better for her to live away from me.

But what does anything matter now? You have grown up so happily and I am sure your life will be like this forever. Even Amna has found someone to love and care for her and it won't be difficult for me to say goodbye to life now. The only thing that's left is for you to forgive me.

But yes, before I say a last farewell, there is something I would like to ask you.

Can you come here to Nainital? I'll be happy if you do. (There's no hurry; you can come whenever you like.) But remember, it would give my soul peace to see you here one day. I want you to come here to see the place you were born in and stay for a few days in the same house where you opened your eyes for the first time (it has been full of memories of the little time you spent here.).

I would also like you to see how it is to live here, to see everything that I loved, the lake and the flowers that grow along its edge, and the trees that seem to remind us of life and its loneliness. I would like you to climb the mountains with their meandering, difficult paths and to see the beauty of this place that is tucked away in the hills.

I would also like you to come and see the shop here that

my father left me, and which now I am leaving to you. Do what you like with it. Once, very long ago, it was full of books and people and we used to be hard pressed for some respite from the work it gave us. I am sorry to be leaving it almost empty and desolate for you. I hope you'll forgive me for this too.

My dear Tahmina, I don't know how to tell you how much I have loved you. And don't think that I didn't love Amna too. If only I could go back to those days again, to live my life once more so that she would be here with me once more....But, please, don't bring her here again, for it's better to forget. Do not even talk to her about me.

But you must come here and when you do, you'll find that everything here will speak to you. Yes, everything will speak to you about me, about you, about life and its myriad joys and sorrows. And I am sure you'll discover something new in yourself and find the happiness that's hidden here.

Finally, let me confess that a sense of irreparable failure haunts me and I feel ashamed at not being able to leave anything of value or foundation for you, something that would have made you grateful and proud of me. All I have are a few things to say to you. Perhaps they'll be of some help to you in some way.

So listen, never feel afraid of life, let your thoughts roam free and don't give up your dreams easily.

Never make the mistake of believing we love anything because it is good or beautiful. Things and people are good and beautiful if we love them.

Be generous to others and keep reminding yourself that

The Shadow of the Clouds

there is luck in sharing.

Don't ever forget that there are always things we don't know. Things we do not understand. There is always some hidden truth behind everything that happens to us. So do not blame people, do not judge them; instead, try to help them.

And remember, not everything bad that happens to us is deserved, and every little bit of happiness is only a gift.

And yes, if your own heart asks something of you, don't refuse. We are always punished by our refusals. If ever you do not know what to do, then listen to your heart and let it take you anywhere it wants to. Put your trust in God and follow your dreams.

Last of all, remember, sorrow always comes unsent for. Do not fear or grudge its lodging in your heart for it is a friend, while happiness is nothing but a shadow of the clouds that fly away.

And before I end let me tell you God always finds some way of giving back to us whatever life may have taken away. For me, it would be your happiness.

With all the love of my heart I now say goodbye to you. May God bless you and keep you in His refuge.

Your father,
Imad Ahmad.

Note: I must tell you about Mr. Pandey. He has been with us since my father's time and has stuck with me through thick and thin. It's he and his family that have looked after me during my illness. I am going to leave everything in his charge and when you come here, he'll look after you and help you. There would have been nothing to worry about even if he wasn't here, because Nainital is as safe as a church.

Nine

She had made her promise to him right away, promised him in her heart not once but a thousand times, "Yes, I'll come! I would have come even if you hadn't called. I would have come anywhere for you!"

Later that night, when Faisal had returned to sit near her on the bed, she had closed her eyes, pretending to be asleep. And so he had left after a while, switching off the lights as he went. She had waited for some time before putting on the lamp to read the letter once more, lingering at each word. And afterwards, she had pressed her face into the pillow and wept again, softly and secretly, easing her sorrow before giving herself away to sleep in the hushed and comforting light of the lamp.

Waking up in the morning, she had guessed by the light outside her window that it was still very early. She had noticed that someone had switched off the lamp during the night and her fingers had instinctively fumbled for the letter she had put under the pillow. Yes, it was there. But she hadn't opened it again; instead, she had continued to lie in bed, mulling over everything again.

What was she going to do now? She had wondered. Yes, she was going to Nainital, that was decided, but....It was then that the first doubt had raised its head in her heart. Not a doubt really, it was more of a vague foreboding, a faint voice telling her not to go, for nothing good would come of it. She had felt a little afraid then and her resolution had wavered a little. But then she had argued with herself and driven the fear away.

She had also wondered how her life was going to change after all this. Perhaps nothing would happen; she would simply go there and return home after a few days and life would go on as before. But no, the real change would come, had already started coming, inside her, in the places that were hidden and vulnerable. She could even feel the difference in the way she was relating to Faisal and Amna, with their presence in her heart giving way to the imperceptible presence of her dead father.

Yes, she had felt irresistibly drawn to him, trying to form a picture of him, yearning to go wherever she could find some trace of him. And then there had been that nagging question, the strange, compelling urge to learn what had happened between her parents, to find out why she had to grow up thinking she was someone else's daughter. This question would perhaps never leave her heart until she learned the truth...

Yes, I have to go, she had thought, because no one here was going to tell her all the truth. Amna was the only person who could do so, but she didn't expect her to tell anything real. Perhaps, I would be able to come to know more in Nainital and that was why I want to go there so much, she had thought.

But hadn't her father asked her not to come in search of any answers, she had recalled the words in his letter. Why had he said so? Was there something he wanted to conceal from her? If so, would it be right for her to go in search of that? And so she had thought and thought but there had been no denying the compelling urge to go ....

The Shadow of the Clouds

But how was Faisal going to take it? That was the thing that had troubled her. He loved her so truly, as if she were his own daughter, she had realised with bewildered gratitude, and yet now she was going to hurt him. But I'll try to mask my feelings as much as I can, she had resolved. I won't let him see how desperate I am to go there to see my father's house and his things, his clothes that must still be there and some photographs too. That was something she wanted to see most, for she had tried to imagine how he must have looked....

Yes, she would not let Faisal see how her heart longed for someone who had gone away forever, without even letting her see him even once. Whether it was wrong or right, but the truth was that, however impossible it was now, she still longed to give her dead father the happiness of loving his own daughter, of playing with her and taking her to school and telling her stories and buying presents for her. She would have liked to see him laugh at her tantrums and chide her when she was stubborn and then wipe her tears. She would have liked to put on airs with him, to comfort him when he was sad.

How strange life is, she had thought sadly, and stranger were the ways of the heart; here was a man she had known and loved all her life, who, in a sense, had been the only man in her life; she had never felt the need to hide anything from him and would never have dreamt of giving his place in her heart to someone else. But then, what could she do, her heart was a heart like any other, fickle and capricious, and though her love for Faisal had not become less in its measure, it had nevertheless changed.

It had been difficult for her to comprehend the change but she had understood that from now on there would be some artificiality between them and she would have to take as great care not to hurt him as she took of the stained glass lamp on the table beside her bed. Yes, however much they would try but the fact that he was not her real father would henceforth always ring a false and incongruous note between them. And that would be a loss to her, a loss of something real and tangible for the sake of a love foregone and never really known.

Ten

Her feelings for her mother had been more troubling, muddled as they were by all sorts of conjectures and doubts that were riling her heart. One moment she would impulsively want to reach out to her out of a shared sorrow. But then, just as suddenly, a feeling of incoherent anger and resentment would well up in her with such intensity that she could barely stop from clutching her shoulders and shouting at her....

She had realised, of course, that she had no right to sit in judgement over her mother but it had still been impossible to absolve Amna of any guilt. She had remembered reading somewhere how men felt more insecure and lonelier than women, of how they created more complications, but if there was a woman to love them, then she could so easily simplify things for them. So, whatever the difficulty between them, Amna could have found a way, as women can always do. But perhaps I am being cruel, she had thought, perhaps she had tried and failed....And so she had continued going from this end to the other, sometimes kind and sometimes cruel towards the woman her father had loved and lost.

She had also wondered whether she would have felt the same love for her father if he had re-married and had other children. Yes, perhaps her feelings for him would have been different then though she would still have loved him.

But the real thing was that he had chosen his own difficult path and tried to live with his memories, however difficult that may have been, and for this alone he deserved all the love her heart could find for him.

"Did you sleep well?" Faisal's voice had broken into her thoughts. He had been leaning against the door. She had looked up towards him, hurriedly adjusting her dupatta. "I came to your room in the night but you were asleep. How are you feeling now?" He had come to sit beside her.

"I'm all right, Abbu, don't worry, I'll get over it. I have you, haven't I?" She had put her head affectionately against his shoulders and they had sat in silence for a while.

"How's Ammi?," she had asked after a while.

"She'll be okay," he had replied softly, "But we'll have to be careful. You remember, don't you, what I asked you yesterday. Try not to talk to her about old things."

"Yes, I understand, Abbu. Don't worry."

"And you too, don't think too much about it. It's all in the past and there's no use making yourself unhappy about it."

"I won't, but there's...." She had stopped in hesitation.

"What is it? Tell me," he had said.

"Abbu," she had somehow found the courage. "Abbu, I want to go to Nainital..." Her voice had wavered. "I want to go there....Just to see his house...You know, he asked me to do so in his letter..."

"I see." That was all he had said and then added after a pause. "What else did he write to you....I can ask, can't I?"

"Yes, why not. Nothing's separate between us." She had said in an effort to make amends. "He's written about himself and Ammi, and about you, too. And he has asked me to come

The Shadow of the Clouds

to Nainital, to see the house I was born in and take possession of his shop. He has also asked me to forgive him," she had replied softly, barely able to stop her tears from welling up again.

"All right, I'll take care of that. I'll take you there myself," he had replied, holding her hand in his. "But could you wait till Amna's recovered a bit?"

"Abbu....I would like to go there alone," she had blurted it out and only afterwards realised that they were possibly the most difficult words she had ever spoken in her life. She had looked up at him, trying to see if the hurt showed in his eyes.

But he had averted his face and gazed silently through the window while she waited, thinking that yes, I have gone and hurt him badly. But even at that moment she had felt the stubborn resolution of her heart. She had waited and waited and finally, unable to contain herself any longer, she had asked him, "Have I said anything wrong, Abbu?"

He had turned towards her then, shaking his head, and looking at her with eyes that she was suddenly unable to read. Confused and afraid, she had looked imploringly at him.

"How can you go alone? It's so far away....I mean, how can I send you alone?"

She had felt such a relief that he had not asked why she wanted to go alone, because she wouldn't have been able to explain that to him. There were no words in her to spell that out. Perhaps he understood, or perhaps he didn't, but there was nothing she could have done about it.

"What's there to worry about, Abbu? I can take care of myself, can't I?," she had said. "And then Mr. Pandey will be there and I'll be staying only for a week or so," she had mumbled, but it had been difficult to convince him. In the end, she had put her arms around his neck, as much to cajole as to console him, and had compelled him, like always, to yield to her request.

So, finally, he had asked her to wait a few days for Amna's sake and, in the meantime, he would make arrangements for her journey. Two days later, he had told her that her plane seat was booked. She would be landing at Delhi where her uncle, his brother, would receive her and put her on the night train to Nainital. He had even phoned Mr. Pandey to inform him she was coming over, asking him to look after her. She was to leave a week later.

After that they had not talked about the subject even once, though Faisal had spent most of his time at home. And though he took them for a drive every night, he had not visited that favourite place of his near the sea again where he had taken her on that morning to tell her the bitter truth that he was not her real father.

Eleven

Since that night, Amna too had remained sad and pensive, and even Faisal, whose presence always lighted her up like a smile, wasn't able to make any difference to the way she had shut herself off from the world. However, her concern for Tahmina had been evident by the way she would make her sit close to her and then keep running her fingers through her hair. And though they had talked little, the silence between them had not been a silence at all.

It had been so difficult for Tahmina to still the many questions that came to her lips; they were searing her heart but remembering her promise not to ask Amna anything, she had sewn her lips and God had given her the patience. But one afternoon, when Tahmina had come to sit beside her on the bed, Amna herself had asked, "What did he write to you?"

Tahmina had been so surprised that for a moment she didn't know what to say. Misconstruing her silence, Amna had added. "I just wanted to ask if he had written something about us, I mean, about me and him?"

"Yes, Ammi, But....He wrote so little and he asked me not to think too much about it."

"Yes. But you must be wondering what happened between your father and me, isn't it? And, in a way, you do have a right to know about it but.....But it's all so difficult to tell....Did he ask you to visit Nainital?" she had asked abruptly.

"Yes," Tahmina had replied, her heart thudding against her chest.

"And you are going?" she had asked in that sudden, strange, cold manner that came over her sometimes.

"Yes, I was thinking of asking you," she had mumbled, somewhat disconcerted.

"You can go if you like, but don't be too charmed by the place," Amna had said in the same hard way.

"It's a very beautiful place, isn't it?" Tahmina had asked with interest.

"I don't know, and I don't want to remember. I wasn't happy there, you know that."

"What happened, Ammi?" she had asked nevertheless.

"It's not a happy story and I don't want to repeat or remember it. Even otherwise, you won't be able to understand," Amna had replied without any trace of feeling in her voice.

"How can you say that?" Tahmina had asked sharply, all her resolutions and promises breaking down. She had suddenly felt so angry with her mother then.

"No, you can't, because you don't know what it's like to be trapped in a cage. That's what it was, that house, with his mother hanging like a curse upon us. It was all her fault! Yes, what a woman she was! God knows what drove her to be like that but her mind was a dark maze, and she hated both of us." Tahmina had been startled by the vehemence in Amna's voice, by the gathering storm in her eyes...

The Shadow of the Clouds

"You can never imagine what sort of a person she was and the strange sort of relationship they had.....I have never seen a mother that loved her son so little. And because she hated him, she hated me too..."

"But what did she do?"

"She made life miserable for me the moment I stepped into that house. There were so many petty rules and regulations! I needed her permission for even such small things as what dress I should wear, or what time I could go to my room. Even that would have been tolerable, but what she wanted me to do was to be a slave to her, even wanting me not to like people whom she disliked. And because I refused to be involved in the petty disputes she was always having with the servants and in her other sordid games, she made me pay with small cruelties. She was an uneducated, uncultured woman who had a stone for a heart and I had my self-respect too ....It was only for your father's sake that I suffered all that for so many years...."

Tahmina had just sat there, too appalled to utter a word, while Amna had continued, her voice trembling with repressed rage. "You can never understand how she was, cursing and making snide remarks and it was really amazing the way she turned white to black and pink to purple! And though she would often help others, she never did so without hurting them with her words at the same time. If anything bad or unfortunate happened to anyone, she would say it was nothing but a retribution for their sins. That's what she used to say for your father too when he was in trouble...."Her voice had become so hoarse that she was almost rasping the words out, but she hadn't stopped for a moment; it was as if a storm had broken in her and there was a wildness in her eyes and face that Tahmina had never ever seen before in anyone.

"Please, Ammi, stop it!" Tahmina had not been able to bear it any longer. "Forget all that."

"No! Let me say it! Let me tell you all the things that happened to me in that house." She had become almost hysterical by then and there was no stopping her. "She always believed the worst of everyone and was so suspicious and petty, sowing discord between her children and how she used to taunt him and blame him for everything that went wrong with him. She would say such terrible things sometimes like, 'You have destroyed the shop your father left you', or 'Go and kick your father's grave'. That is what hurt him the most, for he really loved his father and that bookshop of his."

"But.....But why was she so cruel to him?" Tahmina had asked, bewildered.

"She knew or God knew," Amna had replied, somewhat tenderly this time. "All he told me was that she had always been like that towards him, even when he was a small child. He told me that he didn't have a single memory of ever being hugged by her, of ever having raced, as children often do, into the calling arms of his mother. He used to long for her love as a child, more so as he used to feel so troubled and afraid, but she never cared to visit the house of his heart to see how dark and unkempt it was. If she had done so, then perhaps she would have tidied things up and put on the lights for him. But she never did that. Instead, she used to keep on repeating that he wouldn't be able to do a thing in this world and those words of hers followed him like a malediction all his life. 'Can you realise what a house is without a woman,' he had whispered to me on our wedding night. 'That is how my heart has been for so many long years.' He waited till the end to hear one word of comfort from her, but it never came... Yes, she hurt him terribly, even more than before because she saw how he

The Shadow of the Clouds

loved me. And he couldn't do anything because, after all, she was his mother. Oh, God! How she tormented us. Those wounds will always fester and go with me to my grave."

And the tears had flowed from her eyes like rain and Tahmina had rushed to get a glass of water, her hands shaking like a leaf in a storm. Forgetting everything for the moment, she had tried to comfort Amna, had hugged and kissed her, mingling her tears with hers, till at last she had calmed down and her voice had become as soft and tender as the whispers of a bride.

"You know, I had come to care for him so much, but life in that house had turned me so bitter and I used to take it out on him. I know that was wrong of me, for he was always trying to console me and make amends for his mother's behaviour. I never meant to hurt him. All I wanted was to change him, to make him find some way for us to escape from that house, but he couldn't do anything. He was so broken and crippled inside and wayward too. Besides he was so dreamy, almost like a poet, and had no sense of how the real world worked. He kept being lost in those books of his. And he was so obstinate too, never listening to me and there was no way for me to do anything practical, for I had to wear the veil all the time because his father was so strict about that. I couldn't step out of the house without being covered from head to toe. Oh, how I hated it! You know, he took me to so many out-of-the-way places, places where we wouldn't run the risk of meeting someone who knew us, so that I could put away those black folds of the veil and wander about with him freely, but we would still feel like thieves. But he couldn't do anything more than that, because he loved his father so much and there was no question of defying him."

"But then…..But then why did you leave him alone like

that?" Tahmina hadn't been able to stop herself from asking that and Amna had turned vehement once more.

"Don't ask me that! I asked him so many times to take me away somewhere far away, somewhere we could forget everything except our love for each other, but he was caught in a trap, dependent on his father and working away at that damned bookstore of his. All I wanted was to have a house of my own, to be able to go out now and then and to live with him in peace. That's all I wished for and so many times I asked him to put away his books, to do something practical, but he wouldn't listen to me. Hadn't I put away my desires for his sake? My eyes had shed their dreams like leaves because of him and yet he wouldn't do a thing for me…. And then when his father died, I thought, perhaps, now we would be able to do whatever we wanted with our lives, but things only turned worse for us……."

"What happened, Ammi?"

"That was such a bad time for us. As soon as the old man was in his grave, his mother insisted on a settlement between everyone in the family and that was when I put my foot down. I told them I would only agree if his mother left to live with his brother and we got to keep the house. It was all so sordid and painful but, finally, she agreed and a major portion of the shop was sold off to pay for their share and we had to give up all the cash savings. But nothing bothered us because, at last, we would be going to have a house of our own. We were sorry though for all the bitterness…But it was entirely that woman's fault; nothing gave her more pleasure than to create bad blood between her own children. Your father loved them so much but no one ever cared to help him out."

"But what did all that matter, you had everything of your own by then, didn't you?"

"Yes, I thought so too. I still remember how happy we were when we had the house for ourselves but as fate would have it, very little of happiness was left to us."

"Why? What happened, Ammi?"

"I don't know, perhaps it was all due to the fact that we had so little money. He used to keep so worried, trying to make ends meet, trying to keep on all the people who had worked for the shop, trying to keep it all going somehow. I even had to sell my jewellery to help things out. But he kept ignoring my warnings, never stopping to listen when I told him to close the book business once and for all, to start something new, until there was nothing left to us. And it was just then that I became pregnant with you.....You know, I hadn't been able to conceive all those years and it was something of a blessing that you came along and I thought God would change things for your sake....."

"Didn't he feel happy?"

"He did but not as much as when you were actually born...Both of us were so happy and for a while we forgot everything in the joy you brought. But things only went from bad to worse and all those difficulties made us so depressed and irritable and we became sort of weary. He started to keep cold and distant and would lie and stare at the ceiling in silence and wouldn't tell me anything. I think it was the failure of his bookshop that broke his heart finally and the way he was misunderstood and hurt by his family. I would have done anything to make him happy again but I felt so alone and despondent too. I did try to tell him sometimes that this was no way to face life, that God would find some way for us, that, together, we would make the best of things. But he wouldn't listen to anything. It was as if he believed that everything had been carved in stone for him." She had stopped to catch her breath.

"I can't tell you how lonely I used to feel then, and, perhaps, he felt even lonelier. No one can understand how much we needed to love each other but all we did was to hurt each other and somehow we started to move away from one another. I guess I was to blame too, for I was never able to fully understand what went on inside him, or what he searched for in me.....In the end he just changed into a stranger, almost cruel and indifferent....I can't tell you how I lived through those days, being alone all day and then having to live with his silence through the night. I don't know what would have happened, perhaps I would have gone mad if I didn't have you to love and care for, If only....." And the words had dried up in her all of a sudden.

"If only what....?" Tahmina had asked, intrigued.

"Nothing," she had replied flatly, her voice becoming hard and flat once again.

"You are hiding something from me, aren't you?" Tahmina had said, clutching Amna's hand.

"I said nothing, didn't I?" Amna had replied, almost in anger.

"But then what happened to separate you two?"

"I don't know and I don't care now. Perhaps we weren't made for one another and never found what we searched for in each other."

"But you liked him, didn't you, you loved him...."

"I don't really know. In my time girls accepted to like

and love the man they were married to and there was nothing in him that would have made me feel otherwise. All I know is that I suffered so much for his sake. Call that love if you may but perhaps sometimes even love isn't enough of a glue to keep two people together….."

"But I don't understand all this. I mean, there must have been some specific reason for you to leave him?"

"Maybe, maybe, I don't know, it all just happened. I never thought too much about it. It was too unbearable as it was. It was such a shock to learn he was divorcing me, and something inside me died forever in that moment. It was as if everything that had gone before did not exist for me. And then I remarried so quickly and the only way I could live was not to think about all those things."

"Did he stop loving you?" Tahmina had asked finally, going to the heart of the matter.

"No, I can't say that too," she had replied with a faraway look in her eyes.

"Then what did he do?"

"Don't ask me that, now or ever again. Please…" And Tahmina had seen the tears welling up in her eyes again and it was only later, long after her tears had gone dry, that Amna had spoken, stroking her hair once again.

"I'm sorry if I hurt you. I didn't want to tell you all this…I had forgotten it all and now it has all come back. It was all so unfortunate, for in many ways he was so kind and gentle and he loved me so much. I don't know what happened to him afterwards for he was so tender and dreamed such beautiful dreams for me, though he couldn't make them real… And then,

I'm so grateful to him for not taking you away from me. But..."She had paused to look at her and suddenly her face had turned hard once again. "But don't ever talk to me about him again." And turning her face, she had covered her eyes with her arms.

And then, many days later, when she had come to see her off at the airport, she had clung to Tahmina and wept quietly and said, her voice broken by her sobs, "Why did he have to do this, why couldn't he have gone away silently? He was always giving sorrow....."

"Don't say such things, Ammi!" Tahmina had started to protest, but controlling herself, she had continued to hear her mother's whispered ravings in silence. "Don't stay there too long, it's not a nice place, you understand, come back quickly," she had said at last before releasing Tahmina from her embrace.

And Tahmina had promised her too. "I'll come back soon, Ammi," she had said, wiping her tears. "Don't worry, I'll come back soon."

Twelve

Suddenly everything changed.

The mountains were no longer silent. There were people on the road and the bus had come to a stop in front of a small building perched on the very edge of the mountain. The conductor was busy collecting the toll-tax from the passengers and some of the men had started tidying up their luggage while the coolies were at the sides of the bus, shouting for attention and thrusting their small metal tokens through the windows. Watching the others do so, Tahmina accepted a token from one of the coolies too. Most of her luggage was piled up on the roof and she had kept only a handbag and her purse with her.

"Have we arrived?" Tahmina asked the woman sitting across her.

"We'll be there in a few minutes," she replied, smiling at her and Tahmina felt her heartbeats change.

The bus started again. The road had become narrow now, hemmed in on both sides by all sorts of buildings. There were small, bare houses, stacked like boxes on the hillside, shops, eating joints and hotels, most of them appearing cheap and seedy. Climbing the twisting and turning mountain road for a few more minutes, the bus wound up suddenly into the valley set so high up in the mountains.

She felt the lake even before she had a glimpse of it, for the cool breeze had the whiff of water on it. She had a fleeting view of it before the bus turned sideways and stopped behind another one. The coolies were swarming over the bus now and everyone was in a hurry to get down. Stringing the handbag over her shoulders and clutching her purse, she was the last one to step down. The coolie whose token she had accepted was beside her in a jiffy.

"I'm going up, memsahib," he said, pointing towards the roof of the bus. "You tell me which things are yours."

There were people all around her now and she could see the shops across the wide clearing in front. Someone put a sort of flyer in her hands; surprised, she saw it was an advertisement for a hotel. And before she knew it, she was being accosted from all sides.

"You want a hotel? Come to the Alka, it's the best..."

"No, no, Ma'am. Come to the Majestic. We have running hot water..."

"No, no! I have my own house here," she all but yelled as she tried to literally push her way through them, making her way across the length of the bus to turn towards the lake.

And Oh, God! What a sight it was! She was wonderstruck, almost dazzled by the sheer audacious beauty of it, for there, right before her disbelieving eyes, cradled in the mountains, lay a lake, its dark, green waters sparkling in the winter sunshine.

Surrounded by mountains on all sides, and graced by an utterly blue sky, with the clouds seeming to float upon its water, the lake seemed unbelievable to her. She had never imagined there could be such beauty in the world, and she closed her eyes for a moment, as if trying to capture and keep the sight of it in her forever. Re-opening them, she looked at

The Shadow of the Clouds

the lake again. Whatever she saw was beautiful. Everything had a touch of paradise.

There were boats on the lake, and, far off, she could see a couple of yachts gliding lazily on the water, their red and yellow sails puffed in the breeze. It was a very large lake, almost filling up the whole valley, fringed by trees and patches of flowers. Nearby, many boats were moored along its edge, with the boatmen waving and shouting at people to have a trip around the lake.

"Are you Tahmina?" a voice, soft and lilting, asked her.

She was as much surprised by it as she had been by the sight of the lake. Turning to look, she saw a petite girl standing beside her. She must have been about her age, or perhaps a little older. She was fair and slender, wearing a sari with a dark, maroon shawl wrapped around her shoulders.

"Yes," Tahmina replied, looking at her hesitantly. She wasn't beautiful, her features flat and ordinary, but the brown eyes sparkling under a cloud of hair were more than compensating.

"Hello!" the girl said. "I'm Anjali, Anjali Pandey, and there's papa," she said, pointing towards an old man standing near the bus.

"Oh! Mr. Pandey!" She hadn't thought he would be here for her, at the bus stand.

"Memsahib, Memsahib!" The coolie was calling her from the top of the bus. "Come here and look! Are these your bags?"

Taking Anjali's hand in hers, Tahmina walked back to the bus and pointing out her bags to the coolie, she moved towards where Anjali's father, Mr. Pandey, was standing.

He was an old man, wearing a long, buttoned woollen coat, a muffler wrapped round his neck, standing there with a wooden cane in his hand. He seemed so much like a doting grandfather to her, with his white hair brushed back above his ruddy, wrinkled, smiling face and his large, brown eyes overflowing with affection. She greeted him by folding her hands in the traditional Indian way but he came forward and hugged her, embracing her with such heartfelt affection that she was overwhelmed with emotion and felt her eyes becoming moist again.

"You didn't have any trouble on the way? "he asked, his hand around her shoulders. "Where's your luggage? Anjali will look...." But the coolie had already come down with her bags and was standing beside them. Meanwhile, Anjali had taken her handbag and given that to the coolie too.

"Come on, let's go, beti," Mr. Pandey said, addressing her as a daughter. "You and Anjali take the boat while I'll come with the coolie. You must be feeling tired, uh!" he asked, ruffling her hair.

"No, uncle, I'm all right, but....But where are we going?"

"You'll come to my house first and have lunch with us and then I'll take you to your hotel."

"Oh, no,! Please don't mind, but the first thing I would like to do is to go and see my house.....I mean, my father's house. Is it very far?"

"Yes, it's across the lake. But, beti, listen, you must come to my house first, have lunch and then rest for some time. Anjali's mother will be waiting to welcome you."

"No, uncle, please, please take me to my house first. I'm

The Shadow of the Clouds

not hungry or tired at all," Tahmina pleaded, though she was afraid that she was hurting his sentiments by insisting. But the old man had understood her need, for he ruffled her hair again with affection. "Yes, yes. We'll go to your house first. Okay!"

"Thank you, uncle. I'll come with you to your home after that, but what were you just saying about the hotel?"

"Well, you'll have to stay at a hotel though you are welcome to stay at my house too. But it's a poor man's dwelling and I thought perhaps you won't feel comfortable there."

"No, no, I would love to stay with you but...But the fact is that I would like to stay at my own house here, not some other place."

He became lost in his thoughts for a few moments, the wrinkles on his forehead bulging a little more. But then he smiled, and looking at her in the same affectionate way, he said, "All right! So you'll stay at your own house. I'll see to that. But Faisal sahib did ask me to book a room for you at some good hotel and I've done so," he said, patting her hand.

Faisal's name reminded her that in the flurry of arrival she had almost forgotten her promise to phone him as soon as she reached Nainital. So she went to the Public Call Office across the street and started dialling home.

"I can't believe you are so far away, and alone," Faisal said, after she had told him about her journey and how Mr. Pandey was there to receive her at the bus stop.

"Me too," she replied. "And I really miss you and Ammi. But it's really beautiful here..."

She had hung up after a while and strolled to the water's

edge with Anjali, while Mr. Pandey went along the road with the coolie in tow. The boat started to wobble in the water as soon as she set her foot inside and she would certainly have unbalanced if Anjali hadn't been holding her arm so firmly.

"Don't be afraid, Tahmina," Anjali said, as she guided her across the length of the boat to settle on the seat at the far end. "The water's very shallow near the edge, and even otherwise, no one has ever seen a boat taking a tumble in the lake. It's very safe," she said, smiling at her reassuringly.

"Thanks! You know, I have never been in a boat before," Tahmina said with a laugh. She was still feeling afraid but as the boatman started rowing with the long, wooden oars, she forgot everything else except the wondrous beauty around her. Dipping her hands in the water, which was so cold that it sent shivers all through her, she looked around her, at the mountains and the clouds and the willows along the banks of the lake. There were flowers, yellow and purple and blue all along the way and white swans gliding over the calm, dark waters of the lake. And she just sat there, oblivious of how cold the weather was, feeling so excited and exhilarated, drinking in the beauty, and before she knew, she had fallen in love with this place.

"The end where we took the boat is called Tallital," Anjali told her. "Talli means lower and Tal means lake. The other end, where we'll get off, is called Mallital, or higher end of the lake. And that," she said, pointing west towards the road that went along the side of the lake, following its contours, "That's the main road. It's called the Mall Road and the road on the other side of the lake, the eastward one, is called 'Thandi Sarak'. Its not a proper road really, just a pony trail."

It took them half an hour to cross the lake in the boat and

The Shadow of the Clouds

during the way, Anjali went on pointing out the various sights and landmarks of Nainital. She seemed so warmhearted and lively and went on talking away like the breeze.

"Where's my house?" Tahmina asked her when they were almost across.

"Your house, oh, yes!" And asking Tahmina to turn around in her seat, she pointed out towards the hills across the lake. "It's up there somewhere. You won't be able to find it from here, but when you are up there, you'll be able to see the lake spread below you."

"And the shop?"

"The shop is in the market, just below your house. It's called Bara Bazar, or main market. I'll point it out when we are on our way to your house."

Tahmina wondered if she could ask Anjali about her father, whom Anjali must have known quite intimately, but strangely enough, she wasn't able to bring that question to her lips. Instead, she asked Anjali about her family. Apart from her parents, she had two brothers, Akshay, the eldest, was in the Army, while the second one, Anuj, was studying at the Agricultural University situated in a town in the foothills. Anjali had been through her graduation and her marriage was settled to take place some time in the coming new year.

As the boat was about to reach the Mallital end, Anjali pointed towards a wooden, green building that was jutting out some distance into the lake on the side of the Mall Road. "That's the Boat Club. The British built it and no Indian was allowed inside in their time. It's still very exclusive, for the rich only. And that," she said, pointing in front, "is the Naina

Devi Temple, the Goddess after whom Nainital is named, and adjacent to that is the the Gurudwara."

The boat glided slowly to the edge of the lake and they left it to walk across the gravel stretch towards the stone stairs that led up to the road. A garden sloped down to the lake beside the stairs and Tahmina noticed that it was full of flowers, particularly roses that were in bloom even in winter.

Stepping sprightly, Tahmina reached the top of the steps and found herself on the vast expanse of gravel called the Flatt, which spread out in every direction. A little towards the left, adjacent to the stone railing that bordered the lakeside, was the famous Band Stand, and further on, was the Capitol Cinema, a stately building decked with film posters. There were trees, tall and beautiful, sprinkled all over the Flatt, with the breeze playing through them and tufts of autumn-tinged leaves glimmering in the sunshine and she could see a few hawkers scattered about here and there.

The central point of the town was on her right, where the Mall Road wound up, ending with the lake. There was a little incline there on which a garden had been laid out, and above that, just below the mountain, was a large, hut-shaped, wooden building that must have been built long ago. There was a hotel on its upper floor and below that were shops, with the large signboard of the Modern Book & General Store attracting her attention. In between the incline and the Flatt, the road continued uphill towards the mountain where her house was located.

"In the summer season this area is so crowded you can't even walk freely," Anjali told her.

They went towards the police booth situated at the corner of the Mall Road to wait for Mr. Pandey. And it was a while

The Shadow of the Clouds

before he came into view, with the coolie trudging behind him. Though he appeared tired by the long walk, he declined to stop for a rest and so they moved on.

A little distance ahead, on the left, was the stable from where people hired out horses, while the local hospital was situated on the right, built quite a long way uphill. Here too there were trees, pine and cedar mostly, and the road forked ahead, with one branch leading to the Bara Bazar and the other, narrower one going towards the Post Office.

"Your shop is there," Mr. Pandey said, pointing towards the market. "While the way to your house is by that other path, the one at the back of the market."

Tahmina was feeling tired by now, finding the climbing difficult, and when they reached halfway along the back road, Mr. Pandey asked Anjali to go home and fetch Tahmina's lunch while he would take her to her house.

Thirteen

With Anjali gone, Tahmina walked by Mr. Pandey's side. The old man was having difficulty with each step, stopping now and then to catch his breath. She felt sorry to have given him so much trouble and apologised to him. Though it was difficult for him to speak, he was so breathless, he replied, "I have climbed these hills since I was a little boy. But, yes, age has made me slow." He paused to catch his breath once more. "You are so much like your mother, aren't you? I remember her still. She wasn't as tall as you are though. In that respect you have taken after your father," he said, shaking his head and smiling kindly, unaware of the stab that went through her heart.

A few steps later he stopped to turn, calling to the coolie who was trailing after them, and pointed towards a small path that cut off from the road to go meandering up the hill.

It was a narrow, mountain trail, hedged in between houses on both sides. Tahmina was finding the climb a real task now and she too had to stop off and on to catch her breath. Mr. Pandey, who was a little behind her now, looked up, shaking his head and smiling, both in understanding and encouragement and she stopped to let him catch up with her.

As he came near, he pointed upwards. "It's just round the corner now, in the clearing." And Tahmina felt her heart skip a few beats. Suddenly all her weariness was gone from her and she started to climb a little quicker in anticipation, leaving the old man some way behind her.

A few minutes more of climbing brought her to the clearing. There was a large, cream-coloured building, with a small signboard indicating it was an Army guesthouse. And beyond that she could see a small house, built on a jutting mound of hill and facing south towards the lake. "That's your house up there," she heard Mr. Pandey call to her, breathless as he was, stopping at each word.

And what a welcome and consoling sight it was! A small house with its sloping roof pulled down like a cap. A stone railing fringed the open verandah and she could see some flowerpots on the railing. The plants were growing wild in them with a sprinkling of flowers, mostly white and purple, with a sprinkling of pink. A creeper, growing from the mound, went clinging and climbing upwards to spread all over the roof, with a few stray strands hanging down and swinging in the breeze.

What a lovely little house it is, Tahmina thought happily, just like a house in some storybook. It seemed to have weathered both time and tempest with as much strength and courage as it possessed, having lost its show and pretensions in the struggle. But its beauty had endured and it looked charming and cosy.

Looking around her as she stood waiting for Mr. Pandey near the steps that led to the house, she noticed how quiet it was there, the pure mountain solitude broken only by the sound of the leaves rustling in the cold breeze. The woods on the hill around her were full of fragrance and the air was so fresh and bracing. Quite a few of the trees were singed by the autumn while the others were as they always must have been, their dark green, heavy-laden branches spreading and intermingling with each other. The clearing itself was not large

The Shadow of the Clouds

and was unprotected, except for the two old cedars that stood at its edge.

She could not see the valley below from where she was standing, for the trees grew tall from the slopes of the mountain to rise above the rim, obscuring the view. But she could make out the lake glimmering here and there between the gaps in the branches. Going to peer over the edge, she saw there were clusters of cottages built on the slopes, going all the way down to the road by which she had come along though the road itself wasn't visible from there.

"Won't you come up inside?" She turned back to see Mr. Pandey standing by the railing on the verandah of her house. He had climbed up the steps while she had been busy peering down. The coolie too had trudged up with her luggage and was sitting on the steps.

And so, with the name of God on her lips, she ran up the ten or so steps to open the small, wooden gate and enter the house that had been her home so long ago that even its memory had been effaced from her.

The verandah was partly covered by the hanging slope of the roof and two doors opened onto it. Mr. Pandey was fumbling with the keys to open the locks on them, so she turned and went to stand by the stone railing.

How captivating was the beauty that met her eyes. The lake, with its curve in the middle, was gleaming in the sunlight while the sky on the horizon was light blue, with clouds like tufts of cotton. And on either side were the mountains, as full of trees as houses. One could stand there all one's life and feel no need to go anywhere else.

How could a house be sad and silent, she wondered,

surrounded as it was with so much beauty and peace? But it had been so and she turned towards it, her heart no longer belonging to the beauty her eyes had glimpsed.

Fourteen

The first thing she noticed was the nest some bird had made on the beams of the verandah; it was perched so precariously that it was a miracle it hadn't fallen. She also observed that the house had gone without a new coat of paint for a long time; there were patches where the plaster had all but withered away while at other places it had swelled and darkened from the damp. She also saw the small kitchen tucked in between the two rooms that opened on to the verandah. It was visible through the glass window and she could make out the stove and assorted utensils and jars stacked away inside.

"This used to be the combined living and dining room," Mr. Pandey said, leading her into the room on the left. "But later on it just became useless. He lived in that other room across the kitchen."

The walls were no better inside and the room felt so cold and musty. It wasn't very large, appearing even smaller perhaps because of all the old, broken furniture stacked in it. There was also an oval dining table, set at the far side, standing without its set of chairs. But the room was certainly clean and tidy, because, as Mr. Pandey told her, he had got the house dusted and spruced up to welcome her. A door in the middle of the room led into the kitchen and another one, at the far end, led to a small spare room at the back. She went to peek in there too, but it was empty, apart from a large bed that had been covered with a sheet.

Turning back, she entered the kitchen. What a pleasure cooking here would be, she thought, and opening the windows, she gazed for a moment at the view of the lake from there.

In the meanwhile, Mr. Pandey had picked up one of the chairs and gone to sit outside in the sunlit verandah. He must be tired, she thought, or perhaps he understands my need to be alone just now. Anyway, he was such a kind man, she thought, as she opened the door on the opposite side of the kitchen to step inside the other room, the room where her father had lived all these years.

And as she entered, her feelings stormed back and her heart beat more sadly and wildly than ever before. It was a small, sunny room, its walls painted white. A large table stood by the window, while a bed stood against the far wall. In between, standing beside the wall at the other end, was a wooden rack full of books and beside the bed was a wooden wardrobe. The bed was freshly made, with a clean, brown bedspread, two pillows and a patchwork quilt. There was nothing else on the walls though and nothing was needed, for the windows framed as much of the outside beauty as the eyes and heart could hold.

There was something very peaceful about this room, something very rare and difficult to define. Memories clung to everything, everything reminded her of the past and everything seemed to be full of loneliness. And all the silent objects of the room seemed to be speaking to her, trying to tell her something. She stood there a long time, lost in the little world of her father's room, a man she had never known.

Suddenly a thought struck her and looking around, she went to the table and started opening its drawers. There was a small, leather purse, some pens, a box of pins and candles in

The Shadow of the Clouds

the top one, but these were not the things she was searching for. She opened the lower one, and, yes, there it was!

The wooden frame held two photographs, placed side by side under the glass. The one on the left was hers; a copy of the one Faisal had taken last year. The other one was of him...

His was a thoughtful face with large, dark eyes framed by an unruly mop of hair. The picture must have been taken when he was quite young. He was smiling at her, the shyness reflecting in his face, and she stood with it a long time, looking at it lovingly, not knowing whether to feel happy or sad. And then she took it to her lips and kissed the glass that separated it from her touch.

"Tahmina!"

Anjali's voice from the veranda startled her and the frame fell from her hands, its glass breaking and scattering on the ground.

Fifteen

She was awakened by the cold of the winter evening. It was cold, much too cold and her hands and feet had gone numb, and the bed felt as if it was made of ice. She was lying under the heavy blanket she had brought from Dubai and someone had put the quilt on top of it. The room was dark but she could see the light from the kitchen permeating through the gap at the base of the connecting door. Collecting the blankets around her, she sat up in bed, her teeth chattering, and looked out through the glass of the closed window. The verandah was in darkness but she could see the lights of the town twinkling like fireflies all over the hills.

It was a clear night, the sky full of stars and she would have sat gazing at them if the cold had not made her curl back into bed, pulling a part of the blanket underneath her to insulate her body from the iciness of the bed.

The way the glass of the picture frame had shattered in the afternoon had distressed her, and the first thought that had come to her was that it was some sort of an ill omen. Afraid and heartbroken, she had hurriedly picked up the photographs that were strewn on the floor with the shards of glass scattered over them, and to her amazement, she had found not two but three of them…..

Before she could see and recognise the third one, Anjali had come rushing in, but when she went away to search for a broom to wipe away the broken glass, Tahmina had looked at it. And for a moment even she had been confounded, mistaking it for one of her own, but then, all of a sudden, she had recognised that it was a picture of Amna, her mother.

It must have been taken long ago when she was very young. She was smiling in it, her head flung back, and Tahmina was really surprised to note how much of a resemblance there was between her and Amna. It didn't show so much now, but when her mother was young she had looked so much like her that only someone who knew them intimately could have told them apart. Otherwise, one would have to look very carefully and with great sensitivity to discern the difference in their beauty, for there was a tempting audacity in one and an alluring shyness in the other.

Putting the pictures back in the drawer, Tahmina had not given the matter much thought for she had been too perturbed by the breaking of the glass-frame. Seeing the troubled expression on her face, Anjali had tried to ease her apprehensions. "Don't feel bad, Tahmina, it's good the glass broke. My mother says it's a good omen; it means some coming trouble or sorrow has been warded off." And she had led Tahmina to have lunch.

They had eaten in the verandah, where Anjali had spread a cloth on the floor. The mildly warm winter sunshine had felt good and the food had been delicious, though Tahmina had been too distraught to relish it. But Anjali's friendly chatter and natural warmth had made her feel easy and she had eaten well.

Mr. Pandey had left some time later while Anjali had stayed back. She had helped her to unpack and arrange her things, keeping her involved all the time in her questions and answers. Tahmina had asked her about the keys to the wardrobe, for it aroused her curiosity, but Anjali had no idea.

"Papa will give them to you when he returns," she had said. "Why don't you lie down and rest for some time?"

So Tahmina lay down on the bed, and worn out and tired as she was, she had dozed off into a deep slumber, only to wake up now so late in the evening. But instead of feeling refreshed, the unaccustomed siesta had made her feel sluggish and she didn't feel like getting out of bed. Inevitably her thoughts turned to the incident of the afternoon and she began to think about her mother's photograph.

Why had her father hidden it behind her own photograph, she wondered, for he could as easily have taken it out of the frame? Perhaps he didn't have the heart to throw or tear it away, for his love for Amna hadn't ever left his heart. Yes, that must be it, and she could not help feeling touched and stirred by this. Once again her heart began to ask why they had to break from each other, why had all this happened to rob her of the happiness of loving her father? Whatever Faisal may have given her, and he had given her so much, it was all make-believe, nothing but an illusion. All her joys and contentment with him was nothing but a semblance; however genuine it may seem, it was not real. She felt deprived and felt that she had only been consoled, as girls often are, by dreams and deception, pretence and delusions.

She lay there in the darkness for a long time, with her tormenting questions and tumult of emotions, till at last she heard someone moving about in the kitchen. There was someone else there besides Mr. Pandey and Anjali, for she could discern a new voice mingled with theirs. Getting out of bed, she switched on the light and looked at herself in the wardrobe mirror. Her face seemed older and there were dark circles under her eyes. She had been so careless of her appearance all these days and it showed. Her clothes were all rumpled too but she just brushed her hair and opened the door to the kitchen.

There was another man there, bending over the stove and several plastic bags were stacked on the floor.

"I've brought him to fix the stove," Mr. Pandey said, indicating the man. "And I've brought some provisions too," he added affectionately.

"Oh!" she said, not knowing how to thank someone like him. Later, when the man had left, she offered some money to Mr. Pandey to pay for everything but he refused.

"No need for that, beti!"

"No, please, uncle, you must take the money. Isn't everything else enough that you are doing for me? I'll never be able to repay you for that."

"Don't say such things, beti," he replied, shaking his head. "Whatever I have in the world, it has all come to me through your family. You won't know but I joined the bookshop when I wasn't even married, and then, your father was more like a friend to me."

And so, finally, she asked him about her father. "How did he die, uncle?"

"He wasn't keeping well for years and it was nothing but smoking that got him. That cough of his wouldn't go away and finally his lungs just gave up. I took him to the hospital in the end and pleaded with him to let me inform you all how ill he was, but he simply wouldn't let me do that. He died there, in the hospital, after three days." There were tears in his voice. Tahmina could hardly hold herself back and Anjali put her arms around her and consoled her.

The Shadow of the Clouds

Afterwards, when they had eaten supper and Anjali had gone home, Mr. Pandey said to her, "I'll stay the night here with you."

"Thank you, I am really sorry to give you such trouble."

"No trouble at all, my dear," the old man had replied, his face breaking out in that affectionate smile of his. "And then it's only for tonight because I have found a woman who'll come and stay with you from tomorrow. She's very dependable and will look after you well and what's more, she's an excellent cook too."

"Yes, that would be nice. Who is she, uncle?"

"Her name's Kamla. Her mother works at my house. But, let's get you into bed now because you must be wanting to sleep."

"Not at all. I slept enough in the afternoon," she said. "But it's almost freezing now so I think I'll snuggle into bed. Why don't you come and sit in my room for a while? I have got so much to discuss with you."

"Yes, yes, why not! But let me warm up some coals. That will keep your room warm." And picking up a sack from the kitchen floor, he poured the coal into a burner, and lighting a wad of newspapers, he got them crackling in a jiffy. "Your father used to just sit and watch the coals blazing, watching God knows what is in them. He had an electric heater too, but he never used it. Said it didn't give any real warmth and consumed so much power too and he was right. There's nothing like a coal fire to keep a room warm."

Coming into her room, Tahmina sat on the bed, wrapping herself in the blankets, while he set on a chair near the table, his hands stretched over the coal-fire.

Fahimm Inhonvi

"Where's the key to this wardrobe?" she asked him.

"Yes, I'll give it to you tomorrow. It slipped my mind to bring it today. Actually, all your father's important things, his papers and clothes are in there and he asked me to hand the keys to you only, that is in case you came here. But he was sure in his heart you would…"

And so long into the night, like a grandfather recounting stories to his children, he told her many things about her father, till the warmth of the coals was all spent. And long after he had gone away to sleep in the other room, Tahmina lay awake in the silent, lonely night, gazing at the tiny fading embers in the darkness till the ashes obscured them completely.

Sixteen

She was greeted in the morning by a cold and misty winter day. The fog hung over the peaks and she could see the walls and the trees outside, damp and dripping with the frost. Her bed was warm though and because it was still very early in the morning, and the house was silent, she presumed Mr. Pandey was still in bed.

She was feeling hungry but her body refused to leave the warmth of the bed, so she just pulled the blankets a little more tightly and took out the photographs she had put underneath the pillow yesterday.

He looked young and hopeful in the picture, she thought, gazing at her father's photograph, trying to read his mild and dreamy eyes. He must have been easy to love, and taking her mother's picture, she held them together. For a long while she looked at them, trying to find some clue about their relationship, but she couldn't guess anything, except that they must have looked good together, each one compensating what was lacking in the other.

Replacing them, she let her eyes roam over the room and looked at everything in the stillness of the morning, and once more everything seemed to be full of memories and she longed to trespass on them.

Mr. Pandey had told her so many small details about her father and the picture he had drawn was of a gentle and forbearing man who had tried to work through his difficulties with patience and was always defeated. But whatever he had told her was not so important to her, for what she wanted to know was how her father felt in his heart. She wanted to learn what he thought, his hidden sorrows and all those other things that are invisible and incomprehensible to others. She wanted to speak to him as a friend, to ask him what would have made him happy and what had hurt him and how much and where.

Mr. Pandey had avoided any mention of the relationship between her father and mother, and she too had refrained from asking about that. It would have been embarrassing to both of them. But I must ask Mr. Pandey to get me the keys of the wardrobe today, she thought, as she compelled herself to get out of bed finally, for she could hear him moving about in the kitchen.

The woman he had arranged to work for her had arrived too. She must have been in her thirties, a simple, hardy woman of the hills, wearing a sari and a sweater, with a dash of vermilion paste rubbed on her forehead. Her hands were full of tinkling bangles and she couldn't stop smiling.

"This is Kamla," Mr. Pandey introduced her. "And this is Tahmina. You look after her well, understand?" And turning to Tahmina, he said, "I'll be leaving now. I'll send Anjali by eleven to fetch you over to see the shop. You'll be ready by then?"

"Oh, sure, uncle," she said, accompanying him outside into the verandah and waving him goodbye from the railing.

Kamla had put a bucket of hot water in the bathroom for her after breakfast and what an experience that was. Taking off her clothes, she had shivered in every limb, and as soon as a splash of hot water glided off her body the cold would touch her even more fiercely. Somehow she had washed herself and come out shivering like a leaf, her teeth chattering

The Shadow of the Clouds

uncontrollably and her breath forming wisps of cloud as she ran to snuggle back into the blankets. It was only after she had drunk two cups of steaming coffee that some warmth had returned to her body.

"Wear very warm clothes, it's going to be very cold today," Kamla warned her.

"Yes, I will." And she had put on the woollen slacks underneath the salwar and worn the long coat Faisal had bought her, and when, at last, Anjali came to fetch her, she was standing in the verandah, gazing at the strange beauty of the lake that was shrouded in the mist.

Seventeen

If in summer it throbs like a lover's heart, winter makes Nainital as silent and forlorn as a school during the vacations. It's a time of fastened doors and windows, of wrapped and huddled people, of empty hotels and deserted shops. There are a few tourists and even many of the local people go away to the plains. The three long months of short days and bone-chilling, long and silent nights are difficult to pass, for on many days there is no electricity in the town and the water is like flowing ice. Whatever you touch is as cold as stone and there are days on end when the sky remains overcast and the rays of the sun do not come to kiss the waters of the lake. Often it rains and when the winter is fully settled, there is snow. It doesn't fall too heavily though and afterwards you can see it spread over the roofs and the trees.

And so, when Tahmina came down to walk towards her father's shop, there were barely a few dozen people in the bazaar and most of the shops hadn't opened. The road went uphill and at the end it suddenly branched out, one part going left, down an incline towards the Flatt, the other one going up towards the mountain. Her father's shop was almost near the end of the bazaar, tucked away between a provision store and a garment shop.

It was called the Hillside Bookstore, though the name on the signboard was difficult to make out for the paint had all but faded away. There was a glass enclosure in front, to the left side of the entrance, with a few, dusty books arranged on one of the shelves. Inside, just behind the enclosure, a wooden counter ran the length of the shop, with racks built into the wall behind it. Those racks too were as good as empty but the shelves on the other side had stacks of books lying about in them in a haphazard way. There was a table at the far end, behind which her father presumably used to sit and a door at the back led into a small cabin. The rug on the floor was threadbare and torn at many places and her father's chair was no better.

Tahmina went and looked at the books on the shelves. They were an assorted lot, some fiction here and some textbooks there, a few storybooks for children intermingled with tourist guides. For a moment the bookshops of Dubai flashed across her eyes, with their chic, air-conditioned interiors, the glass sections gleaming and resplendent with the latest titles from all over the world. Oh, father! Why didn't you call me earlier? I would have come and filled your shop with books and flowers, and made you proud and happy. But though this thought went through her mind, as naturally as love makes such thoughts come, she could not help feeling ashamed and disappointed with herself. How would she have been able to do all that? With Faisal's money, of course, she thought ruefully.

"The shop used to be much larger in your grandfather's time," Mr. Pandey remarked. "The adjacent provision store was a part of the shop then."

"I know," she replied sadly. She had known, of course, that the shop was in a bad way, but she hadn't imagined it would be in such a poor condition. It had been lying closed since her father's death and, apart from Mr. Pandey, there was no one else to look after it.

"I don't know what you plan to do with the shop, but it

The Shadow of the Clouds

would be best to sell it. It might fetch good money. Otherwise, it will just lie closed, for who is there to run it any longer, and even if there was, you can see there isn't much to run in any case."

"You, uncle..."

"I can't work any longer, beti. I am too old and broken down. You know I would have retired years ago but I stayed on for your father's sake and perhaps because I love the shop like my own. Your grandfather gave me a job here when my own father had died all of a sudden, and being the eldest, I had to take the responsibility of supporting my family. And then, when your father started coming to the shop, we became friends. He never treated me like an employee and I would have died before I left him, particularly when he was all alone and going through such difficulties. You won't know but on many days we would sit all day with not a customer to serve and it would have been difficult for him to be waiting alone. But don't think that I made any sacrifice; it was the least I could do for him."

"I understand," Tahmina replied quietly. "I wasn't going to ask you to work. The fact is, I don't know what to do and I'll have to ask Abbu to see what he has to say. But yes, one thing I am sure about, and that is I wouldn't like to dispase of the shop he has left me. It wouldn't be right. In fact, it will be very painful for me and perhaps it would hurt his soul too, to see it go into some other hands. In any case, I am going to be here for some time and we'll decide what to do one way or the other, but I would like you tell me about the legal formalities you mentioned last night."

"Yes, I'll explain," he said, going inside the cabin at the end and bringing out some files. "Whatever belonged to your

89

father is now yours, for there's no one else. He made a formal will but even then you'll have to get a succession certificate from the courts here, to transfer the shop and the house to your name. There will be some taxes to pay for that and we'll have to engage a lawyer. I've already discussed the matter with someone…"

"That's all right, uncle. You just go ahead and arrange everything."

"And…." He paused.

"And what, uncle?"

"Well, there are some debts to pay off too. Some outstanding bills you'll have to settle." He was so embarrassed as if they were his debts.

"Oh! Don't worry, I'll settle all that," she replied and then added wistfully, "He loved the shop a lot, didn't he?"

"Yes. And it was not as if he didn't try to keep it going, for he was very hard-working. But the way of doing business has changed so much and it's no longer any good if you are able to work hard at your desk. What's required is to go out and bring in the business, to change and adapt to new situations, and all that was difficult for him to do…." His voice trailed off and from the glum expression on his face, she could see that the old man was saddened by what he had to tell her.

"I understand. Whatever happened was unfortunate and I'm sorry to have made you remember all that. But there was one other thing I wanted to ask you. Didn't he have any other friends? I mean, people to whom he had been close?"

"Well, everyone here knew him, it's not a very big place. But I think as far as real friends are concerned, there was just Mr. Mathew, who lives near the Church up there. Your father used to go up there so often, even attending the prayers in the church, for he used to say he found peace there." He replied, pointing to the road that went up the hill from the bazaar. "In fact, Mr. Mathew was asking about you a few days ago when I met him in the bazaar and I told him you would be coming here soon. I'll take you to meet him."

"Thanks, uncle."

There was not much to do after that and they just waited for Anjali, who had left on some errand after dropping Tahmina at the shop. When she returned half an hour later, Tahmina went to phone home, and after that, Mr. Pandey took her home for lunch.

He didn't live too far away from the shop, in a small flat above some bakeries. Anjali's mother was a frail, little woman who didn't keep well, but she was as nice as everyone else.

It was quite late in the afternoon when she was able to persuade Anjali to escort her home, for she had the key to her father's wardrobe in her coat pocket. But Anjali took her down to the lake and they strolled almost halfway up the Mall Road. There was a shop there, selling some of the most exquisitely embroidered shawls she had ever seen. Looking at them, she suddenly wanted to buy something for Anjali and her parents, for she hadn't brought anything for them from Dubai. So she took Anjali inside and asked her to help choose some shawls and a sweater. But the real task was to persuade Anjali to accept those gifts.

Coming back, they took the boat from the middle of the lake, near the library, and getting off at the Flatt, Tahmina strolled into the Modern Book Depot to look through the books there.

Fahimm Inhonvi

And so, when she finally set out for home, the day was coming to an end and everything was bathed in a strange and rarefied light. How enchanted this place is, she thought, looking around her.

Eighteen

As she walked across the clearing, her eyes lifted to her house and a strange sensation came to her. She felt as if she had always walked this path to her house, as if she had never been a stranger here. And when she had climbed the steps and entered her room the feeling grew more distinct and forceful.

"Will you have tea?" Kamla asked. "If so, I'll give it to you now, for I have to go to my house for a while. I'll come back in an hour."

"No, you can go," she replied hurriedly and closing the door after her, she leaned against it, realising that it was the first time since her arrival that she was completely alone in the house.

For a long while she wandered through it, accompanied by the same sensation of having always lived here. She touched and felt everything, tracing her fingers on the walls and looked in every nook and corner till each and every object had become familiar to her. And later, when she came to sit down by the table in her room and looked out of the window towards the lake, she understood that memories do not live in our hearts and thoughts alone. Like birds, they can make a nest and live in places too, inhabiting and haunting them and crying out to be heard.

So she sat there with her face cupped in her hands, staring into the twilight at the lake and the sky till the darkness had veiled them and the lights had been sprinkled all over the hills and all the memories of the house had been mingled in her.

Nineteen

It was still early in the night and Tahmina was sitting by the window in her room, warming her hands over the burning coals as they crackled and cracked, throwing tiny embers in the air. It was a dark night, with not a star. But the wind had picked up now and it would take away the dense clouds that had been there all day.

Kamla had gone to sleep in the living room. Earlier in the evening, she had prepared supper for her and though Tahmina had asked her to eat together, she would have none of it, insisting that Tahmina eat while she gave her the chapatis fresh off the stove. After that she had made some coffee and put it in the flask beside her bed.

Tahmina hadn't opened the wardrobe after returning home in the evening, deciding to wait till she could do so undisturbed. So now she got up, leaving the warmth of the coals and went to the wardrobe. Turning the key in the old lock on its door, she felt as if she was going to be face to face with the man whose things were stacked away inside.

The topmost shelf had his warm clothes- woollen suits, pullovers, jackets and windbreakers, a coat with a hood lined with fur, three or four shawls, gloves and other such things. The next one was reserved for shirts and trousers, while below that, the shelf was divided into two. On the left, open side were various small things like a torch, an alarm clock, a wallet, a few cigarette lighters and pens. There was a small, carved wooden box too, with a set of tiny bottles of perfume. On the right was the safe and she used the other key to open it.

It was almost empty, except for a file of papers and his bank passbook. Putting aside the passbook, which showed a balance of Rs.3056.00, she started leafing through the papers in the file. But there was nothing of significance or interest. There were just receipts of paid electric bills, the original deed of the house, some other bills and papers. There was nothing personal, no letters or something else that would have given some clue to him. A little dejected and disappointed, she brought out the clothes and spread them on the bed and searched through the wardrobe again in the hope of discovering something else, a diary or an album of photographs perhaps. But there wasn't anything else except for the shoes and slippers in the bottom shelf.

Coming back to the bed, she started inspecting his clothes, even searching through their pockets, but nothing again. So she started to put everything back and it was then that it dropped to the floor from the folds of the sweaters that she hadn't looked through. Letting the clothes drop from her hands, she lunged to pick up the album and took it to the table.

Yes, this was what I was looking for, she thought, turning the cover. But to her utter bewilderment the album was full of her pictures. She looked through it again and again, but there was nothing else in it. And though she could not help feeling touched, she felt somewhat angry too. It was cruel of him, not to have kept any pictures of his own. She would have liked to see how he looked at the different stages of his life. Feeling tired all of a sudden, and becoming conscious of the cold again, she once more rummaged futilely through each and every belonging.

The Shadow of the Clouds

Closing the wardrobe, she came to sit on the bed, wrapping the blankets around her. Why had he done so, she thought wistfully, hiding himself like that? And if he had decided to be so elusive, to be so secretive, then what was the point in asking her to come here? And now there was no place else to search, no one who would give her the answers her heart hankered for. Yes, there was still Mr. Mathew, her father's friend mentioned by Mr. Pandey, but she didn't know what to expect from him.

And then suddenly a thought came to her. Perhaps she was being unfair; perhaps it was she who was being insensitive and heartless. After all, what did he have except memories to live with for such a long time, and memories were such cruel things. Perhaps that's why he threw away anything that would be a reminder of whatever he wanted to forget. Yes, that would have been the only way to keep sane. Yes, memory was a cruel thing and he did the right thing in trying to kill it off.....

And so she sat there on the bed, huddled into the blankets, until sleep came to take her away from her thoughts.

Twenty

It was a clear, sparkling morning the next day. The wind of the night had blown away the clouds and the mist, and as she sat warming herself in the sunshine, Tahmina decided to go exploring today.

But before she set out, she thought it better to wait awhile, for it was certain that Mr. Pandey would be coming along any moment and it would be so rude if he came and she was away. And she didn't have to wait very long either.

She sat with him in the verandah and told him she wanted to go and see as much of Nainital as she could in a day.

"Why don't you wait till afternoon? Anjali will be coming over then. You saw that day, didn't you, her mother doesn't keep well and poor Anjali has to do all the housework. Otherwise she would be with you all the time. In any case, I don't want to let you roam about alone. You hardly know your way anywhere."

"Oh, no, uncle. Don't trouble her so much. I'll just go down to the lake and wander a little though the bazaar. I'll be happy if she can come in the evening though, because I don't think I'll venture out in the cold then," she replied hurriedly. She didn't want him to insist on Anjali accompanying her, not because she didn't like her company; it was just that she wanted to be alone by herself.

Coming down to the road with Mr. Pandey, Tahmina requested him to make an early appointment with the lawyer and he asked her, "Have you thought of anything yet? I mean, about the shop and this house?"

"No, not yet, but I'll tell you soon," she replied and then added, "Uncle, can you tell me the way to the graveyard here, where my father's buried?"

"That's too far off," he replied, somewhat surprised by her question. "Even otherwise, though it's not for me to say so, but I don't think it would be right for you to go there. I mean, I know a lot of Muslim families apart from yours, and I have rarely seen women going there...."

"You are right, uncle," she replied thoughtfully. "Even Abbu said so. I was just wondering where it was, that's all. And," she added, "uncle, please don't think you have no claim over me. You can certainly tell me what's right or wrong for me."

And she could see how happy she had made him by the way he smiled at her.

"Goodbye," he said, as they came on the road and he turned to go away. "Take care not to wander far off, okay, and don't be out all day or you'll get tired again. I'll ask Anjali to come over by five."

And so she had wandered and meandered all over the town. In particular, she had sought out the other bookshops of the town. There weren't too many of them, the largest of them being Modern, which she had visited yesterday itself. Afterwards, feeling tired and hungry, she had come down to the lake and started to look for a place where she could have a bite. There were a string of lakeside restaurants on the Mall Road and she went to one of them that had chairs and tables spread out in the sunshine.

The Shadow of the Clouds

The lunch was delicious, and it felt so lovely too to sit out there in the open, with the cool, lively breeze playing in her hair and the sweet warmth of the sunshine seeping into her while the water of the lake shimmered in the afternoon glow.

Finishing lunch, she went to sit on the wide, stone railing facing the lake on the Flatt. She sat there a long time, watching how the sun and the wind and the clouds touched and caressed the waters of the lake, each in its own different delightful way. Seeing her sitting all alone, some of the boatmen came to ask if she would go around the lake, and, finally, she did. But she didn't make a full round, getting off at the other end at Tallital. There was a small market there too and she explored that before deciding to stroll back by the Mall Road.

It was a long walk but she loved it. The road was at two levels, the lower one being narrow and gravel, generally for people on horses, while the upper one was broader and paved. She came to know later on that during their time, the British ruling class didn't allow the Indians to walk on the upper road, which was reserved exclusively for the British. But for all their snobbery, they had developed Nainital and many other hill stations too, and that was one of the most cherished legacies they had left behind.

About halfway back to Mallital, she decided to give her legs some respite and because she was starting to feel hungry once again, she bought a packet of chips and went to sit down on one of the benches by the lake near the library.

What a Garden of Eden this place is, she thought; the mountain climate was so healthy and stimulating, and wherever you went or whatever you were doing, its beauty did not leave you alone for a moment, hovering like a butterfly in front of the eyes. It must be a blessing to live here, she thought wistfully.

She sat there a long time too, looking about happily, until the fading warmth of the late afternoon sun started to make her feel cold and pensive again. And when, finally, she decided to walk back to her home on the hill, her eyes were full of the beauty she had seen, but the pathways of her heart were somehow still full of sadness.

Twenty One

"Tell me, Anjali, how does it feel to live here?" she asked. They were sitting together snuggled in the blankets. Tahmina had asked her to have supper and Kamla was busy in the kitchen.

"It's a hard life, really. Only the summers are nice, when it's not too cold and there's so much life and excitement all around. You can't even find a place to stand in sometimes, because of the crowds that are here in May and June. And everyone here earns for the whole year in those two months. But once the rain starts in July, it doesn't stop for days and days and everything becomes so clammy; it's a problem to even dry your clothes. And there are landslides too, though not anything serious in the town itself, but elsewhere they are devastating. But it won't take long for something tragic to happen here too, because of the way the trees are being cut away to set up all these hotels on the slopes."

"Aren't there some regulations? I mean, doesn't the government do something?" Tahmina had inquired.

"No one cares in the real sense. It's all about money and that is the only thing that matters these days. But anyway, as I was saying, after the rains we have the autumn season of October and November. That's very pleasant but colder and the tourists are back again though not so many as in summer. Then you have the long, long winter, or perhaps it just seems long. There's not much activity till March, when the spring arrives, which is the most lovely time here, at least for me." Anjali had smiled happily. 'There are so many flowers then…:"

"Oh! It must be beautiful then!." Tahmina had tried to imagine and Anjali had continued.

"But life is hard here, and getting harder by the day. We are having problems with the water supply and electricity, both of them not being enough to go around and the town is getting so shabby and congested. And then there's the poverty! Most of the hill people are so poor because there are so few opportunities, no infrastructure, so few schools, and the only way to earn is through the tourists. It makes the men idle and depressed and they take to drinking, and that makes things more difficult for the women and children…"

"But you just said that during the summer people here earn for the whole year…."

"They do, but that's true for the businessmen, and they are mostly from the plains. They do employ the locals but it's more a kind of exploitation than anything else. The situation's far worse in other places in the hills. There is no development and women have to trudge miles to fetch water and many young people migrate to the plains in search of livelihood."

"But, still, it would not be too difficult to build a life here in Nainital, I mean, it's quite developed here…"

"Oh, well! You build your life wherever you are born, wherever your roots are. But, day after day, it's getting bogus here. We survive on tourists and we should be thankful, but they are as much of a curse as a blessing. Sometimes I just hate them. Most of them don't come here for the beauty, or for the peace of the mountains, but simply to indulge in crass pleasures. They bring so much vulgarity and such ugly things happen. And the lake is being polluted beyond redemption..."

"What about the schools here, they are very good, aren't they?"

"Oh, yes. The schools are good and the boarding ones, like St. Joseph's, St. Mary's and Sherwood have all become so famous that people send their children to them from all over India. In fact, the parents are regular visitors here and that adds to the economy."

Later, Anjali had asked her if she would like to visit the various peaks around Nainital. "I can take you to Snow View tomorrow. You can see the distant Himalayas from the summit, though it would be too misty these days to get a clear view. Still, we'll go by the aerial ropeway and it will be an experience to see Nainital from so high up."

"Oh, yes, we'll go, but Anjali, can you guide me to the church?" she had asked, but observing the look of surprise on her face, she had added hurriedly, "I mean the church Mr. Pandey mentioned yesterday, the one where my father's friend Mr. Mathew lives."

"Oh, so you want to meet Mr. Mathew. We can go any time you want, but not tomorrow, because I want to take you up to Snow View first. No one can say how long this sunny weather is going to last and it would be a waste to go up there when the skies are not clear."

"All right, so we'll go there first. You can pick me up in the morning."

"Yes, sure," Anjali had replied.

"All of you are so nice, Anjali, and I don't know how to thank you," she had stammered.

"But you are nicer," Anjali had said with a laugh, and then, turning serious, she had asked, "I know it's not proper to ask, but how long are you going to stay here? Papa was saying you would go away in a week or so."

"I don't know, Anjali," Tahmina had replied pensively. "That's what I had thought of doing but now....Now, I don't know…"

"Is anything troubling you?" Anjali had asked with real concern, instinctively reaching out to touch her hand.

"Nothing like that….But…." Tahmina had tried to smile reassuringly at her, not having any clue to what was going on inside her. "Oh, well! There's still time to decide," she added lightly and then they had talked of other things.

And that night Tahmina had tried to think about the question Anjali had asked, but the way she had wandered around all day had tired her out, and feeling her eyes becoming heavy, she had dozed off to sleep like a child in her father's bed.

Twenty Two

The next three days went by in a flurry. She had gone to meet the lawyer with Mr. Pandey and he had promised to get the papers ready in a couple of days. And Anjali had taken her up to the summit of Snow View peak too. Going up by the aerial ropeway had been an experience by itself and what a sight it had been to see the whole of Nainital from those heights. She hadn't been able to glimpse the snow-covered Himalayan peaks in the distance though, because of the mist. But the most memorable had been the visit to the church and her meeting with Mr. Mathew and Claire.

Anjali had promised to take her there the day after the Snow View excursion but she had to put it off because of some unexpected visitors to her house, and unable to wait any longer, Tahmina had decided to set out alone, asking for directions along the way.

Mr. Pandey had told her that Mr. Mathew was a retired head master of one of the boarding schools and had his own cottage near the church on the hill, so she was sure she would be able to locate him. It was a long, tiring trudge among the woods on the hill and she even made a few wrong turns before someone guided her. But the effort had not been wasted.

The church was set far back in a lawn fringed by a narrow strip of wild flowers and it looked so quaint, standing in a grove of stately oaks at the far end. She had looked all around to see if she could locate any cottage nearby but there was only the church in that spot of clearing. *Perhaps I can ask* someone, she had thought, glancing at the small group of men and women standing in the ground near the arched doorway.

But as she stood hesitating at the edge of the lawn, she noticed one of the men coming across the ground towards her. He was a tall, slender man, walking with the slow steps of old age.

"Hello!" He called out and coming nearer, extended his hand to her. "I'm Foster Andrew. Is there anything I can do for you?"

"I'm....I'm a tourist," Tahmina had replied nervously, suddenly losing all her poise. "I just came to see. It's all right...."

"Well, that's nice. But won't you like to come and see the church from inside?" Mr. Andrew had asked with a smile. "As a matter of fact, we were just going in for the evening service and you're welcome to attend."

"I'll be happy," she had said, not knowing what else to say. "But I was trying to find Mr. Mathew's cottage," she had added hurriedly.

'Oh, so you have come to visit Mathew, or, is it Claire you are looking for?"

"I...I just wanted to meet Mr. Mathew." She had been feeling so nervous. "Actually someone told me he lived near the church but I can't find...."

"Don't worry, my dear," Mr. Andrew had replied, taking her by the arm. "His cottage is just around that bend. It's hidden by that clump of trees, but you don't have to go there. Mathew's here just now." And he had turned to point at one of the men standing near the door. "Come, I'll introduce him

The Shadow of the Clouds

to you." And as he turned to lead her away, she saw one of the girls coming across towards them.

Catching them midway, the girl looked at her seriously with her dark eyes and then, smiling sweetly, she extended her hand to Tahmina. "Hi! I'm Claire, Claire Harding. Pleased to meet you......"

"I'm Tahmina," she had replied shyly, looking at Claire, who had a sultry air about her. Her short, thick hair framed her dark-complexioned, oval face like a pair of hands and her lips were as heavy as her eyelids. Almost as tall as Tahmina, there was a bewitching suppleness in her movements and her large breasts swelled through the black high-necked sweater she was wearing over blue jeans.

"You are from......" Claire had let the question hang in the air.

"I've come from Dubai," Tahmina had replied.

"Wow! That's far, isn't it? You have come with...."

"You have a nice way of asking questions. Like a fill-in-the blank exercise..." Tahmina had said, laughing lightly. Claire's presence appeared to have put her at ease by then. "I've come alone."

"That's nice." Claire had smiled back teasingly. "And you are staying...."

Tahmina had laughed again. "I've my own house here. And before you go on further, I have come here to meet Mr. Mathew..."

"Oh my goodness!" Claire had cried, her whole expression changing into one of amazement. "You...You aren't

109

Fahimm Inhonvi

Imad Uncle's daughter, are you?"

"Yes," Tahmina had replied, "But how did you guess?" She had been so surprised that someone had recognised her like that.

"Oh my God! Tahmina! Yes, I remember now, that's what your name was." Claire had clutched her hand and was gazing at her, her eyes full of warmth. "Come on, come on, let's see what Dad has to say about this….." And she had almost dragged Tahmina towards the group of people near the door. "Look, Dad, guess who's here?" she had shouted and Mr. Mathew had come forward to meet them.

He was a small man, frail but sprightly, wearing a dark suit. His features were quite sharp and the eyes that gazed at her could only have belonged to a head master who had years of experience in sizing up people in a glance.

He had stood there for some moments, just looking at her, puckering his eyebrows and tilting his white head, searching her face and those moments had seemed an eternity to her. She had felt so shy and embarrassed, conscious that everyone else was staring at her.

"Hmmm, so you are Tahmina from Dubai. I'm Mathew Deacon." He had spoken, at last, his face breaking into as many smiles as his wrinkles. "You are more beautiful than those pictures Imad used to show us." And coming forward, he had hugged her and then turning around to everyone else, he had said, "Well, folks, this here is Tahmina, old Imad's daughter and isn't she a welcome sight?" And then everyone had milled around her and she had become the star of the evening.

"You know, your dear father was a great friend of mine and as he came to the church as often as he could, attending prayers with us, everyone here knows all about you. We were all so sad when he died, for he was such a good man," he had said, his voice turning a bit soft and sad, as he went on introducing her to everyone.

Later on, Claire had led her inside the church. It was the first time she had stepped inside one but it took her only a moment to realise why her father must have felt peaceful in there. It was so silent and cosy with its arched roof and slanted, wooden beams and the light filtering in through the stained-glass windows in a hushed way. Claire had taken her to sit in the front row and the priest's sermon that day had been nothing more than an evocation of the fond memories all these people held of her late father.

After the service everyone had been so nice to her, offering any help she required during her stay and inviting her to their homes. Finally she had bid everyone goodbye and Mr. Mathew had asked her to come over to his house.

"I'll be late, Uncle. I don't know the way properly and it will soon be getting dark," she had said, looking at the gathering dusk in the sky.

"Oh, don't you worry about the dark or anything else, my dear," he had replied. "You aren't amongst strangers now. Come and have tea and Claire will escort you back." And so she had strolled with them to their house, a small, stone and wood cottage, with a little garden of its own, set behind some trees along the mountain path.

Claire's mother was away to visit her ailing brother in Mussoorie and so she had sat with Mr. Mathew near the blazing log fire in his living room while Claire had gone off to make tea. The old man had been full of instinctive recollections about her father, mingling his reminiscences with questions about her and Amna.

Later on, after tea, he had asked her about her stay in Nainital.

"I came here for a few days but now....I don't know how to describe it but it feels as if I have fallen in love with this place and it seems my heart would break if I went away," she had said, trying to articulate her confused feelings.

"Hmmm! I see," he had replied, looking at her in an intense sort of way, and she had once again been struck at how deep his eyes appeared. "It's just a few days that you have been here so it's too early to start wondering about when you are going back. But if you ask me, it would be a pleasant change to have you here for long, you're so pretty to look at..." He had smiled at her, but seeing how serious and troubled she appeared, he had added, "Listen, don't get confused. Just try to listen to your heart and it will guide you. In any case, whatever happens is nothing but a fulfilment of what has gone before and a foreshadowing of what is going to come later."

Twenty Three

Claire had come to see her home and Tahmina had asked her to stay back for a cup of coffee. As they sat talking in her room, Tahmina had found herself becoming more and more attracted towards her. She had never met a girl like her.

Her sexuality hung like the fragrance of a rose around her and her eyes kept their depth and seriousness even when she smiled or laughed in her natural, easy manner. Tahmina was also captivated by the way she carried herself with such ease and poise in her jeans. How fetching and free she appeared, she thought with envy. And she seemed such an understanding sort of person and was such a delight to speak to. For a moment, Tahmina thought of opening her heart to her, but she held herself back somehow. Even then, by the time Claire said goodbye, they had become friends.

She had gone to bed early that night, feeling tired from all the activity of the day, but she had also felt somewhat inwardly restored by all that had happened in the church. How nice everything and everyone was here, she had reflected, even dear Kamla. And this little house on the hill....How it had welcomed her, as if it had been waiting for her for years and how easily it had given her a place in its heart....

Next morning, she had made that day's phone call to Dubai, talking with both Faisal and Amna, telling them about her meeting with Mr. Mathew and how the paper work for the succession was moving ahead. After that she had gone up to Mr. Mathew's cottage once again, for Claire had invited her over for lunch. But before all that, Mr. Pandey had come huffing up the hill in the morning to see how she was.

Kamla had told her last evening, when she had returned from Mr. Mathew's place, that Mr. Pandey had come around to see her and had appeared quite upset to learn that she had gone up to the church alone.

" You shouldn't have gone so far off without informing me," he had remonstrated. 'You know I am responsible for you…" And feeling ashamed for getting him so worried about her, she had asked the kind, old man to forgive her, for his concern was very precious to her.

It was a clear morning that day, but by the time she had arrived at Mr. Mathew's cottage, patches of dark, ominous clouds had started to gather over the sky once again and the wind had almost died down. It was quite cold too, particularly inside the woods, but Mr. Mathew's cottage was so full of old furniture and rugs that it hadn't felt so chilly inside.

Claire had also taken her to her own room at the back, just at the edge of the woods and Tahmina had been surprised to see the large, framed, wedding photograph on the mantelpiece.

"Why, that's you!" she had exclaimed, for it was indeed Claire's wedding picture.

"No, that's you! Where do you keep yourself, Tahmina? I told you didn't I, that I am Claire Harding, not Claire Deacon," she had said, laughing happily.

"Oh, well! This is a nice surprise. And you couldn't have been a bit more lucid last evening. You saw I was so disturbed then…."

"All right, I'll be as lucid now as you may wish. I was married to Henry, my teenage love, six months ago, but we just had two months to start regretting before he ran off to New Zealand for a year- he works for a telecommunication company and they have sent him there to head a project. No wives allowed! And so I am putting up with mom and dad till he turns up again, with eight months still to go. Perhaps he'll be here for Christmas but I fear to hope," she had rounded off morosely.

"I hope he does…" Tahmina had said, affected by the glum expression on Claire's face.

"I hope so," she had replied. "You'll be here till then, won't you?"

"I don't know," Tahmina had stammered again.

"Is anything troubling you?" Claire had asked, "What do you keep on thinking, Tahmina? Anybody can see that you are perplexed about something. It reflects on your face, you know."

"Oh, it's really nothing, Claire," Tahmina had said softly.

"Well, you can keep your sad feelings to yourself, if that's what you like to do. But I always felt that two brooding hearts are better than one."

But as she didn't know what to say, Tahmina had kept silent and Claire had left her alone to go and see to the lunch. But perhaps she had said something to Mr. Mathew, for he had come to sit with her and started talking about Dubai, and then, somehow, the talk had veered around to her stay in Nainital.

"And, if I may ask, what do you plan to do with yourself now that you are here?"

"I haven't thought anything, Uncle," she had tried to be honest with him. "I came here thinking I would stay for a few days and go back home. But now I don't know…."

"Why did you come here, Tahmina?" he had asked her, surprising her with his question.

"I just came to see. I mean, my father had written to me to visit this place some time and I felt I should do so right away. Perhaps that way I would be able to make his soul happy."

"I see. Yes, I can understand what brought you here and you did the right thing that way. But what's troubling you now?"

"I don't know, I really don't know," she had replied. "I don't care about myself, about what happens to me but I'm…I can't really tell you because I don't know what's going on myself," she had concluded with despair.

"I think it must be the shock of learning about your father, so sudden and unexpected. But in any case, it's all over now, isn't it? He has gone away and all his sorrows are nothing but dust now. You must think of the future, about your own life ahead…."

"That's what's troubling me…." She had broken off.

"What do you mean?"

"I can't describe…"

"I understand," he had interjected. "I can surmise what

you are going through and I believe one should never try to find words for something that's difficult to express. But it would be helpful to try just now."

"Well, the whole thing is that from the moment I have come here, this place has tugged at my heart. It seems as if I have lived here all my life, as if my heart would die if I went away from here again. And then I keep thinking about my father...I went away once, leaving him alone and now I'll go away again. I know he's no more, here or anywhere else, but everything seems to remind me of him. And...:" She fell silent again.

"And yes..." He had prompted her.

"And...whenever I think what he suffered, it seems as if my soul is on fire and....And I don't know how to describe it, but I sort of feel compelled to do something for him, something that would make him happy, but I don't know what that would be...But a voice inside me keeps on telling me to stay here, not to go away from here and I would love to do that but...."

"Yes, yes, go on," Mr. Mathew had said.

"But my father, I mean Faisal Abbu in Dubai, he loves me more than you can imagine and it would break his heart if I didn't go back soon. He would never allow me to stay here more than a few weeks, and then there's Ammi..."

"So, that's it. But there's no need to get so bewildered. Instead, give yourself a few days time and God will guide you."

"Thanks," she had replied, pausing before giving voice to what she had wanted to ask him all along. "There was one other thing. I wanted to know what really happened between my parents."

"Hmm. But does that really matter at all?" he had asked, looking at her, but she hadn't replied and so he had inquired, "Didn't your mother tell you anything?"

"Just a few things. Nothing meaningful, or, real, I mean, she was very incoherent, and though I know it's wrong of me to pry into their lives, there are questions that keep on coming into my mind all the time...."

"Perhaps there's nothing more to it than what your mother told you."

"No! I can't believe that....I am certain she was hiding something of the truth from me and I want to learn about it, whatever that may be..."

"I don't know if I can help you there. But still, we can have a talk about this. I have to come down to the town tomorrow morning and perhaps we can go and sit by the lake....."

Later on, when lunch was over and Mr. Mathew had retired to rest for the afternoon, Claire had taken her out for a stroll among the woods. They had come to sit on the trunk of a fallen tree in the glade behind Claire's cottage and Tahmina could view the cluster of rhododendron bushes beside the church wall in the distance, their white and pink flowers looking prettier against the faded grey of the stone.

Claire had been wearing a low-neck sweater that day, with a gold chain dangling around her brown neck and she had prattled about growing up in Nainital, about her school, St. Mary's, and most of all about how much she longed for her husband.

And then all of a sudden she had surprised Tahmina by

taking out a pack of cigarettes and a heart-shaped lighter from her pocket. "I have to light one of these," she had said, lighting the cigarette. "To burn off my desire now and then."

And though Tahmina had been able to persuade her not to take the trouble of escorting her back, Claire had still accompanied her and she had felt sorry that she wouldn't be able to see her for the next few days, for she was going away to Mussoorie the next day.

Reaching the valley below, she had stood for some time besides the lake, watching how the breeze was playing with the willows at the water's edge and the way the twilight was descending on the valley. And walking back to her house she had wondered about what Mr. Mathew would be saying to her tomorrow morning. Maybe he would be able to give her some clue about why her father had to lead such a sad and lonely life in a place that seemed to have been made for lovers.

Twenty Four

The weather had changed overnight and dark, heavy clouds hung over the peaks, cloaking the hills and the lake in mist. Her bed was warm though and she had to literally force herself into leaving it, because she didn't want to be late for her meeting with Mr. Mathew.

"Don't go too far today," Kamla cautioned as she waved her goodbye in the veranda. "It may start to rain any moment."

Silently praying that the rain would hold for a while, she hurried down to the Flatt and went to stand under the large elm, her hands tucked inside the pockets of her long coat, as she waited for Mr. Mathew. And it wasn't too long before she saw him coming towards the Bandstand, glancing here and there to spot her.

As she walked forward to meet him, the old man's face lit up. Greeting her warmly, he took hold of her hand and said, "Come, we'll stroll along the lake for a while. It wouldn't be sensible to go too far though. The rain may arrive any moment. You enjoy walking, don't you?" he asked.

"Oh, yes! That's what I have been doing since I arrived," she replied.

As they walked along the road, Mr. Mathew started to tell her about how Nainital had developed and changed over the years, and finally, when they came to the Grand, he took her to sit on the stone bench beside the lake.

"Let's sit here for a while till the rain drives us away," he said. "This is where I used to sit with your father." And as she took her seat beside him, he asked, "Life feels different by the lake, doesn't it?"

"Oh yes!" she replied. "It makes everything seem so romantic."

"Your father carried on a silent love affair with it all his life," he observed, gazing at the water.

"Yes, he wrote to me that one of the reasons he was asking me to come here was to see the lake."

"Actually, your father's love for the lake was very remarkable because, generally, people who live here all their lives become sort of inured to its beauty and it loses its wonder for them, and, therefore, the lake too becomes indifferent and no longer speaks to them."

"Perhaps seeing it all the time makes a difference," she conjectured.

"It does. And that's what happens between people sometimes who have been together for years and years," he said, and then fell silent all of a sudden, while she sat wondering how to get him into talking about what he had promised to tell her.

"I would like to ask you a few questions..." She almost whispered, at last.

"Yes, of course," he replied, turning to look at her. "You want me to tell you about your parents, don't you?"

"Yes," she replied simply.

"But won't you accept that there are certain things that

must remain only between the two people to whom they belong, and even otherwise, it's always better to leave a few things vague and hidden. That way we learn to accept how life is full of mystery and no one can ever know or understand it to the depths."

"If you think it's not right for me to know what happened between my father and mother, then forgive me. I wasn't asking out of idle curiosity," she mumbled, a blush coming across her face. Realising she felt hurt, he said hurriedly.

"No, no, that's certainly not what I was implying. What I meant was whatever anyone may tell you, it will still not be enough for you to comprehend what really happened between them. There are so many hidden, intimate things between a husband and wife that no one else can know about and it's sort of unfair too, trying to define a person or a relationship in words. ...Anyway, I am going to give it a try for your sake," he added hurriedly, persuaded perhaps by the look of disappointment that flitted on her face. "So let's talk about what you want to know about them."

"Everything, I suppose, but mainly...." she broke off for a moment. "You see, my mother told me he loved her, and that she loved him too, and yet, something happened to tear them apart.....That's what I want to know about...:"

"Oh, yes! He loved her all right, particularly in the way he couldn't bear to see her suffer," he replied.

"Then why did he let her go away? From what my mother told me that day, I was able to form a hazy picture, but it's still not clear to me, and in my confusion, I can't help feeling that my mother shouldn't have left him alone like that and all this makes me feel sort of bad about her....."

"No, no! You see, whenever something goes wrong in a relationship, it's never good or honest trying to pin the blame on one or the other. You don't try to judge in such matters. What I would say is that it was nothing but the will of God."

He paused and was lost for a while in gazing at the water of the lake like it was a book he was reading.

"Listen," he said, at last, "if you went to a psychologist with this thing, what would he tell you? He would say the roots of our conduct lie in the subconscious, and that what happens in the dark recesses of the mind has the power to unfold reality in such a way that it fulfils our secret desires. And then he would say that their separation was a solution that grew up inside them, like a shoot that finds its way out of the earth into the sunshine. But that is just another way of putting it. In reality it is God who works through us and compels us to do what he deems right for us…

So don't let this bedevil you. Forget it. We are all composed of so many different hues and no one is as good an artist as to paint a perfect picture. And then everything has turned out quite right in so many ways for everyone involved, including you, so you must try to accept their decision and forgive them. You'll do so, won't you?"

"Yes. I am not angry with them. But you must tell me something about why it happened, otherwise I won't be able to rid myself of all sorts of conjectures and misgivings…"

"I can only hint at what I personally think went wrong with their relationship…."

"But you were his friend…" she had interjected.

"Yes, but I wasn't here when all that happened. I was

The Shadow of the Clouds

teaching in a school in Dehradun then and I only came back here to join Sherwood in 1980. That was long after your mother had gone away from his life. So whatever little I know is what I came to learn from him, plus whatever little I could make out by my closeness to him. So I'll try to answer your question if that would be any consolation to you, but I think it would be advisable to go somewhere inside. It's getting too cold for my old bones out here," he said, getting up from the seat.

"Oh, yes, of course," she said, feeling chagrined. She hadn't realised how cold it had turned and how uncomfortable it must be for him to be sitting beside the lake under the dark clouds.

"We'll go to Sacklay. The coffee there is excellent and so are the pastries. You love pastries. Don't you?"

Twenty Five

The Sacklay Restaurant and Bakery was situated in the same building as Modern. It was a small place, with large glass windows that captured a glimpse of the lake, and, with its threadbare but cosy sofas and its wooden floor and ceiling, it was an ideal place to spend a cold, grey winter morning. And the quaint little cups in which the coffee was served really charmed her.

"It's very nice here," she observed.

"So it is. Your father was quite fond of this place too and more often than not we used to have our breakfast here. We would go on having one coffee after another till it was time for lunch. But not in the summer though. It's hard to find an empty seat then. But let's go into the question that's troubling you, of why your parents separated, particularly when they loved each other …Tell me, Tahmina, "he asked, looking at her through the smoke of the pipe he had lighted, "What do you know about love?"

"Oh….." she said, startled. "Well, if you love someone you don't go away from him," she managed to say in a sort of whisper.

"That's a poor answer. Tell me, do you read poetry?"

"Yes, a little…"

"Have you ever read Elizabeth Browning's 'Sonnets from the Portuguese'?

"I don't think I have…"

"You get hold of a copy. Maybe you'll find it among your father's collection; it was one of his favourites. Anyway, read those poems she wrote when she fell in love and you'll understand what true love is and why it always blossoms first in a woman's heart. That was the sort of love your father searched for, love that was as natural, intense and overwhelming as a thunder shower…She couldn't have reached those depths of longing, I mean your mother. She met your father for the first time on their wedding night and who can tell what chords he touched in her. But as girls here take it quite naturally to love their husbands, she must have felt the same too. And like almost every other woman, all she wanted would be nothing more than to have a house of her own and to have an ordinarily happy and secure life with her husband."

"Yes, that's exactly what she told me," Tahmina interrupted.

"Ah! So you see, I am not too far off the mark. But it was different with your father. He craved for something wild and dark and intoxicating in her that would make him forget who he was. You understand what I am trying to elucidate, don't you?"

"Yes, I think so…"

"But let's first try to imagine how your mother must have felt when she was married into his family. She was so young then, and someone who had a normal, happy childhood and all of a sudden she had been thrust into a world where everyone was so perplexing. It must have been bewildering to her…."

"Yes, I know," she interrupted. "She told me a lot about that and it was my grandmother ……"

The Shadow of the Clouds

"Ah! So she told you about her." He shook his head in dismay. "She was a mystery without a clue..."

"In fact, she put most of the blame on her..."

"There's truth in that. You must understand your father had a very unfortunate and cursed relationship with his mother and they both brought out the worst in each other. He rarely talked about it, because it was all very painful and distasteful to him, but it's not difficult to understand how that sort of a woman can blight a child's personality beyond repair. That's what happened to Imad too. Though I must say he was able to hide it all very well because, for all his flaws and failings, he was a man of rugged character." He paused to light his pipe again.

"But let us talk about Amna and him. As I said, she was a very sensible, practical girl, and, in many ways, she was her own woman even then. And though she was very beautiful and your father was happy to have found her, they were very different from each other, as much as frost is from fire. I mean, he was a shy and withdrawn person, lost in his books and the lake here, with such little sense of the real world. He must have been too dreamy for her, and perhaps she felt irritated by the way he went about like a child lost in a crowd....

"But that's how he was even when we were in school, and it was only gradually that I came to realise how lonely he felt and how difficult it was for him to relate to a world that seemed to hurt him all the time. What must have happened, perhaps, was that the more difficult and unpleasant the outside world became for him, the more he withdrew into a world of his imagination, till that became the only way he learnt to deal with life.

"But that's not the whole story about him, because, inside

of himself, he was a very intense person, very impetuous and adventurous. But those natural impulses of his were locked away into the recesses of his being, yearning to break out but remaining a prisoner to the power of despair that ruled over him. He told me so many times how he had to fight the demons within himself and how that inner struggle would drain away all his resources, leaving him little strength to face the problems that confronted him in the outside world."

He broke off again to tinker with his pipe and to order some more coffee.

"However, they seemed quite happy with each other in the beginning. In fact, I still remember the evening they came to my house for dinner, just a few weeks after their marriage, when I had come over to Nainital and invited them for a celebration. She had been looking so ravishing then, with the freshness of a rose. You know, looking at you makes me wonder sometimes as though I was looking at her again." He stopped to gaze at her for a moment. "But no, you are very shy and certainly more beautiful, or maybe that's because I have become old. I mean, age makes a man more sensitive to the inward beauty…" And again he fell silent for a few moments to look at her, his eyes twinkling and his face all broken up in a smile.

"Anyway, they were happy to begin with," he continued, "but, all of a sudden, there were so many problems, problems at home, problems at the shop, but the main thing was both of them felt constricted and helpless. She was a prisoner at home, where his mother messed about with everything, and he was stuck with helping his old father at the shop. And unfortunately, instead of bringing them closer as so often happens, these difficulties only deepened the chasm between them….."

The Shadow of the Clouds

'Initially it was Amna who began to be depressed and he was so sensitive to whatever she had to suffer because of him. I still recall what he said to me once, 'She's like a trapped butterfly, Mathew, fluttering her wings against the windows.' And I'll never forget how his eyes had been full of tenderness. You see if anything hurt her, he felt its pain in his heart in a terrible way. That's how he was."

"But couldn't he rebel against his parents," Tahmina wondered aloud.

"No, he couldn't. Not because he lacked courage, or didn't love his wife enough to do so. The real dilemma was he loved his old man too and didn't want to hurt him, or to leave him alone at that stage; the old man wasn't keeping well through those years and he depended on Imad to look after the shop. But there's no doubt he went through a lot of pain to see Amna suffer like that and there wasn't anything he didn't want to do for her. Do you know what he yearned to do for her?" he asked and went on with his narrative.

"He yearned to make her happy and different, like the girls who came here during the summer, girls whom freedom had given such happiness that it reflected on their faces. He saw them with their hair flying in the breeze, looking so fetching as they roamed freely about the hills. 'They aren't going to become sluggish and cold with age, hating themselves and others because of their unfulfilled desires. These girls will always be as lovely as a stream wending its own way through the woods…' That's what he used to say about them and that's what he wished for Amna too. He didn't want her to become a woman like his mother, going through life caged in that black prison of a veil, with nothing to pass the time except the petty cares of the household. He said that's what turned such women

131

so bitter and he knew, of course, because of the way he had suffered so terribly from the sort of woman his mother was..."

"My God!" Tahmina exclaimed softly. "I could never have imagined there can be people like my grandmother in this world..."

"But you haven't seen anything of the world yet, my dear," Mr. Mathew reminded her. "Such homes still exist and so do women like your grandmother, may her soul rest in peace! But it would still be hard to come by a woman who tortured her son like that," he said, and she could see how perplexed he appeared with that and her heart was once more stirred up in a strange way. Mr. Mathew was silent too, till he glanced at his watch.

"It's forty past one, isn't it," he said, looking startled. "You must be hungry, my dear, so tell me what you'd like for lunch."

"Oh no! I am not feeling hungry at all. But you go ahead and order something for yourself," she replied.

"No, I'm in no hurry too. I was thinking about you. Anyway, let's have some more coffee."

Having called out for the coffee, he started to talk with her again. "So you realise now how your father must have suffered by his inability to alter their lives in any way and that's what ate into him. I think where he went wrong was the way he refused to acknowledge for a long time the power that money has in our lives. There was a time when we were in college when he used to say that a man required nothing more from life if he had a woman to love him and his house was full of books and flowers. He was right in supposing that money couldn't buy you happiness, but he failed to understand that almost every kind of happiness could be spoiled if you do not have the money to support it.

"One doesn't easily realise that the power of money isn't about the false possessions it can buy, or the false security it can bring you. Instead, it's significance lies in the fact that it can give you the freedom and the opportunity to create the sort of life you dream about for yourself. But anyhow, it was such a vagary of fate, because your father was a man who wanted and deserved a simple and regular life but things went on becoming more and more troubled and disorderly for him. And it wasn't as if he didn't try to turn things around, but how do I describe it?" He searched about for words for a while before continuing.

"You see, he was always weaving dreams and coming and going out of his despair with such false and unrealistic hopes that they inevitably came crashing down on him. Or, perhaps, it was just his bad luck that nothing would work out for him. That too plays a part."

"But, everything should have been easy after his father died. Even his mother had gone away after that and they had their own house too and…..and…" She had broken off.

"And…and what?" Mr. Mathew asked her, looking at her searchingly.

"Oh, nothing," she replied, lowering her eyes, but then said it all the same. "I mean I was born too. Children make a difference, don't they?"

"You have something there, I admit, and perhaps if you had come a little early …. Anyhow, from what I could figure out, they fought over the bookshop but your father wouldn't give up putting whatever little they had into it till he was almost bankrupt. And one can't blame Amna too, for like all women, she worried about the future, particularly after you were born. I know women think differently, wanting continuity and security in their lives, perhaps because they tend to look far into the future. Do you do that too?" He stopped to ask and went on without waiting for a reply.

"Well, so things started to go terribly wrong with them at that stage. There's an old saying that the heaviest rain falls on the house with a leaking roof and that about sums it up very well. But whatever the difficulties, the basic mistake was the way they closed their hearts to each other and this meant they could no longer face each other unmasked. And that's always a dangerous thing in a relationship……"

He was distracted by a passing acquaintance who had sauntered inside to greet him. But, thankfully, he was in some sort of hurry and went away declining Mr. Mathew's invitation to join them for a cup of coffee.

"Now where were we?" He put the question more to himself than to her and went on again. "Yes, so as I was telling you, they started to keep silent between them. But this sort of thing can't go on forever. If you let life stand still for too long, something or the other is bound to break and one day she had burst out at him with words that must have been hidden in her for a long time. She had thrown his books at him…"

"Yes, she still hates the sight of them…"

"Hmmm," he said thoughtfully. "And I think her persistent aversion for books is really an unconscious betrayal of the fact that she still has a soft spot for him….Anyway, two years after you were born, she finally left to go and live with her parents."

"And he didn't try to make her return?"

"No. He was convinced he would never be able to give her any sort of happiness. That's what despair does to a man. Even earlier, much before he got married, he used to think there wasn't anything in him that could attract a woman or make her fall in love with him. But he was wrong in that. I mean from what I have seen of life, women seem to have this weakness of falling impetuously in love with the sort of man he was, with those sad eyes of his and that shy smile...."

"But this is all so preposterous. I mean, there are such quarrels between people but that doesn't mean the end of their marriage, particularly when they have children ...."

"I know, but God willed it otherwise," Mr. Mathew said, putting his hand across the table to touch her.

"No, I'm certain there's more to it than all this. I mean, I still don't know what occurred that made my mother leave...."

"Come on, my dear, don't trouble yourself unnecessarily. It's just that their relationship broke down," he said, patting her hand.

"I know and I would rather forget everything, it's all so sad and troubling...But still, I don't know why I can't let go of this feeling as if something is eluding me, as if something is being hidden from me...Can't you even give me a hint?"

"I have told you whatever little I knew or guessed," he replied, gazing vacantly at her. "If there's anything more, then believe me, I don't know a thing about it. All your father would say was it was entirely his fault that she left him."

"I don't know what to believe," she said, feeling distraught and empty. "All I know is I have a feeling my mother was concealing something from me and so are you….." She brought her head up to look at him, searching his face with her misty eyes. "Tell me," she said, a sudden thought striking her. "Was there someone else between them?" She flung an arrow in the darkness.

"What do you mean?" Mr. Mathew exclaimed.

"You know what I mean. Was there someone else?"

"Perhaps, perhaps there might have been," he replied softly, looking away out of the window. "I don't know. But even if there were, it wouldn't have been something meaningful. I mean, your father wouldn't have spent all these years alone if he had someone else to love, would he?"

"Yes, I guess, you are right. I guess I'll never be able to learn the truth," she replied, feeling too tired to go on any further.

And Mr. Mathew had ordered lunch after that and started to tell her how he had met his wife when he was teaching in Dehradun and how naughty Claire used to be as a child and how lonely he would feel when she finally went away with Henry….

It was almost ten past three by the time they stepped out of the restaurant and Mr. Mathew took her for a stroll around the Flatt once again. The weather hadn't broken by then though it had become quite dark outside, with thunder rumbling over the valley. But the surprising thing was that it wasn't as cold as it had been when the sun was out, perhaps because there wasn't even as much of a breeze as to make a leaf flutter.

"I must thank you for spending so much time with me, and for telling me so much," she said as they came to lean on the banisters at the edge of the lake.

The Shadow of the Clouds

"There's really no need to be so formal. After all, your father was one of my dearest friends and nothing would make me happier than to spend time with you, to see you smile and look so lovely," he replied, turning to look at her with affection. "You know, Imad loved you to distraction, even though he let you go so far away from him."

"I understand, and yet, even for my sake..." She had broken off, trying to put an end to talking about those things.

"But he wouldn't have liked you to see them fighting and being unhappy with each other," Mr. Mathew replied.

"But why didn't he realise that times change, things change and perhaps everything would have turned right for him too."

"But you must understand that people learn to make judgements from the moment they are born, judgements like the dark are scary, or that mothers are comforting. And if things go the way you expect them to then it's hard to believe otherwise. If only the shop had run well..."

"He loved the shop quite a lot, didn't he?" she asked.

"Yes, and it was so distressing to see him sitting alone there, with nothing to do in the desolation that time had wrought on it. He felt so humiliated by that, though he wouldn't show it to anyone."

"So you think all this wouldn't have occurred if the shop had run well?" Tahmina asked.

"No, I wouldn't say that, though perhaps it might have made some difference, because, yes, love certainly is a poor thing without money. But the real reason was that there was no magic between them. I mean, more than love it's the instinctual bond that can hold a man and a woman together even when there's no tenderness between them. If the chemistry's right they are compelled to come back to each other again and again, compelled to find some solution to whatever problem life confronts them with. And you very well can't blame anyone if that sort of attraction is missing between two people. I mean, it's not something that's in our hands."

"But that sort of attraction is so rare, isn't it?"

"True, and most marriages do fairly well without it, perhaps because most people can go through life without any intensity or deep feelings. Your mother could have done so too, but not your father. For people like him, people who have been hurt or broken, people who are extraordinarily sensitive, well, they need to find such a bond with someone to face life, to find refuge from the demon of loneliness that haunts them."

"And let me tell you," he added after a few moments of silence between them. "Your father realised this too. That's why he decided to let her go and put his trust in God to bring happiness to your lives and I don't think God disappointed him that way."

And later, before saying goodbye near the path that wound its way to her house on the hill, he said to her. "I hope whatever we have discussed will bring some peace to your troubled heart."

"You have been such a comfort. But….But why do such things happen?" she had asked in despair.

"You must understand life is unfair, or, at least, sometimes it appears to be so." He had pressed her hand and added, "But you can console yourself with the fact that after a

The Shadow of the Clouds

while he found the peace that comes to a man who accepts the sorrow that life has given him."

"Yes, I guess so. " She had sighed and asked him, "There was one more thing I wanted to ask you."

"Yes, yes, my dear." He had smiled at her.

"I was unable to give any happiness to my father when he was alive. Is it possible for me to do something now that would make him happy, wherever he is."

"He had his aspirations for you too," he replied.

"I don't understand…" She had looked at him puzzled.

"You'll have to discover that yourself. All I can say is that he wanted you to be happy, and wherever he is, that's what he would be wanting even now. You know, there was a night in him that never passed and you were the morning he waited for all his life……:"

And the rain had started to fall by the time she reached home.

Twenty Six

The rain stayed for three days. It was a lashing, relentless storm, stopping only for little spaces. Even those interludes had been filled with wisps of clouds that floated all over the hills, shrouding everything in mist. And for all the tightly shut windows, the bitterly cold and clammy wind had penetrated the interior of the house, turning everything damp and the coals had become so difficult to ignite. No only that, but for most of those three days the electricity had been intermittent at the best and it kept so dark that they had to light candles even during the day and the whole house had appeared dim and mysterious.

The rain beat on the roof with such force and clatter as if threatening to break an entrance and the house leaked from so many places that both of them kept running about placing a bucket here and mopping up there.

On the first day, Mr. Pandey had come during a lull in the storm, bringing up some fresh vegetables, eggs and milk. Tahmina had remonstrated with him, ticking him off like a mother for venturing out in weather like that. And though he didn't do that again, Anjali had come over to his place to check out if anything was required. Even Tahmina had ventured out with her once, when the rain had petered out for a while the following day. She had come down to the road to phone Dubai only to find that the lines weren't working and she had got thoroughly drenched while returning, for the rain had picked up again and Anjali's umbrella had proved a poor friend.

For Tahmina, these three cold, bleak days had turned into a revelation and so much had happened to her that she didn't know what to make of it all. She could never have imagined that life could be such a maelstrom of feelings and emotions, each of them so utterly different and yet so entwined that it was impossible to separate all the strands. Why was it so totally unpredictable? And why did it seem a song and a dream when its reality was a stone to grind you with? Yes, life was such a real mystery, hiding so much more than it revealed.

Meanwhile, the rain itself had turned into a little adventure, for it had evoked many new and unfamiliar feelings and sensations, and a spirit had awakened in her that seemed as wild as the weather.

She had been sitting in her room the first morning, watching the mist making patterns on the window, when all of a sudden she had been seized by an urge to go and stand out in the rain. Opening the door to the veranda and stepping out hesitatingly, she had come to stand out at the edge, her arms pressed to her bosom, crossed over her strangely beating heart, letting the impetuous raindrops to touch many untouched things in her. She had watched the trees thrashing about in the wind and the lightning flash across the sky, hearing the thunder crashing and echoing throughout the hills and something akin had stirred and responded in her with equal intensity and passion. And though nothing would have tempted her to go out in that frigid rain, yet her heart had yearned to wander about all over the hills in that windswept storm.

And then during the afternoon, when she had come to lie down with the blankets in her bed, the cold had made her snuggle and rub herself in them and a luminous warmth had spread languorously through her body, touching its every pore.

The Shadow of the Clouds

She had felt a sudden desire run through her veins and become conscious of an unmistakable yearning to be near someone as warm and alive as she was.

It was not as if that desire was something entirely unknown or incomprehensible to her, but the intensity of its longing had surprised and disturbed her. And a sweet ache had filled the recesses of her body, flowing like the rain in every rivulet, pulsating and pausing with the wild throbbing of her heart. She had felt so disturbed that she had sat up in bed to look out of the window but there had been nothing to see really, for the view was blurred by the rain. So she lay down again and had somehow gone to sleep for a while.

Later, awakened by a loud crash of thunder, she had blushed at the sultry desires of the afternoon. How had they happened, she had wondered, for they seemed so out of place, with her heart full of grief....How was she to know or realise that often, confronted with something too painful to bear, the heart finds refuge in such distractions. Emotionally vulnerable and lonely, her desires had been nothing but a groping in the darkness for a hand she could hold.

Getting out of bed, she had made herself busy with more mundane affairs. The house had leaked from so many places and she had helped Kamla shift many things from one place to another and then went to help her out in the kitchen.

But later on, when she had come to lie down for the night, she had turned inwards once more. Like all new things, this place too had changed her. Yes, she was learning to see with new eyes. Nothing in life was simple for her any more and everything was so full of mystery and more difficult.

But most of all she had thought about her dead father, whose presence seemed to her as real and tangible as everything else that she could see and touch here. She had gone over everything she had come to know about him and all the years when she had been far away and he was a stranger to her. All those years of absence had been bridged in that one night. Whatever he may have done and howsoever he may have been, he was someone who had loved her and there was nothing for her to do except to love him back in return.

And then on the next two nights again she had kept awake, reflecting and wondering about everything while the flickering flame of the candle had continued to cast strange shadows on the wall.

Outside the storm had continued to rage and the night felt eerie and chilling though it held no terror for her. And long after the candle blew out, Mr. Mathew's words of had continued to echo through all the empty spaces of her heart...."There was a night in him that never passed and you were the morning he waited for all his life....."

Twenty Seven

Though the clouds still came and went, scattering a shower here and a shower there, the weather was on the mend. It was a different world in the sunshine now, with everything sparkling in the cold and transparent air and the sky seemed higher than before.

Five days had elapsed since the afternoon with Mr. Mathew and except for going down to phone her parents in Dubai, Tahmina had not ventured out at all, even though the rain had petered out over the past two days. Instead, she had kept herself busy, tidying up the house in the wake of all the upheaval caused by the storm and spent some time chatting with Anjali who came over every afternoon.

The long winter evenings had, however, proved difficult to spend so easily. She would ask Kamla to sit and chatter with her around the coals after supper and that helped, but once the dear woman went to sleep in the next room, she would again feel tormented by all sorts of difficult and painful thoughts. She would have liked to while away the night by reading some book and she had taken out a few from her father's collection. But try as she would, the words on the page seemed to blur and so she had taken a couple of sleeping pills that Faisal had put in her bag along with some other medicines. For the fact was that she had got tired of mulling over what she was going to do with her life now and had resolved to follow her heart, wherever it would take her.

Waking up early today, she got ready to accompany Mr.

Pandey to go and meet the lawyer. She didn't wear the warm, woollen overcoat, because it wasn't too cold in the sunshine, though the nights had started to become perceptibly colder after the storm. It had taken an hour to go through and sign all the necessary papers and Mr. Pandey had said goodbye to her near the path to her house. But she hadn't gone home.

She was feeling very light-hearted this morning, though she couldn't guess why her mood had changed like this. Perhaps it was the magic of the serene winter day, with the whole valley suffused with sunlight, or the song of the breeze among the trees. Or perhaps it was the picture-postcard sight of the lake in the distance or the rain-washed colours of the flowers that dotted the hillside. But whatever it was, something was making her feel so happy and adventurous and all of a sudden she was seized with an impulse to trek up the mountain to Dorothy's Seat.

Anjali had told her that the climb wasn't too difficult and that, by foot, it took around two hours to reach the summit. It was one of the seven hills surrounding the lake and there was an old memorial on its summit, from a sorrowing husband to his wife, Dorothy, who was killed in an air-crash. Tahmina had at once been taken by the romance of the story and now her heart was set to trek up to the peak.

So the moment Mr. Pandey bid goodbye to her near the path to her house, she turned to saunter down to the Flatt. The thought did occur to her for a moment to go and ask Anjali to accompany her, or at least to trudge up to the clearing and let Kamla know what she was up to. But she was feeling so happy and carefree today and all she did was to ask for directions and, stopping to buy something to eat on the way, she set out across the Flat towards the mountain trail that led up to the summit.

The Shadow of the Clouds

The climb was easy in the beginning, for steps had been cut into the rocks for a distance, but soon enough she was on the narrow and winding mountain track that was still somewhat slippery because of the recent wet weather. All around her were trees, with the air heavy with their smell and she could hear the intermittent calls of the birds echoing through the ever-responding woods.

Though her legs felt like lead, Tahmina was enjoying the adventure of the trek. It was a solitary climb and she met very few people on the way, mostly porters going downhill with loads of wood strapped to their backs. Only once had a party of tourists surprised her, coming down the hill as they were on horseback. They had been foreigners, probably from France as she had been able to guess from their shouts as they came downhill at a fast trot. The horses had terrified her, passing so near, for the path was very narrow and she had to huddle against the hillside to make way for them. How could anyone ride them on these hill tracts, she had wondered, what if their hoofs slipped or they got wild and threw the rider into the ravine?

She had come to a clearing about halfway up to the summit. There was a water tap there and some houses, built like barns into the hillside. The women had paused from their work to stare at her without any curiosity or interest, but the children waved to her cheerfully. Sitting down on a rock to rest for a while, she had eaten the vegetable burger she had bought for the trip. It was nearly half-past one at that point and when at last she reached the summit, the clock showed quarter to three.

She was feeling terribly weary by then and the ache in her legs made her feel as if she would not be able to walk another step. There was not a soul to be seen or heard and for a moment she stood where she was, feeling uncertain and afraid all of a sudden. But the feeling passed and she climbed the steps to the small, round pavilion on the summit.

As she came to stand by the iron railing that enclosed the pavilion at the edge of the precipice, the whole valley came into view, with the lake like an emerald speck far below in the depths. The sheer abyss made her feel dizzy, and unable to look down any more, she turned to sit on the stone bench that was placed there. She could see the mountain ranges spreading far away into the distance and the clear, blue expanse of the sky seemed like a lake to her, with puffs of white and auburn clouds floating on it like leaves.

Feeling refreshed and composed after a while, she munched on the chocolates she had brought with her and then stood up to explore the glade on the summit. Soft, cathedral light filtered through the trees and now and then a butterfly would flit by, sprinkling a dash of colour through the dark brown and green thicket of trees. It felt so quiet and peaceful there and the only sound was of the leaves rustling beneath her feet.

But as she wandered, she felt she heard a sound somewhere close by and turning past a big elm, she was suddenly confronted by a sight so unanticipated and startling that she stood riveted where she was.

Lying beneath the overhanging boughs of a tree was a man, with a woman lying sideways in his arms, her red shawl flung aside on the ground. They were clinging to each other, like moss to a stone, and their lips were locked in such a tight embrace that she could barely see their faces. They were lost to the beauty of the woods and the sky, lost in the language of their lips.

The Shadow of the Clouds

Her first impulse was to turn and run away but the spell had been cast and she could no more avert her eyes as she could still the wild throbbing of her heart. She had seen men and women kissing in films, had read about it and even imagined it sometimes. But the reality of that man and woman in their passionate abandon mesmerised her and she stood gazing at them. She was feeling intoxicated by the carnal intensity of their kissing, their lips not letting go of each other even for a moment and their arms twisting and grasping each other more and more ardently after every slackening.

She stood there for a long time, turning away only when it finally became unbearable to watch them any more. Half-awake, half-dazed, she ran with wayward steps, searching for the trail that had brought her to the summit.

And it went with her, the haunting image of that man and woman, their profile in the half-light of approaching evening imprinted on her imagination. And all through that night that image continued to hover before her eyes, breaking into her thoughts against her will and she felt those kisses burning on her lips, keeping her restless and awake till a pale rose had turned crimson in her.

Twenty Eight

Waking up a little late in the morning, she had hurried through breakfast to reach the shop on time. Returning from the meeting with the lawyer yesterday, she had asked Mr. Pandey, "Uncle, there were a few things I wanted to discuss with you regarding the shop. Can you arrange to open it tomorrow morning so we that could sit and talk there for a while?' And like always, the dear old man had readily assented to her request and so she was now seated in the bookshop with Mr. Pandey.

"I want your help, uncle," she said straightforwardly.

"Yes, yes. Just tell me what you want," he replied.

"I have decided to stay here,"

"I don't understand." He appeared perplexed.

"I want my father's shop to open again and I will stay here to run it. It will be full of books and people once again," she said simply.

He looked at her for a moment, an expression of surprise and happiness on his face. But then he shook his head sadly.

"No one would be happier than myself to see the shop bustling again. But I don't see how you will be able to stay here and run it. It would take much doing and a lot of money to turn your wish into a reality."

"But..." She tried to explain but he waved with his hand, asking her to wait till he had finished.

"I know, I know. You have lots of money and it's natural for you to love what your father loved, but you have no experience and I am too old and tired. And then it's no longer easy to build or establish anything. Times have changed and they have changed for the worse. There aren't any principles any more, no honesty and the competition is fierce. And I don't suppose Faisal Sahib would ever allow you to stay here to do all this."

"I realise that," she replied with a sigh. "It would take some miracle to convince him. But I think I'll be able to work it, for I know he won't stop me from doing something that would make me happy. And as far as the other problems go, well, I'll learn to cope with all that as I go along. But you are wrong about one thing. The real difficulty is going to be money." And seeing the puzzled look on his face, she added hurriedly, " I mean, Abbu will give me all the money I need, but I wouldn't like to use anyone else's money for the shop. That would pain my father in his grave."

"So how do you propose to get it going again?"

"Oh, I'll think of something, don't worry about that. What we have to do first is to prepare a sort of blueprint that would help us plan its revival."

"That's all right but I would like you to give this thing a second thought. I have no intention of discouraging or hurting you but at the same time, I would like to point out that many things are easy to begin but very difficult to continue."

"I know, and perhaps I am making a mistake by giving in to the rush of feelings in my heart. But I am as stubborn as I am sentimental and so I'll stick to my decision. You know my father wrote to me to trust God and follow my dreams and

The Shadow of the Clouds

that's what I am going to do. And an even more compelling reason is that I didn't have any opportunity to give him any sort of comfort or happiness when he was alive. So I feel that the most delightful and proud thing would be for me to turn the shop into a success. So please pray to God that I succeed."

"Hmmm!" She could see how touched he was by the sad way he smiled at her. "Yes, it would give his soul peace in heaven to see the shop flourish once more. But, then again, I have my doubts, for what appears bright in the morning becomes shrouded by the night. So think well and far ahead before you finally decide anything."

"I have. All these days I have been doing nothing else. And I have tried to listen to my heart too and that is what it has asked me to do."

"Okay!" he said, smiling happily all of a sudden. "So it's decided then. Now tell me what I can do for you."

It took them most of the morning to draw up a plan and to chalk out a rough budget until it was time for him to go home for lunch. As they prepared to leave, she mentioned to him.

"There's one more thing, you must find someone to help me manage the shop—someone young, hard-working and honest who would be able to learn the ropes from you. I'll pay well for the right person and your experience will guide us through."

"I'll see to that," he murmured and then added a little hesitatingly, "But you must get Faisal Sahib's permission before we go ahead with this."

"Yes, I'll do that soon. In fact, I am going to write to him

Fahimm Inhonvi

this afternoon. It won't be possible to tell him on the phone."

"Yes, do that. And there was one other thing. It will start snowing in a couple of weeks for sure and it would become difficult to get anything done during that period. You must keep this in mind too."

"Oh, that would be just a little bit of bother, uncle. I am so excited that nothing's going to stop me now," she said happily.

"All right! All right!" The old man smiled at her affectionately as he hugged her goodbye. "But there is still one thing bothering me," he added before turning to leave on his way. "You say you won't take any money from Faisal Sahib but you haven't made it clear where it is going to come from...."

"Don't worry about that too. Everything will take care of itself," she replied, smiling so sweetly and mysteriously. "You know, there's an old saying I read somewhere, that God always provides thread for the work we begin...."

Twenty Nine

Kamla had ignited the coals in her room for the night and Tahmina was sitting at the table, searching for words to write to Faisal about her decision to stay back in Nainital and re-open her father's bookshop.

How happy he had sounded on the phone yesterday, she thought. She had told him that all the legal formalities for the succession were complete and the lawyer had assured that all she had to do now was to appear in court once when the papers would be put up in a few days.

"That means you can come home after that?" he had said.

"Yes, I guess so."

"So you fix a date and inform your uncle in Delhi. He will get your plane seat reserved. Okay?" he had asked.

"Yes....Yes, Abbu," she had replied hesitantly, feeling ashamed. But there was no way she could have told him then and there that she had no intention of returning home for God knew how much time it would take her to get the shop going again. She wouldn't have been able to endure the hurt and disappointment in his voice and her heart would have melted in a few moments.

But she had to tell him anyhow and the only way she could do so was to write to him, though she dreaded the moment when he would read her letter and come to know she was not coming back any time soon. I should have learnt to mend hearts, she thought, before I went about breaking them. But that was easier said than done.

There had been one option she had considered, of going back home for now and then return again after the winter. Perhaps that way she would have been able to get him to agree without hurting him in such an abrupt way. But she had discarded the thought as soon as it had come, for she knew she wouldn't be able to face him with her decision and would succumb to the love in his eyes.

So she had to tell him the truth now and pray to God that he would not take it as badly as she feared. But how was she going to tell him? That too in such a way that would not compel him to think she didn't belong to him any more. Was she being ungrateful? She wondered. Even her dead father had written that Faisal had more right over her than anyone else and she would rather die than deny him that. But what can I do, she reflected with a sigh, what can I do other than to accept the verdict of my heart?

"Dear Abbu," she began, and then was lost for words once more. She had hardly written a letter to someone in her life and now she had to write such a difficult one.

It took her a long, long time to write it and by the time she had finished, she had torn so many drafts that there were just a few pages left in the pad she had bought in the morning. It turned out to be a long and rambling letter and she had allowed the words to flow with her thoughts, beginning by telling him how she longed to be back with him and Amna....

"But, Abbu, if you were here to see how badly the shop was, you would have been compelled like me to think how much it must have hurt him. You have always told me that a man loves his place of work as much as his home, sometimes

The Shadow of the Clouds

even more, and as he had nothing left at home so all his love must have gone to the shop.......

"I don't know how this idea of reviving the shop has come to mean so much to me, but it has turned into a dream that I would like to make real. I feel so excited and happy and I think this will bring some sort of peace to his soul too. And then I have also fallen in love with this place. It's so different and beautiful here......

"I know how you'll miss me for I am missing both of you just as much. But it will be just a few months because all I want to do for now is to renovate and stock the shop once again and find someone to manage it before I return home. It will also be an experience to me, this whole venture, I mean. I am going to learn to make decisions on my own and manage things independently. I think that is something you have been trying to teach me and this would be such a challenging opportunity to do so.

And further on she had written:

"I would be happy if you came here to visit me, but no, not too soon, for though my eyes are thirsting to see you again, I would love to have you here the day my shop opens again. I don't know if you would bring Ammi here too. I guess she is going to be very angry with me and I think she won't like to come here again and you will have to leave her alone. That would be a problem…..But, Abbu, please, understand that all this is just what I have thought of doing. I would still want your approval. Otherwise I'll not stay here a moment…."

And in the end she had brought up the subject of money.

"I know you would send me anything I asked. But that would be so easy. What I would like to do is to use the money

I earned from the boutique and that you told me was kept aside in my name at the bank. I never thought I would be so thankful for this because it means I will be able to revive the shop with money that I have earned. I don't even know exactly how that much would be but I do recall you telling me once that it was more than 18000 Dirhams. And if it really does amount to that much, then it would be more than enough for me to do whatever I have in mind just now…"

Having finished with the letter to him, she had started to write a few lines to her mother too. And though she found it much more difficult to write to her, she had managed somehow, asking her not to be angry and hurt….. "I am sure you will understand my sentiments and perhaps share them too," she had ended, adding, "If I am able to get his shop going again then that would be the least I could do to pay off a little of the debt a daughter owes to her father."

Putting away the letters in the envelope, she had glanced at the watch. It had startled her to see how long it had taken, for it was well past midnight and even the coals had all but died away. Suddenly becoming conscious of how terribly cold it was, she had switched off the lamp on the table and snuggled into the bed.

What will Abbu think of me, she wondered, tucking the quilts around her. Will he consider her ungrateful? Would their relationship be hurt and changed beyond repair? And what will happen when she would come face to face with him again? Will it be possible for her to hide how divided her heart had become? Oh, God! She had thought, why was it so painful to love?

And there was no way she could tell him or anyone else why she felt compelled to avenge her father's despair with hope and his humiliation with pride. It was all so painful and personal and perhaps she would never be able to lay bare her heart to anyone in the world for this.

But I will have to learn from now on to live with some thorns pricking into my heart, she had resolved, as she closed her eyes in the darkness to make her way to sleep.

Book Two

Thirty

December was coming to an end and Christmas had brought the first snow of the season. It had continued to be overcast and misty for almost a week before that, and then, on that joyous morning, the sky and the hills had mingled in one grey whirl of snow that had fallen all through the day and prevented Tahmina from going over to Claire's house to be part of the celebrations. Instead, she had sat by the window, watching the snow settling down like a blessing on the roofs and trees. She knew that this was a beauty that was not going to endure and so she was happy to see as much of it as she could.

As the days had passed by, she had settled down to life in the cold and silent beauty of the winter. Soon after posting that letter to Faisal, she had initiated some repairs to the house and that had kept her occupied while she waited to hear back from him. The roof had been repaired and she had got a geyser installed in the bathroom, for it was too inconvenient to heat the water on the stove all the time. She had also bought a new dressing table as well as chairs for the dining table and a beautifully carved wooden lamp to put beside her bed. And though she would have liked to give the house a fresh coat of paint too, Mr. Pandey had dissuaded her, saying it would be too much of a bother through the cold.

Most of the days she would set out during the afternoon to ramble through the town and the hills, prying into the hidden beauty of the place. Often she would have Claire or Anjali, or sometimes both, to keep her company, though she had to spend the frosty evenings at home, craving as much for warmth as for someone to share her thoughts with.

She had considered buying a television to spend the evenings but there wasn't enough money to spare and, for some reason or the other, books no longer seemed interesting to her, perhaps because life itself had taken on the twist of a story. So the only thing to occupy her during the long, pensive hours after sunset was the notebook in which she jotted down her plans for the revival of the bookshop.

Yes, that was something that excited and filled her thoughts all the time. She would visit and spend as much time as she could in the other bookshops of the town, noting the sort of books and other things they stocked and then she would sit down in the evening and jot down her ideas.

Mr. Pandey had also given her some catalogues of various publishers to study, as well as lists of textbooks that were prescribed in the local schools. The dear old man had even prepared a sort of project report, complete with even the smallest detail about the book business in Nainital. And so it wasn't too long before she had formed a fairly clear idea of what she was going to do with the shop.

The only thing to keep her waiting was Faisal's reply and the money she had asked for. She had been talking to him almost every day on the phone and three days ago he had told her that the letter had reached him. Her heart had missed a few beats and she had almost felt faint but he had sounded so easy and composed, or, at the least, he hadn't let his voice betray anything.

"Don't worry, I'll write back to you tomorrow." That was all he would say before handing the phone to Amna.

The Shadow of the Clouds

"Hello! Ammi, how are you?" Tahmina had asked, prepared to hear something hard and bitter from her. But, thankfully, she too had sounded normal, asking her to take care in the cold and eat lots of dry fruits.

Still, Tahmina had been unable not to feel sad and guilty about the whole affair, for she realised how lonely they would be without her or Kashif at home. I'll not put too much of a distance in time between us, she had resolved, I'll just wait to see the business pick up by spring and go back. And by that time Mr. Pandey would certainly have found someone to manage the shop in her absence. And that was how far she had thought about the future, for who knew what turn life would take once she was back in Dubai!

And so Christmas had passed and when the snowfall stopped next day, she was inundated with so many cakes and gifts that she didn't know what to do with them. So she gave some of them away to the poor children who came to play in the clearing in front of her house and asked Kamla to distribute the rest among the plentiful needy families that lived huddled in the hills.

And for the next three days she braved the biting cold winds and slippery paths to go up to Mr. Mathew's house and asked Claire to take her around to visit all the families that had sent the gifts to her, so she could thank them for sharing their joy with her.

Thirty One

A small interlude of mildly sunny weather and the sky had become darkly cloudy again. There had been snow through the night and it was almost as dusky as evening when the postman had called during the afternoon with Faisal's envelope.

Tearing it open, she had found a bank draft for one hundred and sixty three thousand rupees along with another one for twenty thousand, with a short note attached to it: "You can spend your own money for the shop," Faisal had written, "but this money from me is for your own personal expenses."

Touched by this gesture and what it meant to emphasise, she had hurriedly opened the letter. It was a brief note really and, strangely enough, she felt a sort of relief to find it that way.

"We were so surprised by your letter and it's still hard to believe that you will be away for so long... But we respect your feelings—in fact, we are proud such a thought occurred to you. And though life seems empty without you and the house seems to have withdrawn into itself, your happiness is more necessary and precious than your presence here. So go ahead with your work. But do remember that you belong to us too and that we trust you enough to let you live alone in a new and strange place. I expect you to take care of yourself and not do anything without asking Mr. Pandey. Your Ammi sends her love and blessings to you."

Smiling with relief, she had dressed quickly, insulating

herself from the cold by putting on her jacket over the two woollen sweaters, and stepped out in the dim, grey light of the afternoon to trudge through the snow to Mr. Pandey's house.

Though she shivered instinctively with the cold, she had never felt such an exhilarating sense of life. In fact, her happiness was making her feel almost naughty. She tried to pour out her breath in as big puffs as she could manage, recalling the image of the way Claire smoked, blowing out large puffs of smoke. She remembered with a laugh how, when they were coming back from visiting somewhere the day after Christmas, her teeth had started to chatter uncontrollably from the cold. Stopping to light a cigarette, Claire had asked her to try a puff. "Come on, Snow White," Claire had said, "It won't do any more harm than to turn you a little purple."

And Tahmina had given in, only to burst out in fits of coughing and Claire had laughed so much it had given her cramps in the stomach. What fun she was, Tahmina thought, and her friendship always seemed to hold out the promise of some daring adventure.

Reaching Mr. Pandey's house, she even forgot to greet him before bursting out with her news and the old man was so happy to hear about it. Later on, as she sat sipping tea with them, she had asked him how they were going to get the work started now.

"First thing, you'll come in the morning to open a bank account in your name. You would need that to deposit these drafts. It'll take three days to credit them in your account and, in the meantime, we'll see what we have to do to start with."

And when she had finally got up to leave, for it was

The Shadow of the Clouds

getting dark and threatening by then, the old man had suddenly remembered to give her a bit of news too.

"Oh yes, I had almost forgotten. Sulaiman will be coming over tomorrow morning to meet you at the shop."

"Sulaiman?" She was puzzled. "Who's that?"

"Oh yes, you wouldn't know. He's the man I have found to help you at the shop."

"Oh!" Tahmina had been relieved to hear that. "That's great. And I am sure he'll turn out good, he's come just at the right moment, hasn't he?"

"I hope so, I hope so," he had replied, ruffling her hair with affection as he bid her goodbye.

Thirty Two

She had awakened very early today. Leaving the warmth of the bed without any regrets, she drew the curtains only to find the fog hanging like a veil over the lake. The sun hadn't come out to greet the first morning of the year.

It was still only a quarter to seven and she had a lot of time on her hands to be prepared to meet Mr. Pandey at the bank at eleven. Even so, she hurried through breakfast and her bath, though she did take her time to dress, trying out three different things before settling on the dark blue silk salwar suit and a pastel-pink cardigan.

Looking at her reflection in the mirror, she realised the mountain air had made her look healthy and lovelier. Her cheeks had turned almost crimson, and her lips were like two petals of a pink rose. And the dark circles under her large, wistful eyes had almost vanished. She had been so preoccupied since her arrival in Nainital that she hadn't paid much attention to her appearance and so, as she looked at herself in the mirror, she felt touched and a little surprised by the beauty that was reflecting back.

Sitting down to pray for a while, she asked God to keep the sky clear today and to keep the sun shining for the rest of the winter, for she didn't want the rain or snow to become a hindrance to the work at the shop. Glancing at the watch, she was disappointed to note that it was still only twenty past nine. She was feeling so impatient today, finding it difficult to keep sitting for more than a few moments. Exasperated and excited, she picked up her purse and decided to wander down to the lake.

Coming out in the open, she glanced at the sky. The clouds did seem to be turning a bit fair and patches of sunlight were breaking out here and there. But there was still a lot of fog over the lake and she regretted at not having worn the long coat, or her jacket, for the cold was sending shivers through her body.

Tired of wandering aimlessly around the Flatt, she decided to go and wait at the bank. It was situated near the bazaar and the doors were just being opened, when she arrived. At last, Mr. Pandey had arrived at eleven sharp and it took another half an hour to complete the formalities.

Strolling to the shop with him, she was surprised to see that someone had already opened the shutters and tidied up the interior.

"Namastey!" A clean, sturdy young local emerged from inside.

"This is Raghu. I asked him to come and sweep the place," Mr. Pandey explained.

"And where's the other man you told me about yesterday?"

"He'll be arriving any moment. But let's go inside and discuss the way you want to renovate the shop." Mr. Pandey replied.

"No, wait a moment," she said. "I want you to look at the shop from the outside here. Don't you think if we did away with the cabin at the end and this showcase at the front the shop would appear more spacious?"

The Shadow of the Clouds

"Hmmm." The old man considered for a few moments. "Yes, so it would. But the cabin came in useful for some privacy. You could have your lunch in there or use it when you want to work undisturbed for a while."

"Yes, that's right, but I am going to need more space and that would be the priority. I was actually thinking of introducing some new sections...but let's go and sit at the table so I can explain it all to you," she said, stepping inside with him.

Spreading her notes, she started to rapidly outline her plans to him. "You see, earlier the shop was selling only books and stationery but I would now like to stock some more things like audio-cassettes, greeting cards, gift items..."

She stopped suddenly. Someone was standing, hesitating at the entrance. Following the direction of her eyes, Mr. Pandey turned to look at him.

"Come on in, son. It's Sulaiman," he said and Tahmina looked up curiously at the tall, young man who was coming towards them.

He appeared quite handsome in an attractive black sweater as he walked towards them with his hands tucked into the pockets of his trousers and as he came near, something about him struck a chord in her. He had a strangely arresting face, whose clear-cut, symmetrical lines contrasted strikingly with his mop of thick, wavy hair and the lost vulnerable look in his eyes which were as dark as night.

"Hello, uncle!" he greeted Mr. Pandey. He had a soft, clear voice and yet it seemed as if it was coming from somewhere far away.

Noticing he was looking straight at her with a distant expression in his eyes, she lowered her gaze, even forgetting to ask him to take a seat.

"Sit down, son," Mr. Pandey spoke to him. "This is Ms Tahmina, Imad Sahib's daughter."

"Hello!" he said. "How are you?"

"Fine, thank you!" she replied, an ephemeral smile flitting across her face as she raised her eyes to his face for a moment.

"Beti," Mr. Pandey said to her, "let me tell you about Sulaiman here. His uncle is a very dear old friend of mine and he was also Anjali's batch-mate at the University here. In fact, his mother used to be a friend of Amna when they were both here."

"Oh!" She said, startled at this bit of news, "Ammi didn't tell me about this."

"Oh well, that was so long ago," the old man remarked.

"How's she? I mean, your mother," she asked Sulaiman.

"She's fine, thank you," he replied, with a sort of reluctance in his voice.

"She doesn't live here any more," Mr. Pandey explained. "He has been brought up by his uncle here, who used to teach at St. Joseph's. He's retired now and isn't keeping well since his wife's death last year. And there's only Sulaiman to look after him. Tell her something about yourself, son," he said, turning towards him.

"I am not doing anything at the moment. I finished my B.Com last year and so when uncle told me you were looking for someone to handle the shop, I just wondered if….:" He broke off.

"Yes, you see I want to renovate and open the shop once more and as I won't be able to stay here for more than three or four months, I would be happy if you could manage it independently."

"I can give it a try. But…" He appeared to hesitate a moment. "But I am thinking of going in for a chartered accountancy degree, though there are still at least six months to go before I'll be able to get an admission somewhere."

"But you can continue looking after the shop."

"No, because I'll have to go to some others place to get the CA degree. There's no institute here for that."

"I see," she replied, still looking away from him. "But is there any way you could give me a more long-term commitment? I mean, I would like you to see this through for at least a year."

"I don't know," he replied. "I can't promise. Though it would also depend on how my uncle keeps. I can't go anywhere till he gets well and even then, I don't know if I'll be able to leave him alone."

"I'm sorry," she replied, looking at him shyly.

"Thanks, anyway," he said and the tone of finality in his voice startled her before she realised he had misunderstood her. "I only meant I was sorry to hear about your uncle, not that I wouldn't like you to manage the shop," she added hurriedly, almost apologetically and then blushed too. Why am I behaving like a graceless little fool, she wondered, as she tried to overcome the disconcerting attractiveness of the man who was sitting so quiet and poised before her.

"I'll be happy to do that," he replied simply.

"Good," she said, trying to speak in an impersonal and business-like way. "Then you can discuss everything with Mr. Pandey."

"Yes, of course," Mr. Pandey said, taking out his pen. "Listen, initially you'll have to supervise the renovation work. We'll have to get a mason and carpenters...." And he went on explaining everything to him.

Leaning back in her chair, she picked up her pen and began to draw flowers on a piece of paper in an effort to keep her eyes from wandering to his face. But it wasn't any real use, for he kept on distracting her. The truth was, there was something about him that was making her heart beat in a strange manner.

It was quite a while before Mr. Pandey finally turned to her.

"All right, Tahmina, he'll look after everything now. But you'll have to draw a rough sketch of how you want the shop to be laid out, because the furniture and all will be made accordingly."

"Oh yes," she replied, fumbling about in her purse. "Here it is," she said, taking out a folded sheet of paper. "Here, this is how I want the shop to look now." And spreading out the sheet on the table, she leaned forward in her chair, forgetting everything else in her excitement.

"What would you want a computer for?" Mr. Pandey asked when she told them to make a place for that.

The Shadow of the Clouds

"It'll be very handy, uncle. We're going to use it for billing and correspondence and we can also maintain our inventory on it. Plus, we can generate some extra business by offering composing and printout services. That would not only add to the kitty but will also bring more people to the shop," she explained.

"Hmmm! Yes." The old man agreed. "But who'll handle the computer? Do you know how to operate it, Sulaiman?"

"I have some idea...." He started to say but she interrupted.

"Don't worry, Claire has promised to send a girl who's trained."

"All right. Anything else?" Mr. Pandey asked.

"No, I think this is enough for the moment," she replied.

"So now we have to get down and make a real budget, keeping in mind the money you have..." But the old man hesitated and, after a pause, he turned to Sulaiman. "Okay, son, you can go now. We won't have the money in our hands till Wednesday so you come over at ten on Thursday. And give my regards to your uncle. I'll come over sometime and discuss your salary with him."

Tahmina understood at once that Mr. Pandey didn't want to discuss money in Sulaiman's presence and this was his way of asking him to leave. And she instinctively glanced towards Sulaiman to see if he had felt this too. But his eyes were as empty as they had been all through the interview. Still, she could not help feeling embarrassed for his sake, fretting whether his feelings had been hurt. And so, just as he rose to leave, she spoke up almost impulsively, the words coming to her lips in a torrent.

"Sulaiman, I have a party at my home in the evening today, just a little get-together to celebrate all this. Mr. Pandey, Anjali, everyone will be there and it would be nice if you came too."

"Thanks," he replied, looking a bit surprised at her request and she let him look into her eyes then for a moment before he turned once again to walk out of the shop.

"What do you think?" Mr. Pandey asked. "He's fine and what I like is he's different from the other boys these days. He's very sincere and I know we can also depend on him to work hard. And then, he needs the job too."

"Yes, he does look smart and capable," she replied thoughtfully, "Tell me something about his family, uncle. What were you saying about his mother and my ammi? I would like to meet her."

"Yes, they were friends but she doesn't live here any more."

"Why?" she asked, puzzled.

"It's a sad and twisted story. I don't know the details but it appears his mother made a bad choice, marrying for love." He stopped abruptly and started to gather the papers on the table. Perhaps he doesn't want to talk of such things for my sake, she thought, so she decided to put him at ease.

"So what happened? Were his parents divorced?" she asked.

"No, but it was worse than that. He never let her live in

peace till he was alive."

"So his father's dead?"

"Yes, he died some years ago. But it hasn't made any difference for Sulaiman because he has lived with his uncle since he was three or four years old."

"But why doesn't his mother live with him?" she asked, perplexed.

"She got married again and lives in Mumbai with her new family. Actually, that's where she has lived most of her life because Sulaiman's father was settled there too, though he belonged to Ramgarh—that's a small town in the hills here, famous for it's apple orchards. Sulaiman's father owned a huge one too but he sold it all, piece by piece, to indulge all those vices he had picked up in Mumbai."

"I see," she said and asked softly, "But why did Sulaiman come to live here with his uncle?"

"His parents had made what we call a love marriage but, as I said, his father turned out to be a sour apple as sometimes crops up on even the best of trees. His uncle, that's Sulaiman's father's brother, is so kind and decent, one of the best people I have ever come across in my long life. Anyway, barely a year into their marriage, just around the time Sulaiman was born, his father started showing his true colours. I think it was the bad company he kept in the film world over there. He neglected and mistreated his wife, even beating her up when he was intoxicated, which was often. And the poor girl had nowhere to go, because her family had disowned her for marrying against their wishes. The only place she could live in peace for a while was when she came here to stay with her brother-in-law's family. And, in those circumstances, she thought it best to leave Sulaiman here with them. His uncle didn't have a son, just two daughters and so he was happy to have him."

"Didn't his father object to that?"

"As if he had enough moments of sanity to even remember he had a son! He simply didn't care. He kept his wife with him only so he could vent his frustrations on someone. He dreamed of making a great film but all he managed was to make a tragedy of his life before he got killed in an accident. He was drunk while driving."

"Oh my God! And what happened to Sulaiman's mother after that?"

"She went to live with her family for some time as there was a reconciliation after her husband's death and they got her married again to a widower with three children of his own."

"But doesn't she come here to meet Sulaiman?"

"Very rarely. And even when she does, it's for a few days only. I think she decided to forget that Sulaiman was her son, and I guess it's quite right too, because your real parents are the ones who bring you up in the world," he said, looking away from her.

"Yes, perhaps, you are right," she replied softly, not caring if he was trying to give her a hint or merely stating a fact.

"What about his uncle's daughters? You said he had two of them?" she asked.

"Both are married and his wife died last year too. That's why Sulaiman can't go anywhere, though he'll have to think about his future one day."

The Shadow of the Clouds

"Yes, of course. And what about money, doesn't his uncle have a good income?"

"He gets a monthly pension but that's not enough to go around, particularly because of all the medical expenses. Earlier, he used to do a bit of tutoring at home but that's no longer possible. And all his savings were spent in marrying off his daughters and his wife's long illness. So Sulaiman does need to have a job and I think we won't be able to find someone as good or dependable than him."

"Yes. How much do you think we'll have to pay him?"

"Three thousand would be enough to start with. Then we'll see how things work out."

"Won't this be too little?" she asked.

"No, not at all. It's more than he would get anywhere else," he said with finality and she didn't think it right to argue with him.

"All right, let's go now, you must be tired and it's time for your lunch too. And you have to come for the party in the evening too so I would prefer you have a good rest during the afternoon."

"All right, all right," Mr. Pandey's face lit up with affection for her. "You know what I was saying to Anjali's mother last night?" he asked, his dear face ruddy and glowing as he hugged her. "I was telling her that God has sent another daughter to patch me up and make me live a few years longer than I would have done otherwise," he added, taking away his hand from her shoulders to down the shutter and put on the locks. And this time there was such real sadness in his voice that she stretched out her hand to touch him. "But daughters go away, don't they?" he remarked, "Anjali will be married soon and who knows about you." And there was nothing she could reply to that except to bless him in her heart.

Walking home, her thoughts were all muddled up with the story Mr. Pandey had told her about Sulaiman's family. And she wondered too whether she had invited Sulaiman for the party just to assuage any hurt he may have felt when Mr.Pandey so abruptly asked him to leave. Or, was it something else altogether, like the way her heart was beating differently just by thinking about him?

Thirty Three

It kept bitterly cold all through January even though the winter had been exceptionally mild. As if in answer to her prayers, the weather had been sunny most of the time, and it was only towards the end of the season that dark clouds had gathered to draw a curtain over the valley and some rain had fallen. In fact, one night there had been a hailstorm and its clatter on the roof had woken and terrified her. It had snowed too the next day, but very lightly, as if to touch up the beauty of the place.

The renovation work at the shop was also coming to an end and the parcels of books and other goods she had ordered had started arriving too. Now all that was left to do was to unpack and make an inventory and then start stacking everything on the new, gleaming shelves. Even the computer had been bought and Tahmina had fixed up with the girl Claire had brought to mange the computer. Her name was Sylvia and Tahmina had taken to her immediately.

She looked simple but was so full of vivacity that no one could guess she came from a very poor family. Keeping joyously impecunious, she made everyone laugh at least once every thirty minutes, even managing to bring a rare smile to that piece of wood that Sulaiman had for a face.

For that was how he was, cold and distant and keeping as alone as if there was no one in the world except him. And yet, every passing moment she had come to realise how compellingly attractive this man was.

She remembered that evening when she had invited him for the party at her home the first day she had met him. She had worn one of her favourite suits, the one with shades of silver-grey merging into black, with small white flowers embroidered on it and put on the simple, heart-shaped diamond necklace too. Glancing in the mirror, she had smiled to discover how tempting she looked. Even Claire was so thrilled to see her.

"Why Tahmina, you look stunning! This dress complements your beauty! My God! You were really made for the summer, not for this blasted, dowdy winter."

It has been such a pleasant get-together, and she should have been the happiest of them all. Yet, she had felt somewhat subdued and disappointed because Suleiman hadn't turned up and many times during the evening she had lost the thread of the conversation, prompting the ever-observant Claire to ask why she appeared so distracted.

She had met him again two days later when he came to work for the first time. He had arrived earlier and because the mason and carpenters had arrived too, she had become busy explaining everything to them while Mr. Pandey had sent him off to withdraw some money from the bank.

She had seen him coming back an hour later, as she was sitting outside the shop while the old plaster and racks were being torn down inside the shop. Averting her gaze as he approached near, she pretended to be busy going through the catalogues and he came to sit near her, leaving a chair as a space between them. Without looking up at him, she had asked, "Why didn't you come to the party?" She had said the words in such a way they wouldn't sound a complaint.

"I'm sorry," he had replied. "I couldn't manage it."

"You live very far?" she had asked, still poring over the catalogues.

"No. Can I help with what you are doing?" he had asked.

She had looked up then, but only for a moment. "I am selecting books we have to order, though it'll be Mr. Pandey who'll finalise the purchase. But, yes, you can do one thing." She had paused to look through the bunch in her hands. "Yes, here it is. You go over these syllabuses. We must have all this sort of information on our fingertips from now on." And as she had stretched her hand to pass the syllabuses to him, their fingers had touched each other.

Then, for a few weeks in the beginning when the shop was being done over, she had little opportunity of dealing with him. He was either busy supervising the work with Mr Pandey or looking after errands. Tahmina herself didn't stay over at the shop for too long, as there was no place to sit. She just made a round in the morning and then another in the evening. Otherwise she worked mostly from home.

She had been sitting in the sunshine one day, when, all of a sudden, she had heard someone coming up the steps to the verandah and her heart had missed a few beats to see him standing at the gate.

He looked so handsome then, his auburn skin glowing in the sunshine and his hair falling over his dark eyes. She had welcomed him with a smile but nothing had touched his lips and he had simply handed a few papers Mr. Pandey had sent for her to sign.

She had been alone in the house then, for Kamla had taken the afternoon off. Taking the papers from his hands, she had asked him to sit down, and without saying a word, she had gone inside to make a cup of coffee for him.

Putting the milk to boil on the stove, she had watched him from the kitchen through the gap in the curtains. He was sitting facing her, his head tilted back, gazing at the clouds and she had become so lost for a while that the milk had boiled over and the hissing of the stove's flame had brought her out of her reverie.

He had stood up when she came out with the cup in her hands.

"Have you signed the papers?" he had asked, "Mr. Pandey asked me to hurry back."

"I'll do so while you have the coffee," she had replied, putting the cup on the table.

"Thanks, you needn't have bothered," he had said softly, sitting back again. And so she had put her head down and pretended to go through the papers before afixing her signature while he drank the coffee in silence. He rose after that and she had handed the papers to him without lifting her eyes. And she hadn't looked up even when he had said goodbye.

Thirty Four

January was coming to an end and there was still so much work to do, particularly as they had decided to fix the inauguration for February 19, just a week after Anjali's marriage. She had, of course, informed Faisal about the date and he had told her over the phone a few days ago that he would be reaching Nainital on the 16th.

And so it was a very busy time for all of them and she missed Mr. Pandey, who wasn't able to come to the shop for more than a couple of hours these days because he had to take care of the wedding preparations too. It was in this way that she had come to rely more and more on Sulaiman who worked with her throughout the day.

There was no question he was hard-working and capable and that was what should have been of concern to her. But there were times when she wished he was less remote and would talk to her like a friend. Instead, he acted so downright indifferent, never speaking to her about anything else than work and if she made some out-of-the-way remark, he would not give more than a one or two-word answer, which would leave nothing for her to say further. It was as if she didn't exist for him as a person.

And yet, with each passing day, he seemed more and more like someone she had known for a long time but never understood. And his silence had become like a book she wanted to read all the time, though she couldn't even find her way to the first page. Irritated, she would feel angry with him and sometimes with herself, but the fact was, he was getting into the remotest recesses of her heart and she had started fearing those encroachments.

One day, he hadn't come to work till it was afternoon and it had felt so ridiculous when her eyes would dart to the entrance every minute. He had arrived around three with the news that his uncle had taken ill during the night and he had been busy since morning in taking him to the hospital for a check-up.

"I am sorry," she had said, "How's he now? You must take me to see him today."

"Please don't worry," he had replied, perhaps a little too hurriedly and for a moment she had felt as if he had been horrified she would come over to his house. "He's feeling much better now, nothing serious. Actually it's his asthma which works up sometimes more than usual." And he had turned away to help Sylvia who was unpacking the newly arrived parcel of audio cassettes.

And she had almost hated him then, her fingers itching to throw something at him and shout at him to go away and never show his damned face to her again. Going back to her table, she had tried to immerse herself in work, making a vow never to look at him again. But still, every so often, her eyes would wander in his direction and try to steal a glimpse of his face in the half-light of the shop's interior.

It was more difficult when he was away and she was alone at home after dusk. She would come out to stand in the veranda and gaze at the lake, letting his thoughts fill her as imperceptibly as the night merged into the evening. Just

The Shadow of the Clouds

thinking about him would bring a light into her eyes and she would go on wondering what it was that made her like him so much and why her heart plunged at the promise of his nearness. And why did she at times catch him looking God knew where far away in the distance with those sad, mysterious eyes of his?

Thirty Five

Freshly sprung flowers were beginning to dot the hills as the first sign of defiance to the winter. They were flowers of strange beauty and rare hues and their fragrance hung heavy in the stillness of the afternoons and the butterflies flitted promiscuously amongst them. But the loveliest thing was that Tahmina could now go out during the day without bothering to put on the heavy woollens and her beauty too had burst out like a bud, making her as pretty as a peach flower.

It had started getting slightly warmer every day in February and the twilight also began to linger a bit longer. And the town too was changing before her eyes. Every day there were more people in the bazaar and the shops and schools that had been closed for winter were starting to open again. Even the air had become more transparent and everything shone bright and pure in the sunshine while the water of the lake shimmered with innumerable tiny specks of gold.

Her life too now followed a settled routine. She would arrive at the shop at ten thirty and work all through the day with Sulaiman and Sylvia, returning home just around dusk. With Anjali's wedding just around the corner, she would go to her house almost every evening while Sunday was spent with Claire.

Two days ago, Claire had dropped in at the shop and suggested a picnic as a sort of farewell get-together for Anjali.

"I'll ask my cousin Joe and his wife too," she had said, adding, "And you can invite Sylvia and Sulaiman too."

"Yes, it's a good idea," Tahmina had agreed happily. "It'll be fun and I think it'll make Anjali happy too. She is so sad these days. In fact, last night she was close to tears…"

"Oh I know," Claire had replied, shaking her head. "She's acting up like a typical Indian girl, spraying tears at the thought of leaving her parent's home. But don't let all this drama trouble you my dear, for you can take it from me that secretly she feels happy……"

"Oh, come on, Claire," Tahmina had blushed. "Everyone's not as naughty as you…"

"Baby, you don't know anything," Claire had laughed. "It's the demure, bashful ones who can't wait for you-know-what …." And she had looked meaningfully at her, making her turn red.

"Okay, okay, there's no need to glare at me for discovering a secret," Claire had replied with a wink and asked, "How's the work going?"

"It's all finished, except for distributing the invitations for the opening," Tahmina had told her.

"Ah! That would be the day! You have really worked hard, Tahmina. You know Mr. Pandey met Dad a couple of days ago and he was almost singing your praises. Said you had a natural flair for this sort of thing. You do love the shop, don't you?"

"Hmm! Yes," Tahmina had replied thoughtfully. "Not just the shop, I love everything here. You know, Claire, I sometimes wish I could spend my whole life here. But it all seems like a dream and I don't know why, but sometimes I feel very afraid that any moment I might wake up to find everything taken away from me."

"Oh, don't worry about that," she had replied. "That feeling comes naturally when you are truly in love with something."

Thirty Six

He hadn't come, of course. She had dressed so carefully in the morning, noting with a smile how the color of her face had changed. There was something new too in the way her eyes looked back at her from the mirror. They hadn't lost their shyness but there was a hint of audacity that hadn't been there before and her lips were becoming fuller. In fact, her whole body appeared to have become more succulent and she could feel the sap rising and coursing through her veins. Yes, there was a new sensuousness in her and what a sweet pleasure it was, so much so that she sometimes felt as if it had mingled a new fragrance in her breath.

They had waited and waited for him at the spot where everyone had agreed to collect for the excursion and, finally, they had left without him. And the whole day among the hills and glades had been filled with sadness for her but in order to hide her disappointment she had forced herself to share in the happiness of others.

It was almost evening by the time they returned and the twilight was starting to spread like a purple blush over the valley while the cold breeze that blew across the lake was making her shiver like a leaf. Dropping off Anjali at her home, she started to trudge back towards her house but then suddenly veered down to the lake. Her legs were tired and hurting as was her heart, but she was in no mood to care for anything.

It was a beautiful evening to stroll and a lot of people

were thronging the Flatt. There was a band playing on the bandstand under the elms and the boats were still out on the lake. Skirting the crowd, she started to walk along the Mall Road to the lonely bench near the library where she could sit with her ache for a while.

She saw him then, leaning on the railing near the Boat Club entrance, munching peanuts with some friends. Averting her eyes, she ducked behind a group of people as she walked past him on the road. But she stopped angrily a few steps later, asking herself why she wanted to hide from him. It was he who should feel ashamed to face her, not holding a promise and keeping others waiting for him. Who does he think he is? He didn't even have the courtesy to inform them that he would not be able to make it. Fuming, she stopped to glare towards him, but he was too preoccupied in talking and laughing with his friends to notice her and it was the first time she had seen him laugh.

So, she thought, he knows how to laugh all right! And just look at the way he is talking so freely now when all the time at the shop he went about as stiff as a rack of wood. And turning her face away, she set off towards the Library once again. The bench there was empty and she sat down to gaze at the shimmering reflection of the lights in the water of the lake.

I mean nothing to him, she reflected sadly to herself. I'm just someone he works for a specific period of the day, for a specific salary, and that doesn't mean he should like me as well. He's not my slave, after all, that he would accede to my every wish and command and talk when I want him to and come for parities and picnics when I invite him. Perhaps, she reflected, I wouldn't even like it if he started to be free and casual with me.

The Shadow of the Clouds

But what does he mean to me, she wondered, plucking some leaves and throwing them in the water. What explanation exists for my feeling hurt if he doesn't talk with me like a friend or if he refuses to be touched by my beauty or is insensitive to the pangs of attraction that I feel for him? I don't even know where exactly he lives and he's almost a stranger to me in many other ways too.

But then why does he awaken such irrational romantic longings in me and why am I always trying to capture that look on his face when he is sitting lost in his work? And what is this pain and what does it mean? If this is what love is, then it's nothing but grasping for shadows.

No, this could not be love at all, she decided. It must be something else that has come to me in its guise. Perhaps I have been too lonely, lonelier than I have cared to acknowledge, and this sudden, inexplicable rush of emotions towards this man is nothing but beguilement. Yes, my heart must be trying to distract me from the trauma I have gone through, she thought. Yes, he doesn't have any music in him and it is nothing but his outward appearance that tugs at my heart and makes me strain to hear the beating of his heart.

Anyway, whatever it was and however much it hurt, she would keep it hidden from him and wait to see if he can look past clouds. Yes, I'll never let him learn how much he hurts me, she decided, or how much my eyes seek his face. And from now on, I'll also see through him as if he were a ghost and make myself more distant than the hills and the stars.

And with this stubborn resolve in her heart, she stood up to walk back to the lonely night that awaited her. He wasn't there any longer and that relieved her. But when she had climbed the steep road that led from the Flatt towards her home, she turned once again on the slope of the hill and looked back at the twinkling lights of the town beneath her.

Thirty Seven

Sleep hadn't come easily to her that night and she woke up feeling tired; her legs were still hurting from all the activity of the previous day. It was a beautiful morning though, and a fresh cluster of flowers had sprouted outside on the veranda, but even they had failed to cheer her up.

Walking to her shop later on, she was feeling unnaturally moody and sullen and her anger at him hung like a morning cloud over her. Going straight to her desk without even a glance at him, she was surprised to find a bunch of flowers in the vase on her table. They were white and lilac and had a strange wistful smell.

"I brought them for you," Sylvia called out to her.

"Thanks! They are beautiful," she called back and sat down to work. But it was no use really, for she wasn't able to concentrate on anything and her heart started simmering again. He doesn't even have the courtesy to come and apologise for yesterday, she thought.

He went away after a while to start distributing the first lot of invitation cards and she went across to Sylvia to get some tips about the new software until Claire arrived to go with her to do some shopping for Anjali's wedding.

"Let's have a cup of tea before we venture out," she said, flinging herself on the chair by Tahmina's desk. "And yes, where's that 'Silence Please' signboard of yours?" she asked, looking around.

"What do you mean?" Tahmina asked, puzzled for a moment before she understood she was referring to Sulaiman.

"He's gone to distribute the cards," she replied carelessly.

"Doesn't matter," Claire said, opening her purse and handing an envelope to Tahmina. "When he comes along, ask him to drop this letter of mine at the Post Office. It's for Henry. And why didn't he turn up yesterday?" she asked.

Feigning indifference to hide her feelings, she replied, "I didn't ask."

"But you should have. It was really rude of him," Claire said and then almost whispered, "But all the same, he's attractive, isn't he?"

"I don't know what you mean," she replied in a huff only to make Claire burst out in laughter. It was a relief to see Sylvia come over at that moment and the conversation veered round to what would be the best gift they could buy for Anjali.

Later on, after their shopping was done, Claire suggested they go over to some restaurant to have lunch.

"Okay, I wasn't in the mood for work anyway," Tahmina replied morosely.

"Oh yes, I was going to ask what's the matter with you today. Is something vexing you?" Claire had asked.

"Why, nothing at all!" Tahmina had replied hurriedly, for she knew that once Claire got a scent of something she wouldn't leave her alone till she had got to the heart of it.

"You didn't tell me before you had a degree in the dramatic arts too," Claire said drily. "You should realise by

The Shadow of the Clouds

now that you have as much ability to conceal your feelings as I have for pole vaulting."

"It's really nothing, Claire. I'm just feeling tired from yesterday."

"No! You are looking as troubled as you looked the day when I met you for the first time," Claire said, and added, "Don't feel I am intruding but I have come to care for you so much."

"I know," Tahmina smiled pensively. It's so difficult to bare your heart to anyone, she reflected, and I'll have to be more careful. If she can see everything written on my face, so can anyone else, even him....."

"You are happy here, aren't you," Claire asked. "Not missing home?"

"Oh No! I mean, I do miss Abbu and Ammi, but all the same, I am happy here," she replied hurriedly. And why shouldn't I be, she thought, this place has everything that makes my heart beat. "In fact," she added, "I wish I could live here always."

And suddenly the cloud had lifted away and she ceased to be sad any more. And coming back to the shop, she called Suleiman to her desk on some pretext and when he started to go back, she asked him, "Why didn't you come for the picnic yesterday? All of us were waiting for you."

"Yes, Sylvia told me," he replied. "I'm sorry for that."

"What happened? You forgot like last time?" she asked, looking up at him.

"No. It's just that it was Sunday and I woke up late. And

yes, please remember to ask Mr. Pandey where he has kept that list. I haven't been able to find it."

"I will," she replied, and smiling secretly as he turned away, she whispered inaudibly, "And one day I'll steal the sleep from your eyes too."

Thirty Eight

The next week saw her plunge into the celebrations of Anjali's wedding and it was such fun too. It was the first time she was participating so intimately in a traditional Hindu wedding and its romance was entrancing. Every day there was some or the other pre-nuptial ceremony and everyone would laugh and sing while poor Anjali had to bear it all, sitting decked up like a doll in their midst.

And how gorgeous she had looked as a bride, glowing from the week-long massage of the paste that was made by mixing saffron and sandalwood powder with honey, gram flour, milk and aromatic oils. It had turned her skin so smooth and radiant and its heady smell had got rubbed into her body. And mingled with the fragrance flowers that adorned her hair that night, it had imbued Anjali with an intoxicatingly seductive smell. It had affected Tahmina too, permeating her senses. Her heart beat wildly as she searched the throng of guests for a glimpse of Sulaiman.

She had herself looked stunning in a turquoise blue chiffon sari she had bought specially for the wedding, though she did feel a little awkward too as it was the first time that she had done so in her life. And like always, it had been Claire who had been the most effusive and insightful.

"Why, Tahmina!" she had exclaimed, "You look really sexy in this. It falls so well, hugging your contours. You know, that's why I love saris, though I don't wear them myself. They are so good in hiding and revealing the body at the same time . . .

The only disappointment had been that she hadn't met Sulaiman at the party. He must have been there, most probably hanging at the very edge of the crowd while she had remained at Anjali's side all the time, the cynosure of all eyes. But he must have seen me, she had thought consolingly.

Anjali had departed next morning and she had been saddened to see her go. She had been such a comfort in a hundred small, happy ways, and the tears had come unbidden to her eyes when she had hugged her to say goodbye. And afterwards, she had sat with Mr. Pandey and tried to console him because he was looking so distraught and heart-broken.

"Don't be sad, uncle. She's going to happiness."

And the old man had wiped his eyes and putting his arms around her, whispered, "Don't worry, these are tears of joy. Just pray she finds happiness in her new home. And then God is so kind, isn't he, sending me another daughter who'll be near me now," he had added, hugging her.

The next two days saw her busy sprucing up the house to welcome Faisal. She hung the new curtains she had bought and put a bed for him in the living room. And she also hid the picture-frame with her and her father's photograph, afraid that it might hurt him to see it.

She also didn't go to the shop much, except for some time in the morning. There wasn't any work left to do anyway and she wanted to relax a bit to overcome the fatigue of the past week. After all, she knew that Faisal's arrival and the shop's inauguration were going to plunge her into one whirlwind of activity and excitement once again.

It was difficult however to go to sleep the night before Faisal's arrival, for the old doubts returned to trouble her once more. For the past month and a half she had kept herself distracted with the ongoing work at the shop, or by musing about Sulaiman. But now, with Faisal's impending arrival tomorrow, she wasn't able to stop thinking once again about all that had happened to her and how her life was going to be affected by her decision to stay back in Nainital for some time. It was all right for the moment, keeping happy among the hills and the trees, far away from what she had been, but what about the future? Who was going to tell her what was going to happen in the distance?

It had been so easy to promise Faisal earlier that she would come home in a few months once the shop was set up. But deep in her heart, she had known all along that it was a promise that was not going to be easy to keep. Yes, tearing herself away from this place was going to mean another wrenching for her, as painful and stormy as when she had learned the truth about herself some months ago.

The problem was, she had not been able to come to terms with the decision she had made, but it was time now to reach some definite conclusion. And so, letting the night to stand still, she started searching for some answers in the dark.

What would it mean if I went back to Dubai? What will happen to the shop? Will Sulaiman be able to look after it for long? What if he had to leave at the end of the year? It would mean that the shop would be closed once again. And what about this house? This house in which she had been born in some rare moment of love and beauty and which she had come to love so much, almost like a place in someone's heart. What would happen to it? Its doors would be locked away and its windows will not open again to let in the sunshine and the sight of the lake. The walls and furniture would be covered with mildew, cobwebs would spread on the ceiling and the plants in the veranda would grow wild again. And her father's spirit would be left alone and forsaken once more. And she couldn't let that happen....

But then how would she be able to make such a choice alone? How long would Faisal and Amna allow her to remain tied here and how could she just wipe away the fact that she, like other girls, was expected to get married one day and settle down?

Unable to think any more or settle on something, and too worn out finally to grope about for any answers, she tucked the blankets a little more tightly and snugly around her and closed her eyes. But as she drifted to sleep, she felt herself looking into a pair of eyes that held no answer either.

Thirty Nine

"What a happy surprise Abbu's going to get, finding me here!" she remarked to Claire as they entered the small railway station at Kathgodam.

Faisal had specifically asked her not to come down here to receive him at the station. "I'll catch a taxi and reach the shop," he had said on the phone from Delhi but Tahmina had decided to come all the same. Once again it was Claire who had come to the rescue, asking Joe, her cousin, to bring them down here in his jeep.

"We are exactly on the dot," Claire said. "Let's go and see if the train's arriving on time."

But it was half an hour late and so they strolled around the platform and finally sat down on a bench while Joe sauntered about the station.

"How does it feel Tahmina? I mean about going to face your Faisal abbu after such a long time?" Claire asked.

"Can't you read my face any longer?" Tahmina asked, less playful than she usually was.

"That I can," Claire answered with a laugh,

"But I can tell you, you can't read my face all the time."

"Now why would she say that?" Claire wondered aloud and turned on her with surprise, "Hey, what's it that I have failed to grasp? What's it that you are taunting me with? Come on, tell me…"

"Nothing, Madame Claire," Tahmina smiled, biting a little bit of her lip, "I was just testing the water."

"So, the heart is learning to keep its secrets, is it? Well, you'll soon discover that Madame Claire has the eyes to see through seven veils. And to give a small exhibition, I can tell you that though just now you are feeling very happy that your Abbu's coming, there's still something gnawing at your heart too!"

And turning serious, Tahmina had confided, "Yes, there is….I am wondering whether he'll understand that my expression of happiness is real, I mean, after what I have done—staying back here and re-opening my father's shop. I go on and on praying he would understand that I still love him like I used to."

"I get it, Tahmina, but there's no real need to fret. The way you have described him, I think he would understand that we could love two people in the same way at the same time. Don't parents do so with their children?"

"I hope so, but, perhaps, some loves can't be divided….And then, he's human after all and I cannot shrug off the fact that somehow or the other I must have hurt him…"

"Hey, the train's arriving," Joe called out to them and forgetting everything, Tahmina ran towards the edge of the platform. And a few moments later she was running like the breeze into his arms.

"Oh, abbu! How are you?" Tahmina whispered urgently.

She had stood there, clinging to him for a long time and

he had wiped away her tears. It was some time later, when they had come outside, that she remembered Claire. Looking around, she saw her and Joe standing near the jeep and she introduced them to him.

Faisal was looking very fit and when she remarked about that on the jeep, he told her he had joined a gym. "And you are looking more beautiful than I could remember," he had returned the compliment, making her blush happily. But it was Claire who had been at her vivacious best, making Faisal laugh as much during the one and a half-hour trip up the mountain than she had seen him do so in years.

So it was only after they had reached home that she had been able to talk with him properly.

"How's Ammi?" she had enquired after he had changed his clothes and they had sat down to have an early lunch.

He had looked up seriously from his plate and said, "She's all right. But she's not too happy you have stayed here so long…"

"And you Abbu? Are you angry too?" she had asked with trepidation.

"No," he had said firmly, "I told you, your happiness means more to me than anything else. And then, he had paused to look towards the hills from the window, "You have to do what you have set out to do and I can wait."

And though she had wanted to say so much to him then, she had kept silent. Sensing, perhaps, that he had made her feel sad, he had immediately tried to make amends. "I am very eager to see your shop. When are you going to take me there?"

And she had been so happy to do so. She had proudly

introduced him to Sulaiman and Sylvia and he had gone through everything, asking questions and making suggestions till it was evening. Coming back to the house, he had unpacked and given her all the gifts he had brought for everyone like she had asked him to do, and, after that, they had gone out to have dinner at one of the lake-side restaurants.

"What are your plans now?" he had asked, lighting a cigarette.

"Oh, nothing," she had mumbled.

"What do you mean, nothing? Now that you have opened the shop, you can't leave it in the lurch. You have to think ahead."

"I don't know," she replied simply and truthfully.

"Of course you cannot go on staying here indefinitely. But you can't leave the shop alone too, otherwise all the effort and money would be wasted. That's something we have to solve while I am here. Have you thought of something?" he had asked.

"No. ...I just thought I could leave it to Sulaiman, that is, till he can continue in the job. And Mr. Pandey would be here too."

"Hmm!" he replied thoughtfully, "Let Mr. Pandey come back from Anjali's reception and then we'll discuss it. You know, the first thing I thought about when I read your letter was what would happen to the shop in the future. I saw no point in getting it going again when there wasn't any way you could settle down here. But I let you go ahead because I thought, after the trauma you had gone through, this was the best way to keep you distracted and busy."

The Shadow of the Clouds

She didn't know what to say, so she had kept silent, keeping her eyes averted.

"But I see now," he said after a pause, "that you have become serious about this venture and I know how one can get attached to something that one has worked hard to build. So I can't let your efforts go waste, or let you break your heart over this. But you must understand that I can't figure out how you can continue to live here alone so far away from home. You do understand, don't you, how afraid I sometimes feel for you?" he had asked.

"Yes," she had replied pensively, and then she had tried to make light of his apprehensions, "But you must not worry at all. It's so safe here and everyone is so unbelievably nice and helpful. I think it's the air and the beauty of this place that makes people so good and different here. Meet Mr. Pandey and Mr. Mathew and you'll understand how well they take care of me."

He had looked at her silently for a moment before replying back gently, "Even the sun casts a shadow, Tahmina, and sometimes the fragrance of a flower can lead you more astray than wine. So don't think I would ever be able to stop myself from worrying about you. But anyway, this is not the time to ponder over all this. What's important is for you to concentrate on making a success of the shop. That would be some consolation for the way I keep searching for you at home..."

Forty

It was February 19, a time when often the winter turns back for a last hurrah before receding for good. But this year the spring seemed to have arrived a bit early. She too had woken up early in the morning, just as the dawn was hesitantly breaking over the valley. She had been lost in the beauty of those moments for a while looking at the light spread over the lake.

Jumping out of bed, she flung open the windows and stood shivering in the cold, watching the scene outside, with the lake and the hills looking so beautiful in the faint darkness of the morning.

She had turned after a while to switch on the geyser in the bathroom and Faisal and Kamla had woken up by the time she had finished her prayer. Barely able to contain her excitement any longer, she hurried through breakfast and started to dress for the inauguration, picking up one of her favourite suits, a red and olive-green silk ensemble with fine crystal embroidery and a matching net dupatta. She had even experimented with her hairstyle, before applying a little pink blush and a light, wine coloured lipstick. And, finally, she had taken out the fresh bottle of L'Air du Temps that Faisal had brought for her.

Its perfume always reminded her of the sweet inimitable scent that escapes from a night-old bouquet of flowers that has been left lying around near the bed, and often mysteriously provocative.

"It's almost ten now," Faisal had called out to her, "I think we should leave now."

"Yes, Abbu," she had replied, darting a final, hurried look at herself in the mirror. But as she turned away to leave, she had remembered something and going to the wardrobe, she had taken out her father's picture and whispered, "Bless me, abbu, and please, be happy." And all of a sudden her eyes had clouded and a drop of rain had come to linger on her cheeks before falling down somewhere. Fighting back her tears, she had put the picture back and touched up her face once more.

"What do I prepare for lunch today?" Kamla had asked as she entered the kitchen to go through to the living room.

"Nothing!" she had replied, "I'll order something from a restaurant. What I want you to do today is to clean up quickly and come to the shop."

"Is there some work?" Kamla had enquired.

"No, Kamla, no! Don't you know it's the shop's opening today? So I want you to come for that. And wear the new sari abbu has brought for you."

"Oh, yes, memsahib!" Kamla had beamed back happily, "But don't leave at once, I have something for you," she had said, fumbling with a knot in her sari. "Yes, here," she had added, taking out a piece of vermilion thread, "This strand of thread is very auspicious," she had hesitated, "Can I tie it to your wrist?"

"Why not!" Tahmina had said, extending her hand and suddenly the momentary sadness had left her and she had been filled with a sense of happiness that had remained with her like a lyric all day.

Forty One

It was a day full of promise, full of the sights and sounds of spring. The clear, golden sunshine was warm and the colour and scents of the trees and the flowers hit the senses with extraordinary vividness. And as she descended the narrow, fern-lined path to the road and walked up through the bazaar towards her shop with Faisal, Tahmina let the beauty of the hills and the sky be absorbed into her soul.

Sulaiman had arranged a florist to string tresses of rose and marigold flowers at the entrance and as Tahmina approached near, she saw him standing outside, tinkering with the coffee machine that was placed on a table at the side of the road.

"Hello, good morning!" Sulaiman wished them, shaking hands with Faisal, who moved inside while she deliberately lingered for a moment near him. And perhaps, at last, her beauty touched him, for he looked at her with a smile and she didn't prevent their eyes from holding on to each other. It was a moment as fleeting as a heartbeat and yet she would have willingly given away half the world for it.

"Beti!" Mr. Pandey's voice took her away from him. "He was coming towards her slowly, his face lit with happiness. "Feeling happy and proud, uh?" he asked, holding her hand and gripping it with affection.

"Yes, uncle," she replied happily and walked inside with him, where Faisal was standing with Sylvia.

"Good Morning, Tahmina!" Sylvia cried, "You are looking as beautiful as these." And she had extended a bunch of the same white and lilac flowers that she had brought some time earlier.

"Thanks!" she replied, looking around the shop, which was decked up with ribbons and flowers. "It's looking great, isn't it?" she asked aloud.

"Yes, as good as you all have made it," Faisal said. "And now, tell me, who's going to do the inauguration?"

"Oh! I hadn't thought about that," she replied, realising she had goofed up, but all at once the answer came to her lips, "You! Yes, Abbu, you are going to do it."

"Oh, come on now! It wouldn't look proper. You should have thought of this earlier and asked somebody special, but it's too late to do anything now...."

And then, all of a sudden, it came to her and she whispered something to Faisal, who nodded his head in appreciation. Turning away, she went to the corner where Mr. Pandey had sat down.

"What's it, beti?" he asked.

"Listen, uncle," she said, leaning with her hand on the chair. "You have to do something very important, so get ready!"

"What?" he asked, perplexed.

"You are going to do the inauguration at eleven!"

"I don't understand," he said, but she could see that he was pleasantly surprised and touched by what she had said.

"I mean, there is no sense in asking me," he continued to protest, "This sort of thing is done by someone big and important..."

"No one is more important to me than you, you understand?" she said with finality and Faisal too came up to back her. "Yes, Pandey sahib, she is right! No one deserves this honour more than you."

And so the old man reluctantly agreed and hugging her, his voice husky with emotion, said, "Okay, I'll do it. May God bless you!" And in a strange way that blessing seemed to come to her not from him, but from someone else, someone whose voice she had never ever heard and would never ever hear again.

Forty Two

The day was coming to an end and the shades of evening were beginning to steal over the hills.

Tahmina was sitting behind her table at the end of the shop, looking at the new, gleaming books in the racks, mixed up and disarrayed by hands that had sorted through them all day. And that's how it was with the racks of audio cassettes, greeting cards and the jumble of gift items. The floor was littered with pieces of the coloured wrapping paper and the broken petals of roses and marigolds. And on one side of the shop were stacked the bouquets.

She had received so many of them, accepting and strewing them all over the place, while Raghu, the peon she had hired, went about picking them up and adding them to the pile. In fact, there was such a stack of them now that it wouldn't have been amiss if someone had come and thought that the Hillside Bookstore had branched out into being a florist too. And it was not a bad idea too, she thought, mentally noting down to do something about it. What was more, the mussed and mixed up myriad fragrances of the bouquets had mingled with the peculiar misty smell of the new books to make the shop redolent of the woods up in the hills.

But there was one special bouquet that she had kept apart from others, one that had found a place in her heart. What did it matter if he hadn't handed it to her himself, leaving it secretly on the table for her to discover and wonder over it. She had seen it soon after Mr. Pandey had agreed to her proposal for doing the inauguration. Claire too had wafted in just then, as ardent and lilting as the sunny, spring morning.

Wearing an alluring black dress and looking as sinfully beautiful, she had flung her arms around her and kissing her softly, she had made her blush by whispering, "You are delicious, Tahmina." Coming to sit at the table, Claire had found the bouquet peeping out from under a file. It was not a proper bouquet; instead, different flowers had been bunched by a piece of string. There had been sixteen of them (for she had counted them just now), each of them of a different hue and smell.

He must have gone around like a poet, picking them from here and there, and that's what had touched her. In a way, he had tried to gather all the beauty that nature had sprinkled about in the hills and brought it for her on a day that was as so special for her.

Claire had picked it up and said, "Now, this is a real, romantic way to express your feelings! Just look at all these flowers, Tahmina, especially this white one .....Who's composed this poem in flowers?" She had wondered.

"I don't know," she had replied. "May be Sylvia, but no, she brought some other ones and no one else has come in yet except…"

"Except who?" Claire asked and seeing Tahmina look towards Sulaiman, she had called out to him, "Sulaiman, come here, please." And when he had done so, she had asked him, "Have you brought these?"

"Yes," he had said, as simply as always.

"Why isn't there a rose in this?" Claire had asked him again, almost accusingly, and it had been so difficult for Tahmina to keep her face straight as she observed the look of astounded bewilderment on his face. At a loss for words, he had just stood there, looking at them with those silent, faraway eyes of his.

"Perhaps you don't believe in giving a rose to a rose," Claire had observed dryly, her eyes twinkling with mischief. With a rush of embarrassment he turned away hurriedly to go outside where Faisal was standing.

"Really, Claire!" Tahmina had said, after they had laughed and laughed.

"Did you see that look on his face? Seemed as if someone had pulled a cap over his head." Claire had continued to laugh. And then a little while later, when they had been sitting talking with each other, he had come over again, to ask for some money to pay for the pastries that had arrived. She hadn't been able to meet his eyes then and as he turned to go away, Claire had whispered, "You know, Tahmina, seeing him makes me regret that my heart's been rented out. He would have been irresistible otherwise." And Tahmina had looked up hurriedly to see if he hadn't overheard. Thankfully, he was out of earshot by then.

"Why are you blushing like this, darling?" Claire had caught on at once. And Tahmina had blushed some more and given away so easily what she had tried to hide all along.

Soon after that, people had started arriving and Mr. Pandey had cracked a coconut and lighted a lamp in the traditional Indian way of making an auspicious beginning to something. And after that she hadn't had a moment to think about anything else. She was particularly happy that her visits to the schools had paid off and a lot of teachers had come to wish her good luck.

But the real surprise had been Sulaiman's uncle, Mr. Riaz. He had come around twelve, a frail, old man, walking with the help of a cane and Mr. Pandey had introduced him to her and Faisal, and she had asked about his health.

"Yes, I haven't been keeping well lately and because of the asthma it's difficult for me to move about much or else I would have come to meet you earlier," he had replied and she felt so ashamed then. I should have gone to visit him myself and, she thought angrily, it was all because of him, he had never invited her to his house till now.

"No, no, uncle, please," she had said. "Actually, I should be apologising. I did want to come to see you many times but …"

"I know, I know," he had smiled in understanding. "Sulaiman never invited you, isn't it? He is like that, somewhat undemonstrative and reserved. But don't mistake his shyness. He's always telling me how good you are. In any case, my daughter, Naila, is coming here in a few days and you will come for dinner then."

Just then Sulaiman had come into view, milling around with the customers. How handsome he looks in his charcoal-grey suit, she thought, and started to get distracted again.

Later on, when she was saying goodbye to his uncle at the entrance, he had come to stand beside them.

"You bring her home when Naila is here next week," Mr. Riaz had said to him, somewhat sternly.

"Yes." That was all he had said.

But she hadn't cared, for she had been so happy today, happy beyond words, and even his silence seemed a song to her.

Forty Three

It was night now and a sweet feeling of weariness was spreading through her, prompting her to go to sleep. But reluctant to let go of the day so easily, she got out of bed and tiptoed to the window. It was a night full of stars and she wondered about the world that lay beyond them, or perhaps it existed somewhere between the darkness and the radiance....But wherever it was, whether as near or as faraway as those stars, her father must be happy there.

Yes, he must be happy to see how happy she was here, in this place of beauty that had kept him so sad all his life and how proud he must be today....And the tears had welled up in her eyes just like they had in the shop...

She wasn't going to forget those tears too. It must have been around eight, after everyone had left and she was alone in the shop, sitting at her table waiting for Faisal, who had gone to escort Mr. Pandey to his home. All through the afternoon she had observed with a growing concern how tired the old man had looked, his face glum and thoughtful as he sat down to rest in between. She had even gone over to him to ask whether he was feeling unwell, but he had put on that affectionate smile of his and waved her away, "It's nothing. I'm just a little extra tired after the wedding."

"You are missing Anjali, aren't you?" she had asked.

"No, why would I do that? You are here, aren't you?" He had replied. But he had been worn out by evening and Faisal had insisted on accompanying him on his way home.

Sylvia too had taken leave by then while the peon was away to fetch some of her clothes from the laundry. Even Sulaiman was away, gone to purchase some medicines for his uncle before coming back to let down the shutters.

And so Tahmina was sitting alone then, wondering how happy her father would have been if he had been alive to see the shop now and then all of a sudden, she had started crying. She had let her tears flow, losing all sense of time and place until she had heard Sulaiman's voice and realised she was no longer alone.

She had looked up and saw him standing before her, his tie a little askew and a rose petal sticking in his hair. But she hadn't cared at all and went on crying while he stood there, looking at her with his eyes that seemed to be trying to say something that she hadn't been able to comprehend.

Her tears had dried after a while but she had let him gaze at her, letting their eyes hold on to each other, until nothing had existed in the world except those eyes of his. She didn't know when or how the spell had broken and what it had wrought in them but she had wiped her face with the handkerchief he had extended and lowered her eyes. And he said to her then, said it like a truth he had experienced, 'There's no happiness without tears, is there?'

"I'm sorry," she had mumbled. "I shouldn't have been crying like this."

"There's no harm in crying and letting go of some of your pain," he had tried to console her. Just then Faisal had returned and she had hurriedly wiped her face again and started asking Sulaiman if he had counted the cash.

"No, I'll do that just now. Would you like to take it

home?" he had asked and added, " It would be secure in the safe here too."

"I think we can leave it here," she had said, rising from the chair, keeping her head down as she took her time to clear her desk so that Faisal wouldn't notice she had been crying.

"Let's go home, Abbu," she had said finally and they had left, leaving Sulaiman to finish his work. But she hadn't forgotten to pick up the bunch of flowers he had brought for her in the morning. And now, as she came back to the bed, she picked up those flowers again and placed them next to her pillow..

Forty Four

The few days Faisal spent in Nainital went by in such a flurry, what with the rush of work at the shop, where people were still dropping by, and the dinner invitations from Mr. Pandey and Claire. And so he had asked her to take a break from the shop today to spend a quiet evening with him before he left for Dubai tomorrow.

"We'll eat out this evening. There are a few things we need to talk about," he had said and now they were sitting on the bench along the lake.

Earlier, Faisal had shopped around with her for gifts he could take home and even Tahmina had done her bit, buying a sari for Amna and some small gifts for her friends back in Dubai. She had told everyone she was going to visit her relatives in India and now, when she had stayed back so long, all of them kept on pestering Faisal and Amna for some news of her return.

"Everyone's so surprised when we tell them you have decided to stay some more in India. Why don't you write to, or phone your friends?" Faisal had asked the day before..

"Yes, I will," she had murmured. It wasn't as if she hadn't thought of doing so, but the way she had become so involved here had made everything else seem so distant and so unreal.

The twilight was just beginning to set in over the valley and a light breeze was playing around with the trees and the lake was looking lovelier than ever, it's surface shimmering with the reflection of the lights all over the town.

"The beauty here can steal anyone's heart," Faisal remarked.

"Yes, Abbu," she replied happily, "At least, it has stolen mine for sure."

"Hmm!" he replied. "So that's why you don't want to come back?" he asked with a smile, looking at her.

"Oh, I don't know," she replied awkwardly, a nameless dread creeping in on her. She had been so thankful he hadn't broached the subject till now, but she knew all along that the moment would come when she would have to find an answer.

"You know, abbu, I was thinking how wonderful it would be if you bought a hotel here and we were to come and stay here for keeps," she added hurriedly with sudden impetuous hope.

"I would do that too, for your sake," he said with a light laugh. But then his voice turned serious. "But who knows where you'll have to settle after marriage."

"What's the hurry?" she asked quietly. "I don't want..."

"I understand, Tahmina, and if it was possible I wouldn't let you go away for years and years. But there's usually a right time for marriage and we can't delay it too long now. In fact, your mother has already made a short-list of..."

"Oh God! Please, abbu! Please tell her to wait. It's not as if I am getting old, I'm just twenty..."

"Okay, okay," he interrupted her again. "We aren't

planning to ship you out next week. There's still a lot of time. But, yes, you have to come home and there's not too much time for that. What do you think? Can you leave the shop to Sulaiman?" And as she made no immediate reply, he continued, "I have been observing you at the shop and I am sure it would break your heart if something happened to it..."

"Thank you, Abbu," she replied gratefully, a hasty, wild hope starting to beam again on her face.

"And I think I have found a very good way to ensure it chugs along nicely even when you are away." He paused to see if she wanted to say anything but she turned silent and sullen once again. "Won't you like to hear about it?" he asked, putting his arm across her shoulders.

"Yes," she mumbled.

"Listen, I know you want to remain here and though I miss you, I would still let you do that. But perhaps you don't realise how your mother's taking it. I don't know how to explain it to you, but she is feeling sort of betrayed.... She doesn't say so, but I know she feels as if you have forgotten her and gone over to your father's side. I think you can understand what I am trying to say, don't you?" he asked.

"But it isn't like that at all," she protested. "It's just that...I mean, I can't express it in words...But it's just that I thought it would be a good idea to open the shop again and now I am caught up in it. I'll talk to her on the phone tonight and explain..."

"There's no need to do that," he replied and she could sense the tone of finality in his voice. "You have to come back, as you promised. It's not only about Amna. You have to think of your own life, after all. You have to get married in a year or two and then you'll go and live with your husband. That's why we will have to find some way to keep the shop going without your being here all the time. Of course, you can keep on coming here in between whenever you want. You understand, don't you?"

"Yes, I do," she replied, looking emptily at the lake with misty eyes. She had known all along, ever since the moment she had started falling in love with everything here, that one day she would have to leave. Yes, she would have to turn away from the beauty of this place with no choice but to forget that she had all but given away her heart to someone here. Yes, she knew it all along, but till now she had always flicked the thought away like a loose strand of hair that falls over the face. But the moment of reckoning had come now.

"Good," he said, "So what have you decided, when are you coming home?"

"Whenever you say," she replied flatly

"Come on, Tahmina," he said, drawing her closer. "You have always been such a sensible girl…"

"No, please don't worry, I'm not angry or upset. It's just that I wanted to look after the shop for some more time," she said, trying to smile reassuringly at him.

And perhaps he understood her desperate need, for he said, "Look here, I can give you two options: come home with me just now—I can stay back a couple of days for that—and then you can come here again to see through the May and June tourist season. Or else, you can stay here till April and come back to Dubai. Then we can make arrangements for your next visit again. Think about this through the night and give me an answer in the morning. And, please, cheer up!

Everything's going to work out fine, you'll see."

"Yes, Abbu," she replied, trying to smile again for his sake. It had to happen one day, she thought, it was as ineluctable as something written in a book of fate and there was no use crying over it.

"And now, don't you want to know what I have thought about the shop?" he asked.

"Yes, of course."

"Listen, if Mr. Pandey had been younger, we could have left everything in his hands and you needn't have worried about anything. But I don't think he can manage to work full-time any more. In fact, from the little I have seen of him, I feel very worried about his health."

"Yes, you are right. He does appear so weak and haggard, particularly since Anjali's marriage."

"Hmm! Naturally, that must have affected him. Anyway, this leaves us with Sulaiman, at least for now. Mr. Pandey trusts him implicitly and I would say too that he is dependable; you know I can size up people very well. But I don't think he's in this job for the long term. I have been talking to him and he was telling me he has other plans."

"Yes. He wants to be a C.A. It's only because there's no one else to look after his uncle that he is biding his time at the shop."

"I know, Mr. Pandey told me all about him and he is a nice boy really...."

"In fact, Abbu, I forgot to tell you but his mother used to be a friend of Ammi's," she interjected.

"Oh, I didn't know that," Faisal said with a little surprise, "What was her name? I'll ask Amna about her."

"I don't know. I didn't ask him. In any case, she doesn't live here…"

"Yes, Mr. Pandey mentioned that. Anyway, we have to find a way to make him stick with the shop for the long run," he said and she felt happy for the moment to hear Faisal approving of him. If only Sulaiman would agree to go on being in the shop forever….

"And I think I have a proposal that can make him change his mind. You see, we can offer him a share in the shop." He said, almost startling her, "Not now – but, lets say, when you come back next time, you can ask him if he would be interested in becoming a partner. That would tie him to the shop for sure."

"But, Abbu," she stammered, trying to subdue the excitement she was going through, "He doesn't have enough money to buy a share."

"You don't need the money. You need someone to keep the shop running and alive. And so he can get a stake for his commitment."

"Yes, yes," she cried, turning happily to him, "That would be nice." At least this way I would be able to go on seeing him whenever I am here, she thought consolingly.

"But don't say anything to him now. Let's see how he carries along for a while before we decide. But I think this would put your apprehensions about the shop to rest."

And then later, coming back to the house after dinner, he had said, "Tahmina, you know don't you, how I hate to be hard on you? And seeing her nod, he added, "I wouldn't have

The Shadow of the Clouds

insisted on your coming back to Dubai if it wasn't so necessary."

"I know, Abbu," she replied, trying to keep her voice steady. "Don't worry, I'll think about what I would like to do and tell you in the morning."

"It's so difficult to decide sometimes in life, isn't it?" he asked, "That's why I have given you the options, to make it easy for you."

"Yes, Abbu," she replied.

"And let me tell you too that I understand how much you want to stay here and run your shop and you can't know how much I want you to fulfil your every desire. But there are some desires that are not killed even if you fulfil them…."

Forty Five

"It's so difficult to decide sometimes in life, isn't it?" Faisal had said and how true that was, Tahmina thought. It was well past midnight and the moon had drifted past the window, leaving a patch of darkness in the sky. And getting up from the bed, she tiptoed out of the room once again to stand outside in the veranda.

What was she going to tell him in the morning, she wondered. It did appear better if she went away now to come back again in May; in fact, she was sure she would be able to persuade him to let her return even a little earlier. But, wouldn't it be so abrupt, going away like this in such hurry and that too without even getting used to her lovely, little shop here? And what about Amna? Would she let her come back here again? Yes, that was the real question, particularly after the way she was feeling, as described by Faisal. Yes, that certainly was something dicey. She knew Faisal would back her, but if Amna really put her foot down, then....No, that was something she couldn't risk at all.

And what about Sulaiman and her dreams of love? Being with him all through the day at the shop, waiting for some sign that would tell whether her love was casting its spell over him, she had imagined so much...Strolling with him along the lake with their arms around each other, or being with him in the woods up on the hill, where he would stop now and then to gather her in his arms. And then even more in the distance, living with him in this house and making love through the hushed, languid and sensuous afternoons, his lips lingering on her face...All this would just remain a dream if she went away. No! No, that would be unbearable!

And so, long into the night, her mind teeming with confusion, wavering between wild hopes and imminent doom, she went through the pain of uncertainty. Coming back to bed on the verge of tears, she groped blindly for a hand to hold in the darkness, before breaking out into muffled sobs. But tears were useless so she propped against the pillows after a while and tried to think everything out as clearly as she could.

Why do I want to stay back here so desperately, she asked? Yes, there was the shop, of course, and this house, and all the beauty of this place and her feeling of attachment and loyalty for her dead father. Yes, all these things were tugging at her heart, but she wouldn't lose any one of them if she went away from here. Amna could stop her from returning but for how long? Some day she would come back and everything would be hers again.

No, the real enticement was something else, something cloudy and as uncertain as the rain, the vague promise of a happiness she had been able to glimpse for herself here, a happiness that could only be put together by two people in love with each other. Yes, that was it – I may have initially decided to stay here for my father's shop and not to write a love story amongst the hills, but that was precisely what I am trying to do now.

But was it something real, she wondered, or was she chasing a cloud? It was so difficult to say and it was all her fault really. She had been foolish enough to start falling in love so rashly....But no, I'll not be afraid, she resolved. I'll be brave and reckless and try my luck in love, even if that would mean breaking my heart forever. Yes, I'll wait to see how long he'll be able to resist me or how long it would take me to rustle up the audacity to tell him myself how blindly and recklessly I was falling in love with him.

So that's decided, she thought. I'll tell Faisal in the morning that I would prefer to stay here for now. Yes, that would be the right thing, for to go away now would mean throwing away the opportunity of being near Sulaiman that she now had. Yes, yes, the best thing to do was to linger here through the spring, to hear the intimations of approaching summer. And if by then he still pretended as if no flower bloomed on the hills here, she would pluck her heart and take it elsewhere.

Yes, that's what she was going to do. There were almost two months to go till April and she would let his thoughts twine like a creeper around her. She would let her longing for him dig a well in her heart without caring what the future had in store.

Book Three

Forty Six

March is the best time in the hills before the onset of summer. The sky keeps clear and the soft and cheering spring sunshine is a real treat; meanwhile, the whole valley turns prodigal with flowers and the woods become so fervent and fragrant. But it's the evenings that are really beautiful with the lake shivering with flecks of sunset light that lingers for a long time, while the night languidly loosens its dark, thick tresses over the valley.

It didn't take more than a few days after Faisal's departure for Tahmina to gather her misgivings and pack them away with the heavy woollens. It may have been the golden sunshine or the flowers dappling the hills, or the fact that she could now venture out without shawls and sweaters, or, indeed, it may simply have been the gay abandon of happiness, but whatever it was, it was transforming her, changing her in infinitesimal ways.

On the face of it, her daily routine went somewhat like this: she would rise around seven, say her prayers, and reach the shop at ten-thirty. It was generally a busy time there till two, after which she shared lunch with Sylvia, while Sulaiman went home for his food. The afternoons were dull though, and Claire would often drop in around three to liven things up and they would go out for a stroll around the Flatt. After that it was work again till eight, when the shop closed and she came home, where she would watch the TV for a while (Faisal had bought a set for her) before having supper and finally going to bed. She had even picked up her reading habit again and would usually skim the pages of a novel before falling asleep.

Sundays, however, were for lingering in bed, having a leisurely bath and then going out in the veranda to soak up the sun. Later on it was either a trip to Claire's house or dropping in on Mr. and Mrs. Pandey and this was convenient for Kamla too, who could take Sunday off to be with her family. And then, in the evening, she and Claire would go to a movie or do some boating on the lake to round off the day.

The only discordant note in all this was Mr. Pandey's health. He came to the shop religiously every day, from ten to lunch, but it was very clear that something was missing: he walked more slowly, even stumbling sometimes, and he got tired more easily, and often he would lose his concentration, forgetting what he was going to say a moment ago.

That was why Tahmina had started pestering him to see a doctor, but the old man would simply brush away her concern and it was only when Anjali came for a visit after the honeymoon that they were able to drag him for a check-up.

"There isn't much wrong with him, though he's weak, of course," the doctor had said. "And he has to take care of his blood pressure." And from then on she had made it a daily ritual at the shop to ensure that he took his daily dose of medicines before her eyes.

But this predictable and prosaic routine was as deceptive as appearances usually are, for, as the days were passing with Sulaiman in the shop, she was becoming conscious of a hidden understanding between them that work inevitably breeds. But it must be more than work, she lliked to think. She dared to

The Shadow of the Clouds

let her mind go into places she never did before, more daring in her desire for Suleiman.

True that Suleiman's bringing the special bouquet at shop's opening and then later consoling her when he saw her break into tears had not led into anything more intimate than gentle compassion. But yes, they had started being more open and friendly with each other, though most of the time they talked only about things that concerned the shop. Occasionally, she would ask him about his uncle or he would inquire about Faisal. One day she had asked him who cooked the meals at his home.

"A maid comes around every day to clean up and cook," he had informed. "And she remains all day to look after uncle till I am home in the night."

"How is her cooking?" she had probed.

"All right, I suppose. But yes, uncle does miss my aunt for everything," he had replied with a wry smile.

"When is your sister coming? Her name's Naila, isn't it? Your uncle was telling me she was going to come over," she had inquired.

"I don't know exactly," he had replied, suddenly seeming to have been put off by her question. "She's been delayed for some time."

Nevertheless, there were small, scant signs that deluded her into believing her magic was beginning to work a little. She had gifted him a shirt that Faisal had brought and she had noticed that he wore it to the shop quite often. And then again, one afternoon, returning from lunch, he had brought a cake for her, telling her that he knew one of the best bakers in town and had got him to make something special for her. And yes, there had been moments too when she had caught him looking at her in a strange way.

But for all this, it was also true that he was still as far away from her as the blue in the distance across the lake. Yet there was nothing she could do if her heart went on hankering for him, lured by his silence and his shadow, by his silhouette through the haze of her love, by the smile that rarely touched his lips, even by the utter emptiness of his eyes.

And often, when he would be standing close to her in the shop, so close actually that she could feel his smell, she could barely stop from whispering out his name, or repress her desire to touch him. Not only that, but she would suddenly find herself wrapping her dupatta a little more tightly, trying, perhaps to hide her fragrance from him, fearing that somehow it would give her away to him....

But she could not hide those desires from herself and they burned in her without flame, smouldering and tormenting her and making her luminous with their silent, secret fires. And often, when Sylvia was engrossed in the computer and he was busy with his work, she would watch him surreptitiously, calling his name with her eyes, and then something would come back from him to touch her soul like a kiss in a dream.

Forty Seven

"You'll have to go over to the court tomorrow for the succession certificate," Mr. Pandey had informed her the day before. "It's just a formality. The lawyer will be there and all that you'll have to do would be to make an appearance before the judge and sign some documents. And, yes," he had added, "God bless him, the court is quite far off so I don't think I would be able to accompany you. But I'll send Sulaiman with you."

"Yes, of course, uncle," she had replied, eager and expectant. "There's no need for you to tire yourself."

And so that was how they had set out together, walking a little apart, Sulaiman a few steps ahead of her. The court was in Tallital, across the lake, and by the time they came down to the Mall Road she had managed to catch up and was now walking in step with him.

There were not too many people on the road these days though there was a lot of activity in the bazaar, with the shopkeepers busy preparing and sprucing up for the coming summer bonanza of tourists. The schools had, of course, opened, but the boarders came down to the town only on Saturdays and the only tourists just now were mostly newly-weds on their honeymoon, so, though the town had started coming to life as soon as the winter had turned its back, it was still a fairly lonely and peaceful place.

"It's so lovely today, isn't it?" she asked.

It was indeed a serene and sunny spring morning and the breeze was spraying wisps of hair over her face.

"Yes. If you want you can cross over on the boat. I'll meet you at the other end," he said.

"No, not now," she replied, conscious that they had drawn a little closer and for a moment she felt as if she was going to put her hand in his. "When is your sister coming?" she asked in an effort to distract herself. They were now walking along the lake, under the intermingling boughs of the trees, exactly like she had so happily imagined through the night.

"Tomorrow. I forgot to tell you. I'll be a little late for the shop because I'll have to go down to Kathgodam in the morning to fetch her," he said.

"Oh, sure," she replied, happy to hear the news. "And your mother, is there any chance of her coming too while I am here? I would like to meet her."

"I don't know for certain, but yes, perhaps she may be here next month," he replied, stopping to tie his shoelace while she observed him. How every movement of his affected her, she thought, while on his part he still appeared indifferent to what he was doing to her.

"Don't you go over to Mumbai to see her?" she asked as they walked along again.

"No," he replied. "I used to go there during the winter many years ago but since then she comes over to meet me."

"I see," she said. "And what have you thought about that C.A. thing of yours? Are you still serious about that?" she asked.

The Shadow of the Clouds

"I don't know really, it all depends on uncle's health."

Just then a man and a woman walked past them, their arms around each other, and a sudden rush of self-consciousness put her at a loss to say anything further so they walked along for a while, as silent as lovers.

"When are you are going back to Dubai?" he had spoken at last, startling her.

"The date's not fixed as yet, but I guess I'll have to leave by the end of April," she replied with a sigh. "Though if it were in my hands, I wouldn't go away, ever," she admitted.

"Why? Don't you miss home?" he asked.

"I do, but at the same time I wouldn't hesitate to make my home here, in this place that's tucked in the hills like love in a heart—that's how my father so charmingly described Nainital," she said wistfully and suddenly realised that this was the first time she had mentioned anything about her father to him.

"Are you sure about this?" he asked. "I mean I have seen so many people come here and fall in love with Nainital but it wears off after a while and they want to go back."

"I'm not like others," she replied sharply.

"I know," he replied and even stopped to look at her for a moment, a faint smile on his lips.

"No, you think it's a passing fascination, " she said softly, and a little sadly this time. "But I am very serious. I know I'll never be happy anywhere else in the world."

"Well, nothing's carved in stone yet, so maybe your wish

247

may come true after all," he said while she stumbled over a stray pebble.

"Be careful!" he said, holding her arm for a moment.

"Thanks," she said, his touch sparking a blush on her face and they fell silent once again.

"Can I ask you something?" she said finally, desperate to make him talk some more, for they were almost at the end of the lake and she could now see the buses that were arriving at the stand.

"Yes..." he asked.

"Did you know my father? I mean you have grown up here and you must have met him."

"Yes, of course, but not too intimately. I was too small when our mothers were friends so I don't remember that time, and after that..." He paused. "I mean after your mother went away there wasn't any real contact between us. In fact, even my mother stopped coming to Nainital around that time so.... But yes, I used to run into your father in the bazaar sometimes, or at the shop, and he would ask me how I was doing and about my mom too."

"I see," she said. "And didn't your mother meet him when she came here to visit you?"

"I don't think so. Her visits are so far and few and she can't stay here for more than a week at a time." He stopped to look at his watch and added, "Let's hurry now. Uncle said we had to reach there by eleven and there's hardly any time left now."

And so they had moved on, across the bus stand and

The Shadow of the Clouds

then a tiring climb up the hill. She had found the lawyer waiting for them at the gate and he had hurried her into the court where the whole process had been over in an hour.

"You must be tired," Sulaiman had said as they sauntered down to the lake.

"Yes. I think we must take a boat now," she had replied, her heart beating wildly.

But once they were at the lake he said, "Let me get a boat for you. I have some work this side and I'll go and see to that."

So Tahmina crossed the lake in the boat, sad and lonelier than ever. She had longed for a boat ride with him for quite a while, and he seemed to dismiss the opportunity without as much as a thought. But she hadn't let him see her disappointment.

He had come till the boat with her and when she had made her way across it to sit down on the seat, he had stood for a moment and smiled at her as before, waving her goodbye. And concealing her hurt somewhere deep in her heart, she had smiled back at him.

Forty Eight

It was Sunday evening and Tahmina was standing in the veranda, gazing at the beauty of the dark clouds that had all of a sudden blackened the sky while the muffled sound of distant thunder echoed through the hills.

The weather had moodily turned sultry and sullen in the morning with not even a whiff of breeze to rustle the leaves. Perhaps that's why I have felt so languid all day, she thought. But the long sleep during the afternoon had refreshed her and the wind had now picked up too; it was cool and moist, laden with the smell of woods, and it appeared as if the storm that had brewed all day was going to break very soon.

Glancing at her watch, she silently prayed it would hold for a while, for Naila would be arriving any moment to fetch her for dinner and she had been looking forward to it so eagerly.

Naila had come to meet her in the shop yesterday and Tahmina had been surprised to see how beautiful she was. In fact, she had a strange, haunting beauty, and there was something enticing in her every little grace and gesture, including the way she looked with those liquid eyes of her. But what had been particularly intriguing to Tahmina was the way she treated Sulaiman, almost as if he was a child to play with. She had stayed quite long, talking about her husband in Calcutta and recounting her school days at St Mary's and the pranks she used to play on everyone, particularly on Sulaiman.

"He's so serious, isn't he?" she had asked Tahmina,

tossing a glance at him with laughter, "Almost like Bugs Bunny!" But he hadn't heard, or at least pretended as if he hadn't. God, what a sister he had! Tahmina had wondered afterwards, she must have pricked him like a rose. And finally she had invited Tahmina for dinner on Sunday.

"I'll come to fetch you around six," she had said and Tahmina could see her now, coming up the path to the clearing.

"Won't you come in for a cup of coffee?" Tahmina called out when she came near.

"No, just look at the sky. If we don't hurry we'll be stranded here all evening," she shouted back.

Going inside to tell Kamla she was leaving, Tahmina stopped for a moment to put on her cardigan, for it was getting chilly now, and then went down the steps to go with Naila.

"These storms don't last long, do they?" she asked as they started down the path.

"Not at this time of the year. But who cares," Naila replied, "as long as we reach home before it starts raining."

Sulaiman's house wasn't too far away, just a little distance from the Post Office, except that it was fairly high up on the hill.

"Abbu rented this place way back in 1963 and the landlord's after him now to vacate it. But I have told abbu to do nothing of the sort. He won't be able to get another place at such low rent." Naila told her as they entered the small garden in front. Just then a loud crack of lightning split the sky and a few drops of rain fell on her.

"Oh my God!" Tahmina exclaimed, "Perhaps I shouldn't

The Shadow of the Clouds

have come today," she added, scampering towards the door with Naila as the rain came down in a torrent.

Greeting Sulaiman's uncle, who had come to open the door, she entered a small room and before she could glance around, the house was plunged in total darkness.

"The power's always switched off in a storm," Mr. Riaz explained, "Just a minute. I'll light a candle."

And so the three of them sat and talked in the dim, flickering light of the candle while the clouds thundered outside and the wind crashed through the trees, knocking at the doors and windows.

"Where's Sulaiman?" she asked at last.

"He went to buy sweets for you," Naila replied. "Now he will be stuck in the rain."

"Oh," Tahmina replied softly, and to hide her disappointment, asked hurriedly, "You'll be staying here long?"

"No, I am going back on Thursday."

"Uncle and Sulaiman would feel more lonely after that, won't they?" Tahmina asked.

"Not Sulaiman," Naila said with a laugh, "He knows how to talk to walls, but yes, abbu's going to miss me. I tell him to come and spend a few months in Calcutta with us but he doesn't listen."

"Yes," Tahmina turned to Mr. Riaz, "Naila's right. You must go there, the change would be good for your health too."

"No, no," the old man had demurred. "I can't leave the boy alone."

"Oh God, Abbu!" Naila said with exasperation, "He's not a boy any more." And then turning to Tahmina, she added, "That's the problem, Abbu still thinks of Sulaiman as a child."

"He may not be a child any more," Mr. Riaz said in a sort of mild rebuke. "But you know how sensitive he is and I don't like the way you go about making fun of him."

"Oh come on, Abbu! You know I love him too," Naila laughed. "It's just that I get exasperated at the way he acts Mr. Serious all the time. Tell me, Tahmina," she asked, looking at her searchingly, "What does he do at the shop? I mean apart from work."

"Nothing," Tahmina replied, her heart atwitter. "I mean he just keeps busy with the work."

"That's what I thought," Naila said a little thoughtfully, "In a way it's not his fault really that he's like that. I don't know if you are aware but he's not my real brother…"

"Yes," Tahmina interrupted. "Mr. Pandey told me about him. It must have affected him…I mean whatever happened…"

"Yes," Mr. Riaz said with a sigh, "You are right. He was just five years old when his mother left him with us and though he wouldn't say anything, it must have hurt him. I remember how he used to sit quietly in a corner, lost in his thoughts, and if we asked what was the matter, he would just shake his head and try to smile."

"I guess he must be more attached to you all compared to his mother…"

"Yes, naturally. That's why she doesn't come here too often."

The Shadow of the Clouds

"Mr. Pandey was telling me she knew my mother."

"Yes, I remember, she used to go to your house occasionally. At that time she was living with us here. You must ask your mother, she would remember her."

"Yes, I'll do so but I don't know her name...." She stopped. Someone was knocking at the door.

"Must be Sulaiman," Naila said, going to open the door and Sulaiman hurried on inside the house to change into dry clothes.

"I must go and see to the food now," Naila said, following him inside.

"I'll come and help," Tahmina called, getting up.

"No, no, don't bother, I'll manage. And then it's so dark really. You just sit and talk with abbu," Naila called back before disappearing. And so she sat back and Mr. Riaz started asking her about Faisal.

"Yes, Abbu's fine. He isn't in Dubai at the moment though. He has taken Ammi to Malaysia for a vacation. They'll be coming back next week."

"Hmm. And what about you? Sulaiman was telling me you'll be going back in April."

"Yes," she replied.

"And when will you come again?" he asked.

"I don't know," she replied, "In fact that was something I wanted to talk about with you," she said, "I am worried about the shop. Sulaiman says he isn't sure he'll be able to go on working there...."

"Yes, he has set his heart on becoming a C.A. It's only because of my illness that he has been putting it off, though I tell him he should worry more about his future. But he doesn't listen."

"I know, and I think that's very good of him."

"But he has to think about his future too. You know how things are here these days, so many people are unemployed …" He paused. "It's very sad really because if his father—he was my brother—hadn't been such a fool, Sulaiman wouldn't have to worry about anything. There was so much land but it's all gone now….."

"Come on, the dinners ready," Naila called and Sulaiman too came in just then.

"Sorry about the lights," he said. "Did you get here before the rain?" He asked.

"Yes, just in the nick," she replied, following him inside to the dining room.

"We are going to have a real, romantic, candlelit dinner," Naila chuckled. "How's the storm outside, Sulaiman?" she asked him.

"It's still raining," he replied, sitting down across her.

Dinner was a quiet affair, except for Naila who went on saying something or the other. In between Tahmina stole a few glances towards him and once or twice she found him looking back at her too, his face shining palely in the candlelight.

"You cook as beautifully as you look," Tahmina

The Shadow of the Clouds

complimented Naila, "And now I must ask all of you to come for dinner to my house too."

"Thanks, but you know I am leaving on Thursday so there's hardly any time. But yes, when I am here next..."

"Who knows if I'll be here then," she said and looked up at Sulaiman instinctively. She couldn't say if he had caught on to the implication of what she had said, but she did feel as if a cloud passed over his face for a moment.

"I should be leaving now," Tahmina said after the coffee, glancing at the watch. "It's almost ten."

"But it's still raining, " Naila said. "And it's quite dark too."

"Oh, I'll manage. I think it's just drizzling now and I don't have to go very far too."

"Don't worry," Mr. Riaz said. "Sulaiman will go with you with a torch and you can take the umbrella."

"Yes, of course, he'll go," Naila added. "We can't let you go alone on such a dark, stormy night."

"Then let's leave now," she said with a shy, hurried glance towards him.

"Yes, just a moment," he said. "I'll get the torch."

Saying goodbye to Naila and Mr. Riaz, she set out with him in the light rain, clutching the umbrella, while he walked silently ahead, wearing a raincoat and beaming the torch in front.

"Please be careful," he said. "It's very slippery."

"Yes," she replied in a whisper. It was pitch dark and the clouds were still rumbling ominously but the rain seemed to be petering out. For a while they walked silently before she managed to say something.

"It must be very difficult during the rainy season here?" she said, her feet hurrying to catch up with him. "Anjali was telling me it rains and rains for days on end in July and August."

"Yes and it gets quite boring with nothing to do except to wait for the sky to clear. Last year during the monsoons it kept raining for ten days at a stretch."

"But thank God it's stopped now," she said, folding away the umbrella. They were down on the road now and the path to her house was just a short distance away.

"Yes," he replied, looking up towards the clouds. "But I think it's going to rain some more through the night."

She glanced up too but there was nothing to see except dark, swirling clouds. Why can't we discuss anything else except the weather, she thought with exasperation, looking sideways at him in the darkness. He was walking with his head hunched down, half his face hidden under the raincoat cap.

"Oh my God!" she cried as a vicious burst of lightning flashed across the sky and a sudden gust of wind almost snatched away the umbrella from her hands. Almost immediately there was a deafening rumble and the rain began to drive down in a surge.

"Come on, hurry," he said, turning to her. "The path to the clearing is just a yard or so." And seeing her struggle to open the umbrella, he snatched it from her hands, opening and handing it back to her. But just as they started climbing up the path to the clearing, another burst of wind took it away from her hands and it went rolling down somewhere in the darkness.

"Oh my God!" she cried, "It's gone."

He stopped for a moment and started taking off his raincoat. "Let it go," he said, handing the torch to her. "You can wear my raincoat."

"Don't," she said, wiping the rain from her eyes. "I'll just run up to the house."

"No, you can't. It's too slippery and you are already drenched," he said, taking the torch from her again, "Now come on, get the raincoat on and walk very carefully."

And so she put on the raincoat and struggled to follow him but the rain was now coming down in such a frenzy that it was difficult for her to walk unsupported. Sensing her distress, he silently held her hand and she let the storm fling her into his arms, feeling their drenched bodies clinging to each other, till she had no sense of who or where she was, being conscious only of the fire coursing through her veins and her heart thudding against his chest.

He let her go at last as they came to the steps of her house but her foot slipped and she lurched into him again. Trying to hold her, the torch slipped from his hands, falling to the ground, and as he bent down to pick it up, his face brushed against her lips for a moment.

"Thanks," she said, opening the gate to step into the veranda. "The torch's broken, no?"

"Yes," he replied in a whisper. "Drink some coffee before you go to bed. You have got really wet." He turned to go.

"Where are you going?" she whispered back, still standing close to him, reluctant to let go of the wild, exhilarating happiness she had discovered, "You must come and wait inside. I can't let you go in this storm..."

"It doesn't matter," he replied, hesitating a moment. "I'll manage. And you go inside."

It was so dark that she wasn't able to see his face. He descended the steps quickly to disappear in the rain. Running to the edge of the veranda, she tried to peer through the storm but there was nothing to see. Perhaps Kamla hadn't heard her come, otherwise she would have opened the doors and so she had kept standing recklessly in the rain till the cold forced her to flee inside.

Afterwards the rain stopped and the storm blew away, except for the soundless reflections of lightning that now and then lit up her room while she lay in bed, burning with the desire to touch him and somewhat disturbed and confused at his hasty departure.

Forty Nine

Two days went by, two days during which she waited in vain to see if the night in the storm had done something miraculous to him or not. On her side, however, the desires that had been provoked by the touch of his body, by the brush of her lips against his face, had surprised her by their intensity and abundance.

"You reached home safe?" she had asked him fervently the next morning at the shop.

"Yes," he answered and she hadn't been able to say anything else. But all through the day she had watched him working in the shop, looking so handsome, her own smile hidden in the shadows of the corner where she sat behind her desk. And there had been a few evanescent moments too when their eyes had held each other and she had felt as if he was trying to say something, awakening the possibility, however faint, that she might some day hear his heart beat for her.

Next day, when Sylvia had taken the afternoon off and they were alone in the shop, she had asked him to come over to her desk with some files and when he was seated across her, she had leaned forward as they went through the papers and once or twice she had even brushed her leg lightly against his under the table. But she had to let him go after the work was finished and so nothing had come about, after all.

"Daydreaming?" Claire startled her, "Where were you lost?"

"Oh, nowhere!" she replied. She couldn't possibly tell her she had been wondering what else could happen that would throw them together in the intimacy of the night before.

"Well, wake up! I have some interesting news for you."

"Why, Claire, what's up?" Tahmina asked, suddenly conscious of how happy Claire was looking.

"A lot, my dear," she replied, taking out a letter from her purse. "Just have a look at this. Henry's gone and got his company to allow him to fly in his wife for a month and everyone knows that's me."

"Oh my God! Then you will be going away…"

"Yes, I leave in three days. But listen, why aren't you as happy as I would expect?"

"Of course, I am happy," Tahmina replied, smiling at her, "For you!"

"I understand," Claire said seriously, "You are going to miss me, isn't it?"

"Yes, like a candle," Tahmina replied. "And what I am thinking is that I'll be gone by the time you are back and so we have just three days left for each other. It's so sudden, isn't it?"

"That's how happiness arrives," Claire replied. "You know I have been so starved for Henry that I wasn't thinking about anything else except our being together in Singapore. And all our love making!" she smiled mischievously, "But why are you blushing, Auntie?"

"Please, Claire. The things you say and what if he

The Shadow of the Clouds

overhears?" she glanced towards Sulaiman who was arranging books in the racks nearby.

"Ah! I see," Claire replied, raising her eyebrows, "Well, I have a lot to say that you wouldn't want him to hear at all. So, come along, we're going to sit somewhere and talk for hours and hours."

"Why not, let's go," Tahmina agreed readily. "It's so lovely today outside in the sunshine."

"All right, you go and sit under that elm near the bandstand while I'll go and get some chocolates," Claire said when they came down to the Flatt. "I've got to store up as much passion as I can," she added with a wink.

Settling down on the balustrade, Tahmina looked at the lake and the hills and wondered once more how fairy-tale like this place was. If only she could have her prince charming, then it would all end well for her too, she thought wistfully. Lost in her thoughts, she started tearing leaves from a hanging bough and tossing them into the water.

"You are in love, aren't you?"

Claire's voice startled her so much that for a moment she almost lost her balance.

"Oh God!" Tahmina cried. "I would have fallen into the lake."

"Not when you have fallen in love," Claire said, unmoved.

"Love? How do you spell it?" Tahmina asked, taking the chocolate from Claire and looking away in the distance.

"I spell it with lost eyes, stolen glances, scribbling names and crossing them out, smiling to yourself every now and then when you think no one's watching you, tearing and flinging leaves in the water, stealing the colour of roses for your cheeks and by smelling like the lilacs after the rain...:"

"Go on, go on," Tahmina laughed. "Any more symptoms Dr. Claire?"

"These will do for now," she replied impishly. "Now stick your tongue out and ..."

"You are a naughty, nosey, nanny..." Tahmina laughed again.

"That's another give away, I mean when you start talking in rhymes. It's no use, dear. You can't hide it. And let me tell you that I know who the culprit is..."

"I don't know what you are talking about."

"You won't be able to wriggle out. I have been observing you for weeks and I was just holding back to see how long you were going to take to put your head against my shoulders and ruin my handkerchief."

"It's not funny, Claire," Tahmina confessed at last. "Yes, I love him, I love him so much! But what difference does that make when he can't see it."

"Why don't you get his eyes tested?" Claire wondered. "There's a very good optometrist in Nainital...."

"Claire, please."

"I was being serious, really, but if you want me to be funny then I would say you should go on giving him the rope.

The Shadow of the Clouds

But tell me," she lowered her voice to a whisper, "what are you going to do with the body when he finally hangs himself and is laid out on your bed?"

"Please, Claire..." Tahmina said, blushing all over once again.

"Oh God! Just look at you. You cannot even admit your own needs to yourself. But I can bet you are full of hidden pleasures. Now if only I was a man..."

She had turned serious in the end though.

"Don't be disappointed, Tahmina. Perhaps he's as much in love with you and it's just that love makes some men shyer than women."

"I don't know. I can understand his reticence after coming to know he's been like this always, but why can't he say it with his eyes? And even after all the hints I have given him," she said morosely.

"But you must appreciate his difficulty. He can't just come up and say 'I love you' to you, to a woman he works for and that too on the basis of some vague hints." Claire said.

"Maybe," Tahmina said.

"And then even you have come to know him for not more than a few months. In fact, it wouldn't be wrong to say he's almost a stranger and I think you can be a little more careful. A girl always lets her heart take her wherever it wants to and sometimes that's a reckless thing to do..."

"Oh I know," Tahmina replied gloomily, "I feel afraid too and perhaps I am being foolish, letting him deeper and deeper into my heart without pausing to think what would happen in the end. But I can hardly undo it all now. You can't know how much I have come to love him. And it's been going on from the moment I first saw him. I haven't been able to go to sleep easily at night since then. I just lie in bed and gaze at the stars and my heart wanders to him…"

"Yes!" Claire was silent for a few moments. "That's how it happens, it's almost impossible to stop. Anyway, he does seem so simple and sincere and he's strong and handsome too and any girl would slice her heart just for the sake of those eyes of his."

"I was just wondering though what would happen after he comes around. Have you given some thought to that?"

"No, not really. Just now all I care for in the world is for him to reciprocate my feelings Nothing else matters."

"But many things would some day. Love's very nice and it's perhaps the only real adventure of our lives. But it hurts too, unlike anything else. Just think how you'll break the news to your parents. I mean if you are really serious in love—and I think you are—then we must follow the thread to its end."

"No, please. Don't make me think about all that, not now. It would all be too confusing and unbearable and then what's the use really? I don't think he is ever going to be mine…But how I wish it could be! You know, Claire, it's so difficult to bare your heart to anyone but now that I have, let me tell you that all I want in life is to live here till I die, live here with him, in the shop and my house," Tahmina said, no longer able to hold the tears that had been gleaming in her eyes for some moments.

"Don't cry, darling," Claire said, clutching her hand, "I am sorry, I didn't mean to make you do that, really."

"No, it's all right," Tahmina answered. "I am not crying because of what you said. It's just that I have been so happy here and I dread to think how badly I am going to break my heart over it."

"Don't be pessimistic. Love does break our hearts but it also gives us the strength to gather up the pieces and put them back again. You just wait and watch and everything will work out beautifully. I'll pray for that, from the heart."

"Thanks," Tahmina whispered, smiling hesitantly. "Yes, I am still here for more than a month and if I count the moments they would be more than the stars in the sky."

"Yes, that's the spirit. But do tie one piece of advice to your heart. Don't let him guess your love easily, you understand?"

"Yes, I do, and the way he is I won't even have to try too much," Tahmina said, smiling and biting her lip. "But I will go on loving him more and more, even if that makes my heart ache for life. And if I fail and I have to go away with my love hidden like a moment of beauty in the night, even then my love will remain. No one can take that away from me..."

Fifty

It must have been an hour later after she had returned to the shop that someone came hurrying in with the news.

"Mr. Pandey's suffered a heart attack."

"Oh God!" she cried, "Where's he now?"

"At home. We have called in a doctor."

"Let's hurry, Sulaiman, I hope it's not serious," she mumbled, picking up her purse.

"Yes let's go. If it's really a heart attack we'll have to take him to the hospital immediately."

"Oh God," she thought on the way, realising for the first time perhaps how much the old man had come to mean to her, "Please don't let anything happen to him," she prayed silently. And it was so unexpected too, for she had been noticing happily how he was getting back to his old self once again. Even this morning he was willing to go and find out why the phone connection hadn't come through...

He was already being brought down the stairs on a chair when they reached and though it was a relief to find him conscious, the look of agony on his kindly face was enough to bring tears to her eyes. Restraining herself somehow, she rushed to console Anjali's mother who broke down in her arms.

"No, aunty, please, he'll be all right," she murmured,

while Mr. Pandey was seated in a rickshaw and taken to the hospital.

"His condition isn't too good at the moment but hopefully he'll recover," the doctor at the hospital told them after a check-up, and then looking at their anxious faces, he added with a reassuring smile, "There's no need to worry. Though, of course, we'll have to keep him in the ICU for some days."

She had remained at the hospital till quite late in the night, too sad to care for anything, though she had still tried to keep Anjali's mother preoccupied in something or the other until the doctor had finally asked them to go home, allowing only Anjali's mother to stay the night at the hospital.

So it was a sort of comfort to be kept so busy for the next two days, what with trips between the hospital and the shop and going to see off Claire, who had dropped in at the hospital too with Mr. Mathew. Meanwhile Anjali and her husband had arrived after hearing the news and so had her brothers.

But whatever she did, or wherever she went, Mr. Pandey's smiling face kept appearing before her eyes and often she felt her tears spattering her cheeks like a patch of rain from some stray cloud left over after a storm.

How truly he loved her, fretting over her as if she was his own daughter and how his face always lit up to see her. And she knew too that she wouldn't have been able to stay here and open the shop without him. In fact, it was certain Faisal wouldn't have allowed her to stay on if Mr. Pandey hadn't been around to keep an eye on things and take care of her.

But more than anything else, she realised, he was her most precious link to the past, someone who had stood by her father and looked after him when he was ill and alone. Yes, that was the real though imperceptible attachment between them and she wouldn't be able to bear if something happened to him.

And then there was also the question of what would happen to the shop. She would miss his experience and his blessings and a lot of other shadows would be cast over her life too.

So she had tried every prayer she knew, till, at last, he was declared to be out of danger and shifted into an ordinary room at the hospital.

Fifty One

Mr. Pandey was home after a week and a half in the hospital, his face as brimful of smiles as before. He looked weak, of course, and there was no question of him getting back to the shop soon, where Sulaiman had quietly taken over his work. But the real thing was he had survived, another blessing that Tahmina could count for herself..

Something almost as wonderful had happened too and life had suddenly taken on as many hues as a set of crayons. It was the friendship between her and Sulaiman—it occurred without any planning or fuss, as unobtrusively as a bud turning into a flower.

The first night when she had got up to go home from the hospital, he had accompanied her without saying a word. He had come with her till the clearing before saying goodbye and she had been too troubled to care for anything else except Mr. Pandey.

But the next day, after there was every sign that the critical stage had passed and the old man would come through, she had got up to leave around midnight and once again he had come along with her. Both of them had stood hesitating for some moments on the road down from the hospital, before he had spoken, It's quite late so I'll see you till the clearing." And she too hadn't even put on any pretence by trying to dissuade him. They had walked in silence mostly, apart from exchanging a few words about Mr. Pandey before she had waved him goodbye from the steps of her house.

The next night she had been impudent enough to say, "Let's go for a stroll by the lake. The night seems so lovely today."

After that it had become a sort of silent pact between them. She would go home from the shop, have a hurried supper, and then leave for the hospital and Sulaiman would arrive there too. Sometime around eleven they would take leave together and then go for a stroll by the lake, stopping now and then to lean on the balustrade, watching the reflection of the lights shimmering in the water like sequins on a bride's dress.

It was then that they talked, sharing their thoughts, asking and telling each other whatever was on their minds,, getting to know so many of the small details about one another's life.

Talking about her father with him one night, she had asked, "How did it feel when you came to live here? I mean you must have missed your mother?" she had asked, stealing a look at his face.

"I don't know," he had answered. "I think I tried not to think about whatever had happened. And then there weren't many pleasant memories of home... I think I tried to shut it all off."

"Yes, I can understand," she had replied. "You know, there wasn't any thing terrible like that between my parents, and yet, they weren't happy together. That's why my father decided to leave her. He was afraid their misery would affect me...I didn't accept that when I came to know about it first, but now, now I think he was right perhaps..." And she had told him all the things she had come to know about her father and Amna.

The Shadow of the Clouds

"How do you feel about your mother now? Do you resent she left you here or that she has married again?" she had asked.

"No, not at all. I don't grudge any happiness she can find. Maybe if I had grown up with her, I would have felt more attached and possessive, but not now, not with the way there's been so much distance between us. I did miss her for a few years after coming here but then slowly it faded away. And then my aunt loved me more than her daughters. She didn't have a son of her own and perhaps I fulfilled a need in her...."

"Yes. It's just like what happened with me. Faisal loves me so much that I would never have imagined I wasn't his daughter if he hadn't told me," she had replied, then asked, "And what about your cousins ?"

"Both of them are nice in their own way. You haven't met Rahila... She is the silent, serious one. She wouldn't play with me or talk too much, but she was the one who used to comfort me, bringing chocolates and taking care of my things. Naila, you have met..." He had said with a wry smile.

"Yes, she's awfully mischievous..."

"You know the first time I came here when I was old enough to remember anything, it was Naila who had come to open the door for us. We had come in winter and my mother had wrapped a muffler around my face and head and she had started laughing the moment she set eyes on me. Said I was looking so funny, and perhaps I was. And that's what she has been doing all through the years..." His voice had trailed off and she had felt a hint of some incomprehensible sadness in it.

And so the days had passed and the nights had gone on becoming more tender and enchanting and they had come to stroll further and further with each other, or if they came to stand somewhere, they wouldn't care to see how far the moon had travelled in the sky.

One night she had broached the subject of the shop with him, "Isn't there some way you could settle down here and go on working at the shop?" she had asked, her heart beating apprehensively. "For my sake," she had added breathlessly.

"I don't know," he had replied after a long silence. "You know even I have come to love the shop but…" He hadn't been able to say anything further and so she had tried to put his thoughts in her own words.

"You don't think it's going to pay you enough, isn't it?" she had ventured.

"No, I don't care that much for money," he had replied.

"Then what else do you worry about?" she had asked.

"Nothing," he had said. She had sensed he didn't want to talk about it and yet she hadn't let it go.

"There's something I have been wanting to tell you, though abbu did ask me to wait for some time…" She had paused, mulling over whether it would be right to do so now, but she had said it all the same. "I think I'll tell it to you now." She had turned to look at him, "Abbu was saying he would ask you to become a partner in the shop." And she had relished seeing the look of utter surprise on his face. "Yes, he said he'll give you a partnership so you could go on running it without any worry. Won't you like that?" she had asked, smiling happily.

"I don't know," he had replied uncertainly.

"That's all you keep on saying—'I don't know'— but it's

so simple really. It would take care of your financial insecurity and I'll be happy too to see the shop in your hands forever. You know, don't you, that I can't stay here," she had said, stealing a glance at his face to see if that made any difference to him, "So just think what will happen to it if you go away too...."

"You can always find someone else...:".

"Oh I see," she had replied, the hurt creeping up on her face, "If that's how you think..."

"I'm sorry, Tahmina," he had said hurriedly, startling her. That was the first time she had heard her name on his lips. "I didn't mean to hurt you. In fact, I love the shop myself and I'll do anything for it. But I don't have the money to buy a share."

"But who said anything about money? Abbu was meaning to give it in exchange for your commitment to the shop."

"But that wouldn't be fair, would it?" he had said and she had suddenly flared up at him.

"Oh I see! And it would be fair, won't it, for you to leave the shop after we have set it up and go away knowing it will have to be closed again because there won't be anyone to look after it," she had burst out, almost on the verge of tears.

"No, no, please, I didn't mean that," he had said hurriedly, trying to make up. "Don't worry, the shop won't close, ever. I'll think about it," he had added. But she had remained sullen and they had walked home after that in silence.

She had wept that night, almost like a child, and then sat

up in bed wiping away her tears. What did he think of himself, she had thought angrily, as if there was no one else in the world that she could love or who could run the shop for her. Yes, he was right, she had thought after a while, there wasn't anyone else.

She had found a bunch of flowers waiting for her on the desk next morning. She had glanced towards him and he smiled at her, as if to say, 'I'm sorry, I made you cry last night.' But when they went for the stroll that night, she had waited and waited to see if he would say anything about the partnership business, but he hadn't brought the subject up and she had felt too proud to ask him about it again.

Nevertheless, she had been happy, for however tenuous and fragile it was, the incipient friendship between them was still something to cherish for her. And those hours in the night were something apart, something rare and faraway for him too. He talked so freely then and smiled as if he was someone different.

True, there still wasn't any hint of romance between them and perhaps he didn't care to wonder, like she did, at the way life had brought them together, and at the nascent relationship growing like an intricate pattern of embroidery, tugging them nearer and nearer.

Sometimes, as they walked close together in the night, their arms brushed against each other, or, if they were standing leaning on the balustrade, their hands lay so close that just a strand of hair would separate them. And it was so difficult then, to keep her trembling fingers from touching him and her heart would beat so wildly she was certain he could hear it, standing, as he would be, just a heartbeat away from her.

But something always held her back, and it all concluded like a passing cloud that promised rain.

There had been only one moment, that too on their last night together, that seemed different. There had been a sudden, short shower in the afternoon and it had washed the sky even purer. In fact, the stars had a lustre that night she had never seen before. But it had turned the night colder too and she had nothing on other than a light cardigan.

They had been standing near the lake, with the willows silhouetted against the suffused light of the moon, and all of a sudden she had shivered and he had taken off his jacket and offered it to her.

"Thanks," she had said, touched by his gesture and he had gone on looking at her for some moments.

"It's looking very nice on you," he had said softly, peering into her eyes. "I mean you are looking very different wearing the jacket..."

'Thanks," she had answered, looking back into his eyes.

But the moment had passed though she had gone on feeling delirious all through the night.

Fifty Two

A few more days passed during which nothing more significant happened than the phone connection for her shop coming through finally.

She had applied for it way back in February and the delay had got Faisal irritated, for a phone at the shop meant he could ring up whenever he wanted instead of waiting for her to phone from Nainital. Not that she didn't do it often enough, but, recently, when he and Amna were on vacation, it had been really difficult to be in touch. So she hadn't wasted any time in calling up his hotel in Dubai.

"Thank God!" he had said, after he got to know she was speaking from the shop, "That's one good news. And what about the other? I mean when are you coming home? You remember, don't you, the deadline was April, and mind you, Tahmina, there's going to be no putting it off this time," he had said firmly.

"Yes, of course," she had answered.

"Okay! Then I'll see when a seat's available around the 30th and phone you the flight details. And now, how's your shop doing?" he had enquired.

"Fine. Nothing big yet, but the small sales add up…"

She had put a call through after that to Amna too, with whom she could now talk without any trepidation; Faisal's idea of a vacation had, thankfully, done the trick, and she didn't sound sullen or bitter any more. This was something Tahmina felt happy about, because she could now put away those feelings of guilt that pestered her for having hurt her mother somehow.

She had, of course, avoided saying even a word about Mr. Pandey's heart attack, fearing, and rightly so, that it would mean something more for Faisal to worry over. And then Mr. Pandey was recovering so well too; he had even started throwing little tantrums at being forced to stay in bed all day.

In the meantime, some other things were changing—the weather for one, as the summer was settling in. And that was something she welcomed, for she could now wear her light summer dresses throughout the day.

The town too was, on the whole, getting livelier, with all sorts of stalls and hawkers nearly swarming over the Flatt, which was gradually acquiring a carnival atmosphere, even though the rush of tourists was still some weeks away. Indeed, sometimes it no longer seemed to be the same place at all, with its serene and silent beauty. The onslaught of tourists was not something Tahmina was looking forward to, and she sometimes felt glad that she would leave before it came about.

But the thing over which she was breaking her heart these days was that she could no longer go strolling at night with Sulaiman. As long as Mr. Pandey was in hospital, it had been easy, leaving together as they did, particularly as it would be fairly late in the night with most of the shops closed and very few people out at that hour. But all that was over now and they hadn't any further excuse or stratagem to use to make it happen again.

She couldn't say whether he missed the strolls as much as her, but yes, she was certain there was a hint of disappointment on his face when he said goodbye to her after closing the shop at eight and turned to go away for the night. And she would trudge back home, lonely and unhappy at the prospect of another long, brooding night.

The worst thing was, she was convinced something magical was on the verge of occurring between them. She had felt it as surely as one could sometimes guess the coming line of a song or a poem. If only they had been able to go on like that in the night...

In desperation, she was throwing all caution to the winds, gazing at him for long moments in the shop, across the vase of flowers on her desk, without caring that Sylvia was there with them. Or she would call him to her desk more and more, often with excuses that were embarrassingly silly and even go to stand near him when he was sorting books in the racks. She would feel the strange smell of his clothes then, feel it pervading all through her and hurry back to her desk and bask in the pleasure of the desires it provoked.

And the thing that was going through her like a pang all the time was the realisation that it was all her fault only... she had not made much of those nights when they were together... she had let the moments pass... those moments when she could have slipped her hand in his and told him of her feelings.

Yes, she had been awfully unwise.. She could have understood, as Claire had observed, how difficult it must be for him to say he loved her—that is if he really did so. He worked for her, he had to keep in mind the trust Mr. Pandey had put in him and they had only come together a few months ago, with such a difference between their worlds...

And now it was futile to hope, for there was hardly any time left. She would leave in a few weeks and they would part with nothing more than a passing friendship between them, somewhat like the one that sprang up between people during a journey. Yes, she would go away, her heart left behind, but never known.

Unless…Unless, of course, if she decided to do something …Something like asking him to meet her at the lake tomorrow night and confessing her feelings to him.

Fifty Three

The first thing she felt on waking was the smell of the flowers in the veranda sneaking in through the window that she had left open last night. And then came the sound of thunder.

Throwing off the quilts, she jumped out of bed to rush barefoot to the window. Yes, it was overcast and hushed outside, and the fragrance of the flowers seemed to be hanging heavily in the warm, humid stillness.

"Oh my God! It's going to be one of those summer storms," she thought disappointedly. "Now how am I going to ask him to come for a stroll?" But a flash of lightning brightened her up. The rain was a good omen, wasn't it, she reflected happily, recalling that night in the storm when he had brought her up to her house in his arms, almost! And then it was a long time till night and, most likely, the storm would be over by then.

Turning away from the window, she went into the kitchen to ask Kamla for breakfast.

"You are looking so happy today, memsahib!" Kamla remarked, observing her.

"Yes, and perhaps I'll never be happier any other time," she chuckled joyously.

"That's very nice," Kamla said, "Won't you tell me why?"

"Hmm! No, not now!" she answered, "But don't worry. You'll be the first one I'll tell it to. Just pray it happens, I mean ask God to give me what I am going to ask for today."

"Of course, I'll pray. I always pray for you," Kamla replied simply, pouring out some tea for her. "But if you told me what it was, I could say some special prayer…"

"No! No! No! Not now," Tahmina laughed. "Let me get ready now. It looks like it's going to rain heavily and I'll be stuck at home."

And that's what happened. She was just on the point of leaving when there was a loud crash of thunder and the clouds opened up like an umbrella. There wasn't any chance of venturing out after that, so she went to stand by the window and let herself bathe in the feeling of freshness that rain always brings.

It was good in a way, she thought, that the storm was breaking so early in the day, for it meant the sky would clear by evening and there wouldn't be anything to keep them from going out in the night. Yes, she wasn't going to go back now, that was decided. As soon as she managed to get to the shop, she would ask him to meet her at the bandstand tonight. And she was sure he wouldn't refuse.

"But… Suppose he refuses, what then? Oh God!" she thought, "If something of that sort happened, everything would be broken and I won't be able to show my face to him again. Yes, it could even mean losing him forever…" She was filled with such dread that she had to sit on the chair to hold herself still.

She went through their encounters in her mind and decided that he too must love her, though in his own silent,

The Shadow of the Clouds

inconspicuous way. Or she wished ardently that those were the signs that she had rightly read. For other than being in love with him, she also felt secure in his presence, what with coming to work so closely and depending on him.

Heaving a sigh of reprieve, she decided to do something that would take her mind off such questions and her glance settled on her father's rack of books. Yes, it would be a good idea, she thought, to go through it and see if there were any more books by P.G. Wodehouse in there.

Last month, sifting through the rack on a Sunday, she had come across *The Small Bachelor* and started reading it on a whim and it had turned out to be one of the most beautifully funny love stories she had ever read. It had made her wonder too how a man, as gloomy as her father was supposed to be, could have liked such literature. But perhaps that's why he read it, she had thought...

Later, she had come across another one also—a Jeeve's story called *Joy in the Morning* and enjoyed that too. And then she had mentioned it to Sulaiman one night through their strolls and it turned out he was simply crazy about anything by Wodehouse.

"You love his books!" she had been truly surprised. "I could never have imagined! And do you try some of those pranks in real life too?" she had asked somewhat mischievously.

"I wish I could," he had replied very seriously. "But I can't. So I just read about it. There are a few ones I have missed though. Will you check up some time and see if you can find them in your father's collection?" he had asked.

"Why not! You write down the titles and I'll search for them."

"Yes, I'll do that. One of them is easy to remember, *Money for Nothing*. I had it from the school library once, but it got lost somehow and I have been looking for it ever since." But as it happened, she had forgotten, and even he hadn't reminded her again. But I'll search for it now, she decided.

It was while she was sorting through the ones at the back that she came across it—*Sonnets from the Portuguese*—that book of poems Mr. Mathew had mentioned so long ago. Yes, she had forgotten about that too. Forcing it out from the pile, she took it aside to wipe away the mould on its leather jacket and it was then that the picture fell out from between its pages.

She bent down to pick it up, intrigued, and for an instance it seemed as if someone had thrust her over an abyss. Stumbling to the bed, she just sat there, staring at the picture in her trembling hand, her mind in a whirl.

Though it had faded a little from the years between the pages, it was still clear enough for her to make out her father, nestling in the arms of a woman; they were sitting somewhere in the woods, their backs to a tree, the woman's arm around his neck.

What did it mean, this photograph? She asked herself, her head beginning to throb in pain. Who was this woman? And what was her father doing, sitting with her like that?

She wanted to tear it to pieces and yet she couldn't turn her eyes from it, as if it was the most fascinating thing she had ever seen, as if it was pleasure to go on stabbing her heart with pain...

So, after all, my father was as ordinary as anyone else, she thought, wanting to cry. She remained still as she sat listening to the rain.

Fifty Four

It was around eight in the evening and Tahmina was at the railing in the veranda, her face cupped in her hands as she stood gazing at the lake in the darkness.

It had stopped raining some time in the afternoon and the sky was crowded with stars now, except for a few scattered patches of dark clouds. It was getting cold too, but she wasn't in the mood to care for anything. The day had passed off in a sort of haze and all she wanted now was to go to sleep for ages and ages, never to wake up again. And yet she was out there in the cold.

Kamla had come inside some time later in the morning, to see what she was doing in the room for so long, and created such a fuss. "Just look at your face, as if you have seen a ghost..."

"It's nothing, Kamla. I have a slight headache, that's all."

"No, I'll go and ask Dr. Joshi to come and see you," Kamla had insisted, eyeing her with concern.

'Now don't you go troubling the world for my sake. I'll be all right soon," she had said. "But it'll be nice if you would go over to the shop and tell them I won't be coming in today. Wait till the rain stops though, or you'll fall ill too."

She had put away the photograph under the pillow after that, not wanting to look at it any more, and closed her eyes, but it had got sort of etched on her mind, particularly that woman's face—oval, with thick, sensuously curved lips and big, dark, ardent eyes...She wasn't a beauty, yet there was an unmistakable allure; and her long, black hair appeared to have been tossed loose...But the most perplexing thing was her face seemed so familiar, as if Tahmina had often seen her before...

Perhaps she had drowsed off after a while or been simply in a stupor, but the next thing she was conscious of was the wrenching pain in her hands and legs. Noticing dimly that the rain seemed to have stopped, and feeling as if she would suffocate inside the room, she had got off the bed and without caring to look in the mirror, she had picked up her purse and rushed out of the house.

She had wandered aimlessly for some time on the Flatt, like a leaf being swept about in the wind, before going into a public booth and putting in a call to Amna. But she had disconnected the line as soon as she had heard her voice and then went out to roam again, insensible to the pain in her legs, before turning to walk home, no longer able to hold her tears.

"How are you?" Suleiman's voice jolted her out of her reverie.

"Oh, it's you," she said, turning. He was standing a few feet away, looking at her.

"Sorry, I startled you. Didn't you see or hear me coming?"

"No..." She stammered. "I was watching the lake."

"I thought I would look in to see how you were."

"Thanks," she replied softly and turned to lean on the railing once again. "I am all right now."

"You shouldn't be out in the cold like this," he said.

The Shadow of the Clouds

"Yes, perhaps. But I like to stand here," she replied, "Would you like to sit inside?" she asked.

"No, It's all right," he replied, standing near her against the railing, his arms crossed on his chest, while she continued to look far away. "I like to gaze at the stars too."

"Can I ask something?" He broke the silence after a while.

"Yes?"

"What's the matter with you? Has something happened?"

"No..." she said. It was all so unbearable...And then, all of a sudden, she started to sob, her face in her hands, softly at first and then more freely.

"What's happened, Tahmina," he asked, coming nearer, "Please tell me. What's the matter, please..."

And she told him, mumbling through her sobs, while he stood silently near her.

"I see," he said when she had finished and wiped away her tears,   "I'm sorry ...." And he fell silent again.

"There's nothing to say, is there?" she asked, turning to look at him in the gloaming. "It's the same old story of betrayal. I couldn't have ever thought he would do something I would feel ashamed of."

"No, I think you are getting it wrong, Tahmina," he said, and for a moment, she felt comforted just to hear her name in his voice. Her pain sharpened her consciousness, and each word of Suleiman's sank into her with an intensity she had not known before. "It's a mistake to put a moral interpretation on such things. There may have been some compulsions, I mean, some circumstance or the other to explain it. And then, how are you so certain that the conclusion you have reached is all that's there is to it?"

"There's nothing else to it. You just have to look at the photograph to know they were lovers."

"I can't say really. As far as I know, your father didn't have a reputation for that sort of thing. This is a small place and if there was something like that, it would have gone about. And then, what's intriguing me is, if there was another woman in his life, where did she disappear?"

"Yes, I have been wondering too…God knows what happened. But I'll find out who she was," she answered.

"It's not going to make any difference to know that…"

"No, Sulaiman, I have to know who she was, because I would like to go and ask her why they did such a thing…You know I thought of asking my mother…I even went to phone her, but then I thought, no, she would get disturbed again. It was so shocking even when she heard about his death and then I left her alone too—to come here—and that has hurt her too. So if I say anything about this now, she'll get upset all over again…and I can't obviously go and ask Mr. Pandey or anyone else…it would be too dreadful…"

"That's what I am trying to tell you. It'll only get worse if you try to ferret out the past. Please," he said, a sudden urgency in his voice, "Please, Tahmina, try to be sensible. It doesn't matter what your father did or not. What's important is that he loved you…"

"Then why did he do such a thing? I am sure this is why

my mother left him, taking me away from him too...and then, why did he have to leave this picture behind? He had destroyed all the others. Then why leave this one back? Was it so important to him, unlike those of my mother's which he destroyed?"

"Perhaps it wasn't deliberate. Perhaps he kept it in that book and forgot about it..."

"I don't know...Listen, will you help me?" she asked abruptly.

"Why not..."

"But you'll have to promise first, that you won't say no..."

"If you like. It's a promise," he said, looking at her with that peculiar half-sad, half-comforting smile of his.

"All right, come inside then and I'll show that picture to you. After that I'll want you to trace that woman for me..."

"But there's no point," he started to say.

"No, you won't understand. No one would," she interjected. "I must find that woman, even if just to see what my father saw in her. I want to meet and ask her everything she can tell me ..."

"But who knows where she would be? You don't even know her name."

"Yes, but if she's someone who lives here, you'll recognise her. You know, her face seems sort of familiar to me, as if I have seen her somewhere, and that might be because I may have come across her somewhere here."

She went ahead to open the door to her room, switching

on the lights as they entered.

"Where's Kamla?" he asked.

"She goes away for some time in the evenings these days. Her mother's not keeping well so she has to go over to cook supper for the family," she explained, opening the drawer of her table. "Here," she passed the picture to him, watching his face expectantly. But he just stood there, staring at the picture without any sort of expression on his face.

"No, I don't think I have ever seen her here," he said, at last, his voice sounding somewhat distant..

"Are you sure?" she asked, disappointed.

"Yes," he replied, handing it back to her, "Forget her, Tahmina," he added, turning away. "I think I'll leave now."

"No, wait," she said hurriedly. "I'll make some coffee for you."

"No, thanks. It's getting late and uncle will be waiting." He stopped for a moment at the door. "Take care of yourself and don't think too much about this," he said, looking at her with eyes that seemed strangely withdrawn yet heavy.

Fifty Five

"How are you feeling today?" Sulaiman asked, looking up as she entered the shop.

"It's all right," she replied with a hurried, thankful smile, turning to answer Sylvia, who was asking about her too.

"Your father called from Dubai a few moments ago," Sylvia told her. "He'll be calling again in an hour. And there's a letter from Claire too. I have put it on your desk."

"Thanks," she mumbled, going across to the desk.

It was a long, rambling letter, putting a smile or a blush on her face now and then. "And what's going on with that romance of yours?" She had asked in the end, "you are such a dear, giving away your heart so easily, and I hope you don't go away empty-handed…"

Putting the letter away in her purse, she sat playing around with the papers on her desk, pretending to be busy, lifting her eyes occasionally to look towards him, but, somehow or the other, he would be looking elsewhere whenever she tried to search and find his eyes. She was feeling so lost that the phone bell almost startled her out of her wits.

It was Faisal, with the news that her airline ticket was for the 27th of this month.

"Yes, Abbu, thanks," she said quietly.

"You don't sound happy?" he asked.

"Oh no!" she said hurriedly. "Actually, I want to come home too now…"

Putting down the phone, she sat back wearily. So it was final now. She glanced at the calendar. She would be going away in two weeks…She looked towards Sulaiman with a sudden, desperate pang, wanting to rush and cling to him, and cry her heart out…

A little while later, he had gone out, mumbling something about some bills being due and so she left too, to go and visit with Mr. Pandey for a while.

It was almost at the end of the day, when Sylvia had left, as she usually did a little before closing time, that she went over to him. He was sitting behind the counter, doing some calculations.

"Can we meet tonight, Sulaiman?" she asked softly, "There's something I want to discuss with you and I thought we could go for a stroll after supper."

He looked up, hesitating a bit before he answered. "You are still brooding over that, aren't you?" he asked.

"No. It's something else," she replied, looking out on the road.

"Couldn't we talk it over here?" he asked quietly.

"No," she had said, blushing with sudden hurt and anger.

"I was just thinking that might be convenient for you," he said hastily, looking at her anxiously. "Where do you want me to come?"

The Shadow of the Clouds

"Thanks! I think ten o'clock at the bandstand would be okay," she answered and left for home, a rumpled smile on her lips at the thought of how alarmed he had looked at having upset her.

Fifty Six

"Let's go on that pony trail, at the other side of the lake," she suggested, observing the large number of people still milling around on the Flatt. "It'll be quiet and lonely there."

They had met earlier, on the road coming down to the lake.

"It's so warm tonight," she remarked, as they skirted past the Capitol to reach the narrow, dark trail that meandered by the lake all the way to Tallital.

"Yes. And it's going to rain again tomorrow," he replied.

"How can you tell?" she asked.

"There's no breeze for one, and then you can see that halo around the moon. That's always a sign of imminent rain."

"I see," she said, stopping for a moment to look up. Yes, there was a distinct, yellowish halo. "I didn't know this."

They went along silently for a while, before he asked, "You are still disturbed over that picture?"

"I can't say. I am trying not to think about it...I wish it wouldn't have happened, everything was going by so simply," she said wistfully, "You won't mind if I ask you a question?"

"No."

"How would you feel if you came to know something of

this sort about your father?" she asked.

"I don't think I would feel anything at all. I have no memories of him. I don't think about him," he answered flatly.

"I'm sorry," she mumbled, ruing her question.

"And if you are wondering what I would feel for my mother in such a situation," he went on. "All I care for is that she went through a lot of unhappiness and loved me enough to give me up, so that I could grow up safe in a normal way. Wilfully, or in some intuitive, unconscious way, that's what your father did for you too. So don't ever stop for any questions. Just go on loving him like you have been doing and everything would go on being simple again."

"Yes, perhaps you are right," she replied thoughtfully, "I think that's what's been haunting me at the back of my mind since yesterday—that my love for him would change now...Thank God it's so difficult to start loving someone less," she added, a feeling of lightness spreading through her.

"Let's turn back now or you'll get tired," he said after a while.

"Yes," she consented. "In fact I am feeling sort of creepy, it's so dark and shadowy here. Even the lake seems so eerie and forbidding from this side."

Coming back to the Flatt, they went to stand under the elm near the bandstand, leaning, side by side, on the balustrade.

"Look, how safe and beautiful the lake seems from here, with all these lights reflecting in it," she remarked, imperceptibly shrinking a little closer to him.

The Shadow of the Clouds

"Yes," he replied and then asked, "What were you wanting to talk about?"

"Yes, I'm coming to that," she said, her mouth suddenly turning dry. "Abbu phoned this morning to tell me he was sending my plane ticket. It's for the 27th." She stopped to wait and see if he would say anything, but as he didn't, she continued. "I must know your answer now—I mean about staying on at the shop as a partner. You had promised to think it over and tell me," she said, making a beginning.

"Yes," he answered, hesitating a moment, "That's going to be very difficult..."

"You mean you'll go for that C.A. thing?" she asked, biting her lip to quell the sudden feeling of foreboding that was sweeping through her.

"Yes, Tahmina," he said, "I don't like disappointing you, but it'll not be possible for me to do what you want."

"I see," she said, "So you don't think you'll be able to earn as much here at the shop," she added, mockingly, bitterly.

"I told you it's not about money..." he said and she could feel him drawing away from her, no longer leaning at her side. "It's something else."

"It's all right," she said, looking like a crumpled flower.

"I'm sorry, I care for you and I can't tell you how difficult it is for me to refuse you."

"No, it's all right. It's your life and you have a right to make your own decisions," she said, standing straight and looking at him, "I am sorry if I have made you feel bad. It's just that I had set my heart that you would go on looking after the shop. We have come to know and trust each other and I don't think I'll find someone else like you."

"Don't worry. I'll help you find some one better," he replied. "But, please, don't be sad or angry."

His answer seemed like a mockery to her, but "No, I won't," she said, shaking her head. "But only if you tell me why you won't like remaining with the shop." And as he didn't say anything, she added, "I'm sorry. I shouldn't ask perhaps…"

"No, I'll tell you," he said, perhaps alarmed by the whiff of tears in her voice. "The fact is I don't want to go on living here."

"But why?" She was startled, not only by what he said, but also by the sheer intensity of his voice, "It's so beautiful here …"

"Yes, there's so much beauty here. But it can be as heartbreaking as love," he remarked, almost in a whisper.

"What do you mean?" she asked, trying to peer into his eyes in the scattered moonlight.

"Let's go now," he said abruptly.

"No, not till you have told me," she whispered too, her voice wrapped in the same sadness she had glimpsed in his eyes a moment ago. "We're friends aren't we?" she asked, suddenly feeling afraid of losing whatever she had of him. .

"Yes, of course. But there's nothing to tell, really. It's just that I have got bored living here," he said, looking around.

"No, you are hiding something. I can see that in your eyes," she said, "Has someone disappointed you? Tell me," she said, just about managing to hold herself back from clutching his arm.

"Who would?" he muttered.

"Someone you loved?" she ventured, suddenly, maddeningly desperate to know, "Come on, tell me, who's she?"

"Naila," he said, his voice tired and husky.

Naila! Naila! Naila! His cousin! Oh my God! Why hadn't I guessed, she wondered.

"I see," she said, biting her lip. "And didn't she love you back?"

"I don't think she felt the same. And I never told her too. But I loved her from the moment I saw her...And you can't know what it is to go on being in love with someone without ever being able to speak about your love ..." He was speaking so softly, so slowly now. "Knowing that if you did you would be laughed at...We grew up together. I saw her every morning and every night and yet I could never even dream of ever touching her in the way I wanted to. I would get up in the night and look at her, sleeping in the same room, her dark hair scattered all over her face and her beauty would singe my eyes like smoke. But I went on repressing my desire to touch her, to tell her I loved her."

She stood silently, listening to his voice only, his words not touching her heart at all, as if it had suddenly turned to stone.

"But she's gone now, hasn't she?" she said later, after he had fallen silent. "Can't you forget her?"

303

"No. And everything here goes on reminding me of her too. That's why I want to leave," he said.

"But...but why don't you think that some day you'll marry someone else and it would be all right then?" she went on, her voice sounding flat and empty.

"No," he said, looking so unnaturally hard and impassive then. "There's nothing in this world, least of all a woman, that I can love any more."

"But if that's the way you loved her, why didn't you tell her?" she mumbled, turning away her eyes to hide the tears that were beginning to burn.

"To be laughed at?" he asked, mocking and bitter in his turn, and then adding, as simply as if he was telling a truth, "Even otherwise, it's always a mistake to expect to be loved in return..."

"No!" she cried, surprised at her own vehemence. "No! It's not a mistake!" she added, and whirling away from him as if he was a stranger, she walked away from him, walked away without saying even a word of farewell, without any thought of what he would think of her, without caring to see whether he was coming after her or not, conscious only of the pain that was gnawing in her . . .

She was barely conscious of how she reached her house, or opened the door to her room. Stumbling to the bed in the darkness, she flung herself on it with the force of a vehement curse and let the sobs escape her.

Fifty Seven

"So, you'll be going away too," Mr. Pandey said, smiling forlornly at her. "Today's Monday and you leave on Saturday. That's just six days..." He was sitting across the table, clutching his wooden cane with both hands. "I don't know if I'll ever be able to see you again..."

"Why not! I'll be back very soon," she lied. "And you are going to promise to take care of yourself. I must find you looking better when I return."

"Of course, of course," he replied. "But I see that you aren't looking happy these days. What's the matter? Don't you like going home?"

"I am going to miss you," she said sincerely, feeling a sudden rush of affection for him. His simplicity was not something that she ever ceased to find endearing.

"You are worried about the shop?" he asked again, looking at her quizzically with his worn out, brown eyes.

"No, not at all," she answered, "You are all here to take care of everything. But let me warn you. You are not going to tire or worry yourself. I'll be keeping tabs on that, you understand?" she said, trying to laugh.

"As if these two will let me do such a thing," he replied, looking towards Sulaiman and Sylvia, who were busy with some customers. "Okay, I'll be going now," he said with sigh,

"But don't forget I'll be waiting for you tonight. You are going to eat with us every day in the evening till you leave."

"I'll come," she said, watching him struggle out of the chair and shuffle over to give Sulaiman an affectionate pat on the back before wobbling out of the shop.

Lowering her gaze to the table, she tried to concentrate once again on the list Sulaiman had given her in the morning. "Just take a look at it. We are running low on several items and it would be better to place the orders before you leave," he had said, in that impersonal tone he was putting on ever since that night when she had walked away from him…

She recalled how she had sulked at home next day, afraid to hope again and yet waiting for the evening to fall. She had stood for so long in the veranda, her heart beating wildly at the slightest sound or shadow, thinking he was coming up, if for nothing else then perhaps to find out why she had kept away from the shop. But the twilight had merged into the night and the day had passed.

A strange stillness had settled on her since then and time was refusing to grow wings. She came to the shop, trying to appear pleasant and normal and he went about his work too, as if nothing had happened, as if there were no feelings of any sort between them, apart from the usual, ordinary niceties between people who worked together.

Sometimes, when it was no longer bearable to keep her eyes away from him any more—for she longed for him than ever, looking at him every time as if she was never going to see him again—she would simply go out and wander about in the woods, or shop around for gifts to take back to Dubai.

Often she would go up the hill to spend some time with

Mr. Mathew and his wife, both of whom had to suddenly leave for Mussoorie, where Mrs. Mathew's brother's illness had taken a critical turn. They had given a quiet farewell dinner for her and she had missed Claire a lot, thinking sadly of how people went away leaving you with memories.

But the most difficult hours to pass came during the night. Feeling restless and empty, she would come out in the veranda to see how the night was faring, seeking for an answer as to why everything had gone so awry for her, and wishing someone took her away too, just like the night took away the moon with it...

"Where's Sulaiman?"

Tahmina lifted her eyes to see a woman near the entrance, standing sideways, talking to Sylvia over the counter.

"He has just gone out. Who are you?" Sylvia was asking.

"I'm Saima. Sulaiman's my son," the woman replied in a deep, dulcet voice.

"Oh! What a nice surprise." Sylvia exclaimed, "When did you arrive? Sulaiman didn't tell us..."

"Yes, he didn't know I was coming," Saima said, turning and moving forward towards Tahmina, "You are Tahmina, aren't you?" she asked, and all Tahmina could do was to stare at her in utter disbelief.

Fifty Eight

"Hello!" she said, smiling at her, "I'm Saima, Sulaiman's mother. I arrived this morning...what's the matter? Aren't you feeling well?" she asked with concern, moving quickly to put a moist, warm hand to her cheek.

"No...I'm okay," Tahmina stammered, her mind almost numbed by the shock. "Please sit down," she managed to say.

"Why, Tahmina, what's the matter?" Sylvia asked too, "Aren't you feeling well?"

"I'm all right. Just felt dizzy for a moment," she answered with a faint tremor in her voice. "It's passed now."

"But you are looking so wan!" Sylvia said, pouring a glass of water for her. "You really must go and see a doctor."

"Don't worry," Tahmina answered, glancing at Saima again, who was watching her silently. "I'll be okay in a while."

"Have you been having such spells regularly?" Saima enquired. "I think you must get your blood pressure checked. If it's low, then that would account for it."

"No, this is the first time I have felt anything like this," Tahmina answered, "I wanted to meet you so much," she murmured, trying to change the conversation.

"And I wanted to see you too," Saima replied, continuing to look at her with those dark, large eyes of hers in a strangely familiar way and it struck her then, why that face in the picture had seemed so familiar, for there was such an unmistakable resemblance between them, particularly in the way they looked at you with that far, far away expression in their eyes.

"Oh my God! And I showed that picture to him...so that was why..." She thought, strange sensations rippling through her.

"Sulaiman wrote to me some time ago about you and the shop. I was so surprised to know you were here and it was so sad to learn about your father too. I knew your parents, did you know that?" Saima asked, somewhat hesitatingly.

"Yes. Mr. Pandey told me," Tahmina replied.

"Your mother didn't tell you about me?" she asked again and Tahmina noticed the look of relief on her face when she nodded in the negative. "How is she? You have taken after her..."

"Hi, Sulaiman," Sylvia's voice came across, startling her once again, "Look who's here—Your mother!"

He was standing, staring silently at them. Tahmina and Sulaiman's eyes met for an instance before he came forward to wish Saima.

"Why didn't you phone? I would have come down to the station," he said, leaning to hug her.

"I thought I would give you a surprise this time," Saima said. "Now you go and get me some things from the bazaar first," she said, taking out a slip of paper and some money. "And for God's sake, don't forget anything or you won't have your chicken stew tonight," she added with a laugh, and turned to Tahmina again. "I try to cook his favourite food while I am here."

Hesitating for a moment, waiting perhaps for her to look up at him, he turned and went out of the shop.

"There's so much I would like to discuss with you," Saima was saying. "Why don't you come over in the evening?"

"I have something to ask you too," Tahmina said, looking back at her calmly. "Can't you come over to my house for a while just now?" she asked, watching the fleeting expression of surprise on her face, which hadn't lost its allure; the lines had deepened around the lips and eyes but she seemed to have changed so little. Indeed, the languorous sensuality about her that came across in the picture had only got accentuated over the years.

"Why not! You live in the same house, don't you, I mean the one Imad bought later on?"

"Yes," Tahmina replied, picking up her purse and stepping out from behind the desk. "Let's go."

Walking at her side, Tahmina could feel the whiff of perfume she was wearing, something with a smell like orchids, and glancing at her, she noticed that her dark tresses seemed to have thinned out and lost their lustre and she had brushed them back into a neat little bun.

"You came to know about your father only after his death, didn't you?" Saima was asking. "I hope you have got over the shock by now?"

"Yes," Tahmina answered.

"And how did this idea come to you of setting up his shop again?" Saima asked and went on without waiting for an answer. "But I am pleased you did. You know I wasn't able to keep in touch with him after your mother went away - I didn't come here again for some years and then when I did, it was usually for such a short time that I wasn't able to meet him."

"When was the last time you saw him?" Tahmina asked.

"That must have been three or four years ago," she answered, thoughtfully. "We met each other briefly on the Mall Road. He told me about you and Amna then. I felt so sad to see him. He had changed so much..." Her voice trailed off.

They were almost at the edge of the clearing by now and Tahmina stepped briskly ahead to lead the way, taking out the keys from her purse to open the door to her room.

"You stay alone?" Saima asked.

"No, there's a maid. She is away for a wedding today," Tahmina replied, pulling out the chair from under the table for Saima.

"What will you have, tea or coffee?" she asked, drawing the curtains to let in the light.

"Don't bother," Saima replied. "Just sit here and talk with me. You aren't feeling that dizziness now?"

"No, not at all," Tahmina replied. "I think you should come and sit comfortably on the bed."

"Yes," Saima got up from the chair and taking off her sandals, she propped herself against the cushions. "Thanks. My legs are aching after the journey. Anyway, let's hear what you wanted to ask me?" she said as Tahmina went across to the wardrobe to take out the photograph.

She came and sat on the bed facing Saima and, without

The Shadow of the Clouds

saying a word, extended the picture to her, fixing her eyes on her face. Perhaps Saima sensed what it was, for there was no look of shock or surprise on her face as she glanced at the faded photograph for a moment.

"I see," she said, lifting her eyes for an instant before lowering them again, "How did you find it?" she asked dryly, gazing outside the window.

"In one of his books," Tahmina replied.

"Have you told anyone about it?" she asked, looking searchingly at her.

"No," Tahmina lied. "I found it only a few days ago and it isn't something I would be able to show anyone."

"Yes," Saima replied. "He shouldn't have left it behind."

"My mother knew about this?" Tahmina asked.

"Yes."

"Who else?" Tahmina asked.

"I don't think anybody else had any hint. You see we...our relationship didn't last long—just three years—and we were able to see each other only when I was here for a month or two. Nobody would have guessed, not even your mother, if this photograph..." She fell silent for a few moments, lost in her thoughts.

"You know, this was the last time we met each other." She spoke again, "We didn't even know someone was clicking a picture of us until afterwards. They were some tourists...I still remember that man, he thought we were a couple on honeymoon. I was going to protest but the man seemed so pleased, grinning and telling us we looked so good with each other and we didn't think it was going to do any harm. I mean he was just a tourist who didn't even know us."

"But we were wrong," she continued, "He got the roll processed here and then, just by chance, he saw your father in the shop and recognised him. So he came in and handed the picture to him and as God would have it, your mother was sitting across the table in the shop at that moment. I had gone back to Bombay by then. Imad wrote to me afterwards, how your mother had gone away...you must be putting me in the dock for that..." She stopped, lifting her eyes to look at her again.

"I don't know what to think..." Tahmina said. "Why did this happen between you?"

"What can I say?" Saima answered, speaking quietly, stormily, "I don't know what tempted us. We knew it was wrong and illicit and yet we couldn't stifle it... sometimes it happens that way . . . you are searching for something and someone comes along and you think you have found what you have been looking for and love happens, just like straw catching fire."

"But how did you meet him?" Tahmina asked.

"Sulaiman's uncle is my brother-in-law and I used to come here during the summer and autumn. Sulaiman must have been five and you had been born that very year. I had met Amna somewhere and we had struck up a friendship and that's how I came to know Imad. Then I came across him alone one day in the woods and we wandered along, talking with each other. That's how it began..." She stopped again, reflecting.

"Both of us were lonely and broken at the time." She spoke again while Tahmina sat listening, her head bent to one side. "I had always been a little reckless—or I wouldn't have married someone like Sulaiman's father, breaking off all ties with my family to run away with him and then discovering what a mistake I had made. And I did something of the same sort once more with your father...Except that...except that it wasn't a mistake this time...I did find a nice man afterwards and I'm happy with my new family now, but I still crave the happiness we found with each other...You can't know...no one can...how it was between us, that wild thirst for our stealthy rambles in the woods, the way we made love to each other as if there was nothing else in the world...It was something so wild and lovely and unrepeatable. Something even stronger than love, more compelling and more satisfying, and I don't regret it, even though it broke his marriage. He did, of course; he just couldn't accept the grief he had brought to Amna. It did something weird to him. He told me he never wanted to see me again." She paused to catch her breath. She had jerked straight and there were tears in her eyes now.

Getting up silently, Tahmina went to bring a glass of water for her and handing it to her, she felt a momentary surge of compassion for her. Even though she was driven by anger and loathing for the woman who had broken her mother's home and deprived her of her real father, she could not help being taken in by her compelling soul wrenching honesty. Trying very hard to keep herself calm, she asked, "What was he like when you knew him?"

"No one sees you with the same eyes, you know, and to me he was the sort of man who could love a woman to the depths. He made me forget everything. I lost all my pain in his company. And it was the same for him too...I don't think your mother understood ...love can withstand anything except frost—I am not blaming her. Perhaps she never realised what kind of happiness a woman can discover when she gives herself away to someone with absolute abandon...she got too wrapped up in other things. I don't think she ever gave herself to him like a man wants to possess a woman...I am sorry," she stopped suddenly, going on in a tender whisper. "I am sorry, I shouldn't be saying all this to you, isn't it?" She asked, "Please try to understand. We just held each other's hands in the darkness for a while."

"He never meant to hurt his wife," she said after a brief silence and Tahmina caught the sadness in her voice, despite the loathing that was welling in her. "In fact, he loved her more than he ever loved me. That's why he was so desperately lonely. That's why he hated me afterwards, or that's how it seemed...He compelled me to go away too. He simply closed his heart to everything after she went away. And perhaps I wouldn't have been able to wrench my freedom too from that man I had married, so I tried to forget and left him alone. And such things never return again if you let go of them even once..." She fell silent once more twining her fingers while the curtains blew gently in the breeze.

"I think I'll go now. Sulaiman must be waiting for me...is there something else?" she asked after some time.

"No," Tahmina replied.

"You look so young and innocent..." Saima said at the door, touching her cheek once more. "And so lovely too! He loved you too. Don't ever think otherwise. I'll go now," She turned and then faced her again. "Take care, my dear," she added, moving her fingers through her hair, "You'll always be dear to me too."

Fifty Nine

It was a calm night, warm and dark. It must have been an hour, perhaps more, when Tahmina had come to stand in the veranda. The rare, purplish hue of the twilight was still lingering over the hills but it no longer held any enchantment for her; it was just another of those things she would have to forget.

She hadn't gone back to the shop after Saima had left in the afternoon. Instead, she had busied herself about the house, taking down the curtains in the living room and putting them away in the large box she had bought and then messing about with her clothes, packing most of them away too in her travel bag.

But the shocking revelation of the afternoon had continued to gnaw at her heart, forcing her to sit down and face it's implications for her own sweet folly for a man whose mother had been caught in an illicit, passionate affair with her father...

Perhaps that's why Sulaiman had withdrawn even farther from her, she had reflected, it would have been too awful...and yet there was something else too, something strangely compelling...If only he would be hers, she wouldn't think even once...

I'd better leave for Mr. Pandey's house now, he would be waiting, she thought, glancing at the watch. It was almost ten past eight. Turning away listlessly, she started to go inside to brush her hair.

"Are you going somewhere?"

She spun around, her heart racing madly. Sulaiman was standing at the gate, looking at her.

"No…Yes, I was going to Pandey uncle's house," she stammered. "But there's still time. Please come inside."

"No," he said, stepping forward. "I won't stay long. Let's just stand here in the open."

"Okay," she said, moving to the railing, trying to still the growing storm inside her.

Both of them stood silently for a while, till he put a prosaic end to it. "Why didn't you return to the shop in the afternoon?"

"I had to do some packing. You know I'll be leaving on Saturday," she said, not even trying to hide the petulance in her voice.

"You brought my mother here in the afternoon," he said. "What did you say to her?"

"I asked her the truth."

"Was that necessary…"

"Yes, it was," she answered flatly. "I had to ask her. I had to know…"

"And what did she tell you?" he asked and all of a sudden she realised how painful it must be for him too. Turning her head a little, she tried to read his face in the darkness.

"They had been lovers," she told him. "It was something very brief…You won't realise how sorry I am…I should never have shown that picture to you. If only I knew…I am sorry I hurt you," she said in a sudden rush of remorse, wanting to reach out and comfort him in some way.

"No," he said. "It was better like this. It gave me the respite to think over it, to accept it. It would have hurt more if I had come to know of it in some other way."

"You aren't angry with her?" she asked, turning to him, searching for his eyes. "They needed each other…"

"No, I guess not," he said, holding on to her eyes. "I know just how much she has suffered and if she found some little happiness perhaps, then I can't grudge her that…But I can't even say it hasn't affected me, though not in the way anyone would imagine…" He paused to look away in the darkness and asked, "I expect you didn't tell her that I know about this?"

"Of course not," she answered, turning to rest her arms on the railing while he stood lost in his thoughts.

"I should be leaving now," he said some moments later, "But if you aren't in a hurry, there was something else I wanted to say."

"What?" she asked uncertainly.

"You are angry with me, aren't you?"

"Why would I be angry with you?" she asked, her heart like a lump in her throat.

"Because of what happened that night," he answered. "You were so angry then. You still are."

"I am sorry about that night too. I shouldn't have walked away like that but it…it just seemed so wrong what you said and I don't know why it affected me so," she replied, looking away for fear that her eyes would betray her.

"I only said what I felt and maybe I was wrong. I have never talked about those things to anyone in the world…but every moment since then I have wanted to come and say sorry. I wouldn't like you to go away angry with me."

"I didn't know you cared so much for my feelings," she said bitterly and then repented quickly. It wasn't his fault he loved someone else. "I'm sorry, I shouldn't have said that," she added, remorsefully. "In fact I should be grateful for everything you have done for me."

"I don't know what you are talking about …"

"No, really. You have worked so hard for the shop. That's why I have come to depend on you so much…"

"How can you say that when I have disappointed you? I mean by not being able to stay on at the shop…"

"That doesn't matter too much now. I am not even sure if I would like to continue with it any longer…"

"What do you mean?" he asked in surprise.

"I know it's going to be heart-breaking, but what's the use? You'll go away too after some time and I don't know if I will ever be able to come here again," she said and as he didn't say anything further, she added, "I have been so happy in the short while I have been here and you won't even guess how much you have contributed to that."

"That may be the way you look at it," he replied, at last, "But the fact is you are so nice, anyone would love to do

The Shadow of the Clouds

anything for you. And even otherwise," he paused for a moment. "I read somewhere that the fragrance of the rose remains with the hand that gives it away..." He stopped, and though she couldn't see it, she could feel that familiar, sad smile on his face.

"That's nice and true," she said, smiling sadly at him in the darkness too.

"If you are ready to leave now we could go down together," he said without even a slight change of expression.

"No, there's no hurry," she whispered, not trusting her voice, no longer able to hold the sudden, unbidden tears. "I'll go and make some coffee for you," she mumbled, moving quickly to rush inside, ignoring his request not to trouble her self.

Stepping inside the kitchen, she stood with her back to the wall, shutting her eyes, feeling the scalding of the tears over her cheeks. She didn't know how long she stood there in the darkness, for she hadn't put on the bulb, until she heard his steps. He was coming inside, calling her.

Wiping her face hurriedly, she turned on the light and started to fumble with the stove, conscious he was standing behind her.

"What's the matter, Tahmina?" he asked gently. "Are you crying?"

"No, why?" she replied, turning with downcast eyes, making an effort to sound surprised. But it was no use really. He was standing near the door and she could feel his eyes reading her face. And then, all of a sudden, impelled by her grief, she fluttered down the little space between them, hurling her self into his arms, her eyes bubbling over again.

And then, like a fire smouldering beneath the ashes that all of a sudden leaps up into flames, he forced up her face from his chest and sought her lips with his own.

He kissed her again and again. Though this was what she had ardently desired for the past many months, it seemed now as unreal as all that had taken place in the last few days of her life, changing everything in her world. The headiness she experienced came much out of her own sense of unreality than of anything else. Swayed by one strong emotion or another, she thought she must have finally been losing her balance. She had not realised at the time what toll Saima's confessions had taken on her. How the intensity of her presence had drained her. And now she was standing here, in her father's house, held feverishly in the arms of Saima's son. In all these months of girlish longing, much of it the fare of romances she took for her bedtime reading, she had not glimpsed a world like that of Saima's. She felt that she would never cease to be in thrall of that compelling voice, and those dark intense faraway eyes that had now taken posession of her again. Saima's son Sulaiman—the words kept throbbing in her mind as Sulaiman kissed her again and again. Then at one time she abandoned herself to him completely.

The next thing she knew was that he had torn himself from her and started walking towards the door. She stood still for a moment, too shocked to comprehend anything, her eyes gazing dimly at his receding form.

"Sulaiman! Sulaiman!" she cried, her voice like a faint, falling whisper.

"Don't go away, please...:" she cried but he had already disappeared, the sound of his steps echoing in the silence of the night. Rushing out to the railing, she watched him walking away down the path, a dark shadow in the shy radiance of a pubescent moon.

Sixty

It was a bright, sunny, summer morning and looking at herself in the mirror before she started out for the shop, Tahmina was surprised there wasn't even a faint trace on her face of a sleepless night. After Sulaiman had left, Tahmina had spent herself crying feverishly while the night burnt itself out like a forgotten candle.

Coming out in the veranda she stopped, apprehensive of what the day held for her. In the end, however, she somehow managed to walk down to the shop. Stealing a look at Suleiman, she went straight to her desk and started scribbling a few lines on a piece of paper. That done, she sat back, waiting for him to look towards her. She waited and waited and finally called out to him.

"Can you go over to St. Mary's just now, about that matter we discussed?" she asked, delighting in the puzzled look on his face. He was standing across the desk and their eyes met at last.

"I have scribbled down some notes," she said, dropping her eyes as she extended the note to him, asking him to meet her in fifteen minutes on the deserted pony trail at the back of the lake.

"I am going to do some shopping. In the meanwhile, you can go over to the school," she said breathlessly, picking up her purse and leaving the shop in a hurry.

Will he come? She wondered, walking across the Flatt. It

wasn't too crowded just now and half way across, she stopped to look back, but there wasn't any sign of him coming after her. Maybe he has taken some other route, she thought, deliberately slowing down and even stopping for some minutes to gaze at the lake, which was sparkling so brightly in the sun that it hurt her eyes to look at it.

Does he really love me? She wondered, or was it just a rush of passion? Perhaps that's why he had torn himself away from her. And yes, he hadn't said he loved her, not even once. Perhaps the unexpected events of the last few days had worked on his nerves as well, and he had given into an irrational bout of passion, both responding to her signals and acknowledging the strange bond that had developed in them ever since the forbidden photograph sneaked into their lives. But Tahmina was determined to find out if there was more to it than that. She was determined to say goodbye to her girlish flights of fancy, and her coy and reticent behavior, so carefully designed out of pretty pictures of appropriate maidenly passions that the books summoned. She decided to face him and herself squarely before leaving Nainital for good.

The path was deserted like she had wished for, with just an occasional passerby. There was a shabby, wire fence edging the lake and she walked some distance beside it before turning back. He should have been here by now, she thought, searching and finding him coming along the road at the back of the Capitol.

"Thanks," she said, as they fell in step, wanting to slip her fingers into his hand. "Let's go somewhere secluded."

"Why don't you…" he started to say.

"Please," she said.

The Shadow of the Clouds

"Okay," he answered, turning his face to look into her eyes for a moment, their sadness piercing her heart. And suddenly it was if they were alone in the world and she put her hand in his as he led her towards the woods on the hill.

Sixty One

He brought her far up the hill, holding her hand as he guided her along perilously narrow, meandering trails in the woods. It was so silent here, with only the sound of their feet, and the air was heavy with the scent of the pines.

"Let's sit here," he said, as they came to a small patch of clearing, dropping to the grass to lean against a tree and gathering her up in his arms at the same time.

"Why did you go away last night?" she asked, looking him in the eye.

"You can't love me," he said but she could feel his arm tighten around her.

"I already do," she replied.

"But I can't," he said, kissing her hair.

"Why? Perhaps I am not good enough for you?" she asked gently.

"It's not that. You are too rare and generous, so beautiful in everything you do, in the way you look and the way you smile, biting these lips of yours, beautiful in every little thing that you do and say and..." He paused.

"And..." she asked.

"And in the shy, hesitant love in your eyes, in the way you have gone on loving me even as I tried to resist you."

"Then you knew, didn't you?" she looked up, taking his hand to her lips. "And I thought…"

"That I was an insensitive brute." He laughed.

"No…Yes, I did sometimes." She laughed too. "And you were in love with me too?" she asked.

"I tried not to," he answered seriously. "I tried so hard."

"Because of Naila?" she asked.

"Yes. It seemed so absurd to me at first, that I could even feel anything for you and I felt afraid too, for both of us…I thought one day you would go away too …"

"How can you say that?" she asked. "Don't you know how much I love you? Just the thought of going away from you makes me feel as if nothing's left in the world any more…Oh, darling, I love you and I won't ever go away from you," she said, drawing his face to her lips.

"No, you'll have to go away," he said, kissing her back, "You won't be able to defy your parents and they are never going to let you hitch your life to me. Not after they come to know about my mother…Don't you realise that?"

"I do and that's what I have been thinking all through the night. I could never have imagined my heart would be so divided like it is now…I know it's going to hurt my mother and, God forbid, if Abbu starts thinking I wouldn't be defying him if I were his real daughter. It's all going to be terrible and I don't know what's going to happen. And yet," she looked up into his eyes, "there's no other way too."

"Then what are you going to do?" he asked, weaving his fingers through her hair.

The Shadow of the Clouds

"I'm going to marry you and live with you here, running the shop and no one can take me away from you," she said quietly, wiping away the few drops of tears that had rolled down her eyes.

"Don't cry," he said gently, kissing her eyes. "I know it's going to be difficult and you'll get hurt by it all too. That's why I say, forget me"

"Never," she said, snuggling even closer.

"But there are other things too," he said.

"What?"

"Naila, for one," he said softly. "You know how I loved her and it's pretty deep rooted."

"I know," she said. "But I'll accept that."

"You won't be jealous or fight over it?"

"Why? Haven't I already won?" She smiled. "And even if we do, don't people love each other more dearly after a quarrel?"

"Perhaps," he answered with quiet laughter. "But what am I going to do here? I mean I'll have to get a decent job."

"Why? We'll run our shop! That's what I dream of."

"Your shop, Tahmina," he reminded her.

"But I told you, you'll become a partner," she said, looking at him, trying to melt him with her eyes. "For my sake, darling!"

"Hmm!" he said finally, smiling at her. "You know my mother was telling me last night she has been saving some money for me over the years and perhaps I can use that..."

"There's isn't any need," she said. "What's mine is yours too. But you can have it any way you like," she said, rubbing her face against his chest. "And now tell me that you love me. You haven't said it even once."

"Can't you guess?" he asked, stroking her hair.

Sixty Two

They had just three days before she went away and how time flew by! Tahmina would steal away to the woods in the afternoon. They would talk in whispers in the secluded, enchanted silence. They would talk about their childhoods, about places they had visited, friends, families. They talked for hours and realised that they had more to say to one another. In all those months when passion was forbidden to them, they had talked. And now they realised that it was in the talking that they were most intimate.

They met in the night too, after she returned from supper with Mr. Pandey. He would be waiting for her near the lake and they would stroll along, talking with each other.

And now she would be leaving some time in the afternoon today. She didn't want to go, not now; it would have been so easy to write a letter to her parents and tell them she would be delayed here. But Sulaiman hadn't agreed.

"No, Tahmina, I can't accept that," he had said, "you must go back and keep your promise. And it would be better for us too if you went and settled everything at the earliest and then came back, forever."

She had sensed the fear in his voice, had read it in his eyes. And to tell the truth, she was afraid too. She had no clue how she was going to tell Faisal and Amna…she would be so helpless over there and only God knew what she would have to do if they didn't agree. And even if they did, they weren't going to do it happily.

She had thought about it miserably all through the night, asking herself whether she would have the courage to tell them that, though she loved them, she had to follow her heart too and live her life the way she dreamt about it…But it had felt so strange thinking like that…After all parents had their rights too. They brought you up in the world, took care of you when you were helpless and made choices for you when you needed them to do so. And doing that over the years, they got so used to it that if you defied them, they took it to heart, feeling hurt and betrayed when it wasn't like that at all…Oh God! She had thought, love was so simple and yet we make it so complicated and painful.

She had expected to wake up sad today. After all, they would be parting before evening. And yet she was feeling so happy, a happiness she could never have imagined, like the water of the lake sparkling in the sunshine or the breeze amongst the trees or the flowers blossoming in the veranda. Perhaps it was because of what she had decided to do today. Yes, she was going to make his fear go away before she left.

Last night, when he had come to see her to the house after the stroll, she had put her arms around his neck and said, "Leave the shop closed tomorrow and meet me at nine at the bandstand."

"Why?" he had asked. "Sylvia generally comes around by eleven and we can meet then."

"No, go and inform her to come early to the shop tomorrow. Tell her I'll come to say goodbye in the afternoon."

"Okay," he had answered, kissing her, "But I would have preferred we didn't meet tomorrow. It would make it more difficult to say goodbye to you."

The Shadow of the Clouds

"No, we must meet tomorrow..." she had said, kissing him till her lips ached, and finally said, "There's something I have to give you..."

But before she left to meet him, she went to her travel bag that was standing, stuffed and ready, against the bed in her room, and took out her father's framed photograph. Gazing at it for a few moments, she put it away again and came to stand by the window to look at the lake, the hills and the clouds.

"Thank you, Abbu," she whispered. "Thank you for bringing me here. You have done for me what I could never even have aspired for. Thank you for this happiness that will always remain with me, as enduring as your love in my heart or this lake and all the beauty of the hills...Thank you for this small, blessed house and for the life I am going to spend here...I'll never let all of this fly away, I promise, I'll learn to tie the clouds with a knot and keep them with me." And wiping away her tears, she stepped out in the veranda to go and meet him on the Flatt.

"I want to take you somewhere," she said, slipping her hand into his.

"Where?" he asked.

"Up there," she said, pointing towards Dorothy's Seat on the summit of the hill. "There's a glade up there..." She smiled, biting more of her lip than usual.

And so they climbed up the hill and she found the glade where she had seen those two lovers so long ago.

They remained there for three hours, lying down on the grass, making love and talking, their voices echoing through the silence of the trees while the butterflies fluttered over the flowers in the golden warmth of the sun. Later she had wept with fullness and exhaustion.

"Don't cry," he said, kissing her eyes.

"Why? Didn't you tell me once, that tears were like rain. They bring the happiness of flowers afterwards."

"I know," he answered. "But I still can't see you cry…"

"Okay," she said, crying and laughing at the same time. "But remember, you're my cloud. Don't ever fly away."